All the Help You Need
A Vic Pasternak novel

By Sean Preciado Genell

All the Help You Need
Copyright 2015 © Sean Preciado Genell
All rights reserved.

1st Edition

ISBN # 978-0-9764009-6-7

This book is a work of fiction. Any resemblance of characters to actual persons living, dying, or dead, is purely coincidental.

To contact publisher:
PO Box 116 / North Liberty, Iowa / 52317
email: info@slowcollision.com
or visit www.slowcollision.com

Cover design by: Patty Hogan & Slow Collision Press
U.S.G.S. topographic map of Iowa City, 1983. Courtesy of the University of Texas Libraries, The University of Texas at Austin.
Portions of this work have previously appeared in "Haulin' Ass" and "Business as Usual" published by *Little Village*.

Slow Collision Press
Iowa City, Iowa

get ready.

For Uncle Pete and the T.E.

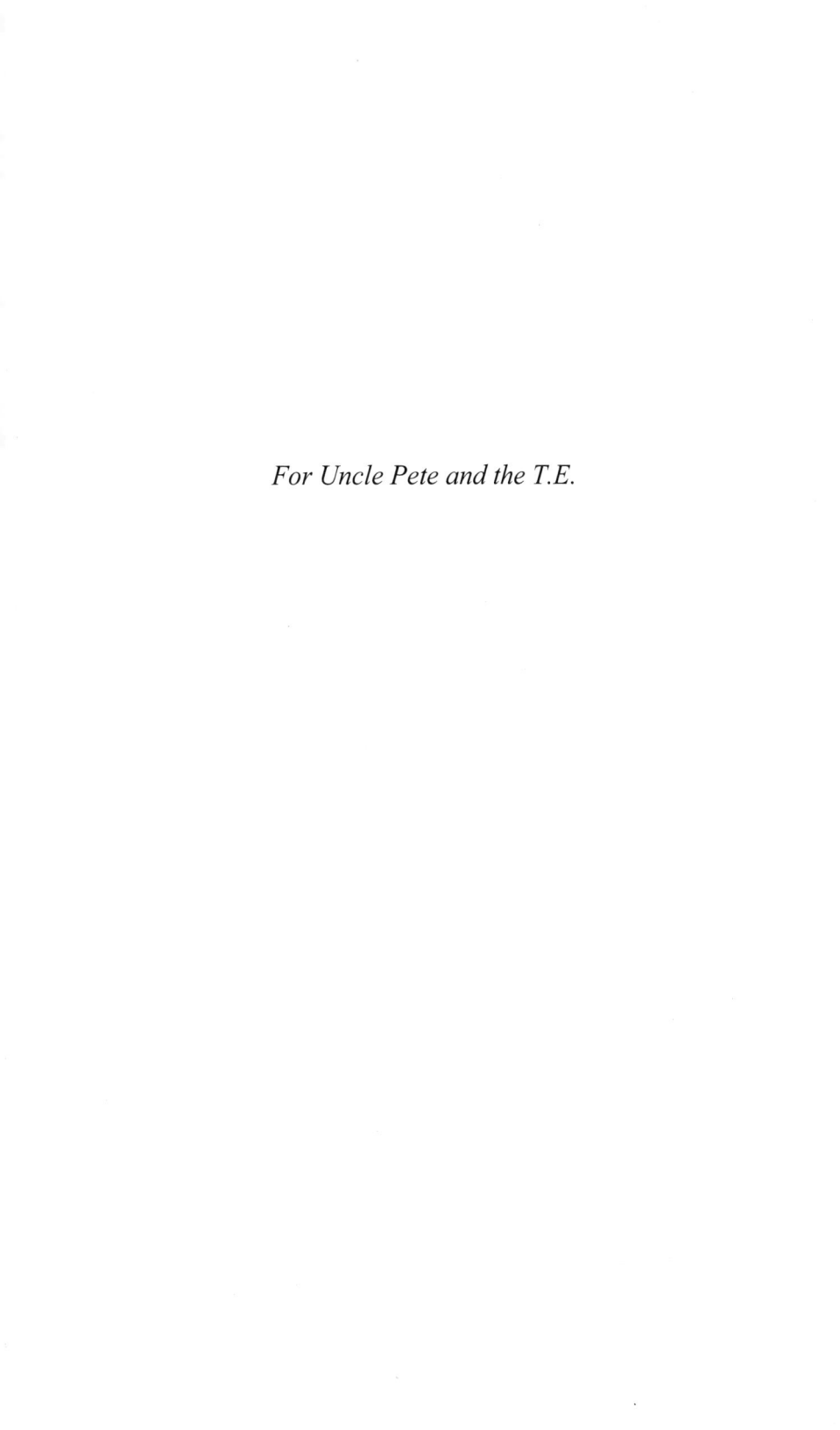

There's nothing but a voice-like left inside
That seems to tell me how I ought to feel,
And would feel if I wasn't all gone wrong.

Robert Frost, "A Servant to Servants"

I

PARTYTOWN U.S.A.

1

THERE ARE NO good taxi stories.
"That's bullshit, bro. Tell me the weirdest thing that ever happened in here."
"First off, tell me where you're going."
"Tell me the weirdest thing. I can handle it."
"Tell me where you're going or you're getting out."

The last time I quit driving taxi was after a courthouse visit to press charges against a regular drunk we call the Sex Dungeon Lady. The arresting officer pulled me aside, gripped my elbow, "Jesus H. Christ," he said. "Did you get a look at the bar?" He was referring to the bar built inside the garage attached to the defendant's home. With all its surfaces veneered in white Formica and matched with white barstools. Its checkerboard floor blocked with mannequins wearing shiny leather boots, rubber gear and zipper masks. A sex swing dangled wantingly from the rafters. Too hammered to use the front door, the Sex Dungeon Lady always carries the garage opener in her purse. So yeah, I've seen the bar.

But try relating any stripe of that weirdness to the backseat kid who demands to know about it. He was poured into my cab, his eyes glossy and his maw sucking at drool.

"You know some fucked up shit. Now out with it. C'mon."

He claps twice, *chop-chop*. Then he takes his window half down and spits on it.

It's my first night back on the job and already I want to choke out a fare.

People always want to hear how girls make out, or about the pukers, or what kind of creepy shit goes on. Taxi drivers, on the other hand, share tricks of the trade and survival tactics. Like me and that courthouse cop. We get off on subtle oddities and unseen dangers and other aspects that don't have truck for most people. Not unless you're a hooker or mercenary.

True story: I once got choked by a dude sitting behind me. He and his pal had come out the bar as if climbing out from under a bridge. Rode-hard white boys high on crystal meth. "How are ya!" He reached around the headrest to pat my shoulder before clamping his hand on my windpipe.

You'd be pissed, guaranteed. And if you're quick, you'd stomp the brake and break his hold and twist in the seat swinging your Maglite with all hope in the world that it'd crush his skull like a fucking piñata. And this while you pilot your taxi through traffic.

Normals think that this is the story.

"So did you get paid?" That's all a cab driver wants to know. Because it's the first rule of the job. We work 12-hour shifts with no hourly and take a 40/60 split with the owners. Or even less. So always get paid. Even if it means checking your swing.

The backseat kid is still asking for it.

"C'mon, biatch. You know you want to tell me."

I've been in this business over 430,000 miles at roughly 200 per night, four to five nights out of seven for 10 years. That much time and energy pushing wheels for money turns you into a good read of people.

This is why I get a psychic pinch when I see the backseat kid peeping in my rearview. I can't say exactly from where this feeling comes. But it is startling. Like hearing the voice of a dead friend. It tells me this jagoff is going dodge on his fare.

I ask for my cash two blocks from the drop.

He lazes over on the bench taking his time about it, wiggling fingers in pockets that come out hooked with pocket trash. We roll into his parking lot as he tosses said trash over the seat. Then he shoves the door open and leaps out as if he's parachuted from a plane, yelling, "Geronimo, motherfucker!" Or most of it before he face plants. Then he gets to feet and skitters off like a wounded deer.

Let's see what he's left: Cocktail napkin, blank; a tobacco cellophane; a matchbook with an unfinished phone number; a mini-Ziploc that appears to have once contained a finely grained white powder; an outsized condom; and a fold of $20s.

To be honest, I spotted the cash first thing and as he plunged out the door I choked back my urge to stop him. Far across the parking square, he gazes at my taxi through the yellow lot lights. Then he hustles into the apartment building and is gone.

I take up my radio and call dispatch. "#22 is clear."

"CLEAR #22. GO BACK DOWNTOWN."

I wheel out of the parking square and take it downtown as ordered, gunning the engine as I fly the chute of student's cars parked on either side of this too narrow of a road. The cash is sweaty from riding in the kid's skinny jeans. I spread the mixed bills in the domelight and count $106 on a $4 fare. Not bad for my first night back.

EMERALD CAB RUNS its taxi shack south of town and west of the river. Back where the county used to weigh its trucks. We got a parking yard, a two-stall garage and 24-hour dispatch. The latest protocol advisory is also tacked to the door.

THERE ISN'T ANY PARKING FOR TAXIS BY TEH DOORS. PARKING IS ONLY FOR DISPATCH. THX, *THE OWNERS.*

I quit on May Day and stormed out of here and threw my taxi keys on the roof then drove my fading F-150 out to Colorado. I hadn't planned any of it save for that an old friend had offered me a job on his medical weed farm. So having a place to land, and with everything else looking bleak, I leapt at the chance. Captain Jerry Nicodemus, smoking, leans on the radio desk, the two walls above him flown with giant maps of town. The rest of us await our next missions. I'm on the arm of the couch occupied by Leon Bath. Quiet Chuck Bowden is wedged in the far end staring at his cellphone. A skinny new kid sprawls in a metal chair unfolded beside the dispatch desk. Next to the kid is Zina Schram, rare ladybird veteran, lingering at the office door pretending to check her schedule. She turned red to see me and hasn't said hello.

The old man tends to forget who's in rotation, which is why we're all in the shack. Leon Bath, who needs one, leans a fart from his enormous ass and barks laughing. He digs an elbow in my hip: "So what happened to Colorado?"

"It didn't flood if that's what you're getting at."

"How long it take you to get back?"

"About eleven hours. I got a bum wheel on the car."

Leon raises his fat face, impressed. "Still pretty quick."

"Distance equals Rate times Time," I shrug. "It's all about keeping a steady needle."

He tips his chins at me. "Bring back any weed?"

Nothing's changed around here but the calendar and the new kid. And because I've mentioned it, Leon wants to talk about the Great Flood.

"Did you see your dad's house got sunk? Totally flooded, man. I seen the roof all caved in."

"A bank owned that goddamned thing," I tell him. "So good for those son bitches."

I'd lost the house to foreclosure four days before blowing off to the Colorado weed farm. Then June swamped the Midwest with the worst flooding in five hundred years. They tagged it #GreatFlood like that thing in the Bible. I saw my dad's house on the news. I could tell it was his house by the tallboy cans left in the chimney pipes and by my message, DOWN

WITH OLD CANOE, rolled out in huge plain block and cleverly color-matched to the shingles. That was the rooftop I had left to peek out of the river.

Zina Schram fires a bullshit grin from behind crossed arms. "You could've told me you were leaving. You lost your house and you said you needed a place to stay. So I kicked out my roommate."

"I never committed to that idea, my friend. I'd issued you a 'maybe.' I also told you not to kick the roommate out."

Zina owns a converted one-bedroom and I don't want to live with her, or her stinky dog. I was already in Colorado when I heard the roommate got the boot. I'd sent her a month's rent to cover any assumed deposits. So I didn't leave her cold.

Jerry's worn laugh gutters like a beat muffler. "We figured you quit for good."

"Sure," Leon goads. "Done with this and 'all of us bitches.'"

"I didn't say 'us bitches.' I said, 'you bitches.' I had a chance to go and I went. The foreclosure of my dad's house took a bite from me. Then four days later, if anyone recalls, I was in court with the Sex Dungeon Lady."

I play the recap as I'd done for the judge. After sucker-punching me from the backseat, the Sex Dungeon Lady had gotten out of the cab taunting a fight before clawing at me through my driver side window. I rolled her arms up in the glass and waited for the cops. In court, she claimed no memory of how she became trapped like that and suggested I might've been trying to kidnap her.

"What'd the judge say to that?"

"He slapped her with a fine and sent us home. But it stings. Like with an accident. When we get hit, we're still at fault. We're supposed to steer around shit like that. Not roll bitch's arms up in the window. So I was done. And I left. And I cut you out, Zina, and everybody else out and I'm sorry for that."

My apology pries a genuine smile out of her. But Zina radiates a shower of mixed tones. She plays more casually annoyed than tuned-up about it.

"So why come back?" asks Jerry.

"Everyone gets everything he wants," I tell him, and leave it at that. Four months to the day later, I'm back at this shit. It's like I'm addicted. That's the only explanation.

"I'm out of here." Zina stabs her cigarette in Jerry's ashtray. Taking up her tripsheet and cash purse, she breezes out to her cab leaving the scent of peaches. "See ya."

She won't look at me as she slams out the door but Captain Jerry makes sure I see his wide eyes.

"We'll be all right," I tell him.

Leon elbows me again. "You hear about Cowboy? He got robbed last Saturday."

Cowboy used to work for us but now runs with our crosstown rivals, Taxi Gold.

"And he's an ex-marine or some shit. How'd that happen?"

"It's the southside," Leon says, shrugging like I might've guessed. "He says they were kids and he didn't feel right hurting them. Come Sunday, the same kids hit another dude." Leon shows the math with a wag of his fat fingers. "That's two robberies in five days."

Through the venetians I watch Zina's cab go rolling out of the lot as an unknown dude creeps on our door. He drops a cig, stomps it. Scratches at his two-week beard. I take him for one of our neighborly hobos. Next, he disappears from the window. I hear him bang through into the garage and then the door from the garage swings into the office.

The creeper stalks inside like a regular of the club. He looks like a hitchhiker that'd eat your brains. Broad-shouldered, tall and lanky, with long arms, hands, fingers and dirty nails. Greasy jeans hang off his butt under an outsized t-shirt. Cap knocked to the side. From his clothes I whiff a peculiar funk like he's been playing in floodwater, or shitting his pants.

The phone blows up and like a pitching machine the old man radios Zina to the Super 8, Leon to Kmart, the greenhorn to the currency exchange, and Quiet Chuck to the Vine. All at once, the room begins to clear as the hobo snoops about. He rubs two quarters between his fingers. "Anybody got a cigarette, preferably an American Spirit?"

"I smoke menthols," Leon says going out the door.

"I got USA Golds if'n you want," says Jerry.

I say, "Lucky bitch gets a preference?"

But Quiet Chuck offers his American Spirits as does the greenhorn. The creeper peels a square out of the pack but Chuck won't take his fifty cents.

"Make that son bitch pay," I growl at Chuck, and I warn the stranger: "Hobos keep it outside."

Hobos and junkies camp behind our yard in the high grass on the river's edge. They usually leave us alone but he isn't the first to storm in here making demands. I glare at the creeper and the creeper glares back at me, dumbfounded.

"I says the hobo camp's out on the river. Now scram."

I clap at him, *chop-chop*.

The creeper thanks Quiet Chuck and goes back in the garage as everybody leaves for calls. The old man bursts laughing until he's whooping with a hand over his mouth.

"Vic Pasternak, that ain't no hobo. Haw haw, that's Billy!"

"That guy's a cab driver? He's one of our drivers?"

Captain Jerry whoops and whoops, firing up a fresh smoke as he answers the phone.

The stranger returns from the garage brandishing a bottle of Windex. He looks at me with flat, cold, crazy eyes and comes at the couch lifting the cleaner like he's going to spray me. I catch another wave of his peculiar musk.

"You using that?"

He points the Windex at the newspaper on which Leon had been sitting.

"It ain't mine."

"I'ma use it for my windows then." His drawl is spiked with brass notes, like Alabam' by way of Boston. "Washing with newspaper makes'm shine like they wasn't there, bubba."

He grins sideways and sallies out the door. I get off the

couch and over to the schedule.

"What's that creep's name?"

"Billy Kinross," replies Jerry. "You remember Frank Boulot? Drunk Frank?"

This town has more than one Drunk Frank. But there's only one BILLY K. on our schedule. Seeing where my name is penciled in, we're set to work the same shifts all week.

"Already put to weekend nights. What a lucky dick."

"This ain't his first rodeo."

Jerry waves me into the folding chair beside him.

"There are two ways to go through life."

"The hard way and the easy way," we both say at once.

I ignore the chair and go to the window to split the venetians. The creeper wipes down his interior windshield with the newspaper, stretching across the dash to get the whole thing.

Taxi drivers are scorned everywhere, unfairly and fairly. This business draws survivor types and other outcasts. The thrill seekers, authority doubters and haunted souls; the dopes thinking they're making real money; street rats that don't give a fuck; musicians, alien hunters, drug addicts, professional students; single dads, the chronically mentally ill and felons. This game is all about putting asses in seats, at least from the standpoint of Thx the Owners. Drivers don't always stick around, good and bad. When our new greenhorn quits, some fool will volunteer for his seat. Newbs always find their way here. As do those that can't work elsewhere, or won't. Even dickheads that throw their keys on the roof get another chance. Our work cooks up strange gumbo and over the long haul we that remain grind on another until we're something like comrades in arms. Or siblings of a proud and dysfunctional family. But this window washer doesn't look like a member of the tribe.

Jerry shifts to a low voice. "Billy's working to get back to the righter side of the pasture."

"He's a jailbird?"

"We always hire jailbirds," says Jerry. "And don't be smart.

I got him the job and he's doing fine. The Christ has personally asked that I shepherd Billy toward a righter path."
He shows this nudging with a tilt of his hand.
The townies call him Preacher, especially behind his back. He's been an abuser of rye and pills and women, husband to four and a five-time divorcé, he who would take dozens of 12-Steps. Ten years on, Jerry Nicodemus is alive and sober and he mashes The Christ button as if keeping his pinball on the table.
"I think Jesus is calling on you, Vic Pasternak. At least be kind to Billy as a favor to me. You'd see he's salt of the earth if you'd just have a little heart."
Billy waves at the venetians. Then he climbs behind the wheel of his cab and drives off, making a big circle out of the lot. He stares at me as he drives off.
"I got a little heart all right," I tell the old man. "And I don't like that guy."
Captain Jerry plucks off his glasses and rubs a hand on his face.
"Billy Kinross has hoed a harder row than you or I, buddy. When he was young, his kid brother got snatched in broad daylight from right out in front of the house. You remember Frank Boulot, the boxer? County champ called Bull Francis? My old drinking buddy?"
"You keep asking like I should."
"We shared a trailer up in Hilltop. Anyhow, Frank was Billy's uncle and Billy was sent to stay with us after what happened to his brother. He was fifteen and all boy. Trouble from the get and with a red mohawk too. Billy pissed in the neighbor's car. Or like when he threw a bully out the window at Westside. Got pinched for drugs, vandalism. For carrying too long a knife. One night, he started every garbage can in the PedMall on fire."
Jerry grins wistful. "But you'd catch Billy helping people in need. You could tell he really wanted to be good."
"Does he still piss in cars?"
"Now look. I'm no longer a man who says anybody deserves what he gets. But the guy who got that was a mean

cocksucker used to beat his dog. And that's why Billy'd done it. Despite all he done, Billy keeps to good reason. He's ethical."

"Ethical, huh. So what ethics got him sent to the jail house?"

"You just best ask him."

"Bullshit. I'm working with the son bitch and enquiring minds want to know."

Jerry Nicodemus rolls his head on his neck like the Christ might be wrestling him one way or the other. But he's saved by the ringing sideline. The old man answers, drags out the call with chitchat, hangs up, says, "Marilyn's ready to go at Dollar Tree."

THE GARAGE WHERE I live is on the south end of town. It shares the apron-way with a Kum & Go. I'd gone to Colorado on the promise of a sure income but hadn't been in a fiscal position to move all my shit. So my buddy Clyde and I did each other a solid and I rented one of his commercial garages. I've stayed current on rent but upon landing back in town I was relieved the key still worked. Turning on the warehouse lights, I was relieved again to find everything just where I'd left it. Which of course meant shoving shit back from the door enough so I could park inside.

I had left Denver in the afternoon driving a '84 Corolla traded for a '83 F-150 that wouldn't have made the trip back. Of course the 'Yota's front-end busted loose before I got out of Colorado. Crawled under for a look and saw the frame eaten by acid from a battery blown up long ago. The axle was, and is currently, the only thing holding the wheel to the car.

At Ogallala the sun was going down on me. By the time I'd refueled in Omaha the traffic had at last surrendered the interstate so it was just me and the big rigs roaring under the interchange lights. I wrestled to keep my needle steady and the wobbly rig straight. Driving 12-hour shifts is ordinary for me but my ass and legs ached, my guts soured with travel center coffee.

Thirty miles to go and a lesser driver would have pressed woozily on for home. I lumped off the big road to make my final approach on the county gravel, and to puff reefer.

The roadway there runs along the interstate until lifting into wooded hills above the lighted cloverleaf. You can see the big roads from Denver to Chicago, and from St. Louis to Minneapolis, and highway lights running to ordinal points like it was altogether a radiant octopus. Iowa City and its neighboring towns spill across both sides of the big road to Chicago.

Jiggety-fucking-jig.

The city lights shone against the outer dark and then I hit blacktop. I kept driving, both hands on the lumping wheel. I'd told everyone I wasn't ever coming back.

Passing beneath the southbound interstate I felt a twinge as the city jumped me at once. Condos and suburban tracts and a valley of wide-lot McMansions. Westside High and the university fields. Everything looked as it had when I left in the spring. All except for one grid of town that stood unlit. Taking the window down so I could smell the funk, I turned north and lumped into the bottomlands.

The river bends around this part of town on an S-curve and it was on the lower loop where the water first spilled over, wiping out an anchor corner. Without electric, the area stood in fell dark but I could make out the burger joint, taco shop and Chinese buffet bulldozed into piles. Roaring against the windows of the Heartland Inn were industrial fans signaled with green gumball lights that shone like diseased cop cars. The roadway was filthy with an apocalyptic haze and crows, picking in gutters, lifted through the beams of my wobbling headlights.

I broke north again into an older quarter, what's hemmed in the upper loop of the S. The Great Flood turned out to be a big fucking deal. Even our illustrious President of the United States made a photo tour. He was shown to walk up to the edge of the water at the corner where our neighborhood began.

Zina emailed pictures when the damage was fresh. The houses can't be seen because garbage is piled a dozen feet high

along the curbs. Ramparts of drywall, carpet and pads heavy with slime, sectional furniture, subflooring, saturated cabinets and wallboard, mattresses. She wrote I would need to see it in order to truly believe it.
No doubt.
City electric burned in the street lights but every house was dark. The walls of garbage had been dismantled and cleared yet every driveway was occupied by a box dumpster piled with ruined food, Hefty bags of clothes and shoes, libraries of books, china collections, waterlogged toys, magazine and record libraries, tools that didn't make it, musical instruments, washers and dryers, refrigerators, ovens. Of four hundred houses in Mosquito Flats, more than a hundred have been torn down. Empty lots stood like teeth missing from the mouth of a giant. The stench clung in my nose, even now, an incredible stew of shit and moldy sweat socks. Still the grass shone vibrant and there were signs of triumph over the ordeal. WE SURVIVED. One house stood jacked up on twelve-foot stilts, garage door and all. So hope was living in this sad place.

A team of dozers was parked at the lowest end. Near to my dad's house, where I lived after he died. Zina's pictures showed its vandalized rooftop collapsed by the weight and heave of the river. Whatever remained of the little ranch had been scraped from the lot and hauled away. I got out of the car and walked to where it had been. The foundation was busted out and its footprint filled. Not a doornail left.

My people had been farmers that survived the '80s by turning into truckers. I remember losing the farm, and Mom and us kids uprooting every couple of years to follow Dad. We'd land in Dayton, Victorville, Anchorage, Omaha, and out to California again. Mom wanted to be buried around her people when she got sick so we returned to Iowa and my brothers ran back west after she passed. But I was done moving. My old man quit the road and settled here too, buying his house in Mosquito Flats.

I imagine that purchase to be his regaining of a lost crown. Buying it back like it might've been in hock. That I fumbled this crown during another economic crisis is not irony lost on me. I'd been willed the house because I was "the real Iowan." As if it was a century farm. Maybe he didn't know how else to handle the property. I should've sold the fucking thing, and didn't. I should've taken on roommates, and didn't. And if I'd held on a couple months I'd have gotten out of that note a lot cleaner than I did. I'd even carried flood insurance.

I drove out of Mosquito Flats and lumped the 'Yota to Clyde's garage where'd I'd stuffed everything when I lost the house. Three warm beers remained from the Omaha truck stop and I sucked one down while kicking the futon open in the back office. I kicked off my Redwings and drank a second beer while digging through Hefty bags looking for a blanket.

Making a christening of it, I lobbed both empties across my new living room.

"Welcome home, asshole. Next time, burn the bridge with fire."

Every morning the road shivers in my hands and legs. The river sludge stinks in my nose. I feel like punching myself in the face. Before I can sleep I puff more reefer than I need and open another beer that I don't and I stay up late to cipher out my every wrong turn.

2

THE INTERSTATE EXITS onto our main road and sends the traffic roaring south two miles into a T-intersection on the Ped Mall, the heart of downtown Iowa City. The university mixes with regular commercial zones inside the square mile. School halls and cafés and law offices stuck in among boutiques and liquor stores and headshops. The dorms and student ghettos get confused for government housing. The tourists all say we look like Boulder, Colorado.

"Yeah but Boulder's crawling with douche bags," I tell them as another drunken hero spidermans across my hood.

Standing beneath the West Bank clock, a shirtless fat guy with a shaved head bellows long singular tones like a Tibetan throat singer. People stare but no one engages. Even the cops whistle along like dude's as regular as a fireplug.

"We're in Hell, keep moving," clucks the girl sitting shotgun.

This gets a laugh out of me. Too big of one. Football traffic louses up good D=RT. I volunteered for Wayne Linder's football shift while he's off getting drunk at his kid's wedding. So I have him to blame for the last 40 grueling minutes inching from the stadium in a parade of Winnebagos, out of state SUVs, Prevost coaches and beer wagons.

Soon as I drop my fare, more folks pile in bouncing back to the game. "It's third quarter and they closed the roads," I advise. "University hospital's as close as we can get."

"And you expect us to pay for that?"

Dispatch yells over the radio like his office is on fire. Might as well be. This is Partytown U.S.A. and on these eight Saturdays of the year we throw our doors wide to mayhem, and allegedly unlike anywhere in America. Tens of thousands swarm our sidewalks and streets shouting and shoving toward troughs of ice-cold beer, turkey legs, barbecued things on sticks. We average more money on a home-team loss so I always know who I'm rooting for.

Drawing into the bus station, my fare blinks at me having just returned from the edge of consciousness where he's apparently seen a revolting horror. "What town am I in?"

"Illinois City, Ohiowa. End of the line, pal."

There is a golden equation at work behind all this disorder and it is pristine in expression, hidden and godlike. It has been quantified by experts that have for us performed the laborious task of Figuring Out How This Shit Works. As such, they have me caring most about the money I carry in my own purse. But the real story is all the money brought in from without. The football program sustains from these eight days $100-million dollars of gross county revenue. Crunching the numbers, $15-million per game. And that's just the white market money. That doesn't include city and state revenues collected by tax and fine. Nor the uptick in energy and cell usage, or the gray dollars made by market vendors and lawn parking sales and Mexicans blowing through our lots in midnight vacuum trucks. That $15-million per game also doesn't count the underbelly revenue dragging in. And you'd better believe it snows in August around here.

Four hours into shift an emergency call comes over the radio.

"IN NEED OF ASSIST SOUTH FIRST AVE CARWASH."

I volunteer because I'm close and if I needed it I'd want somebody to jump in and help me. Plus I've been on high alert since starting back. The cab robberies have me on an edge and right now I'm holding a stack of paper worth $500. All night thinking what I'd do to somebody that would try to rob me. The Maglite is wedged firm under my leg and I grip its knurls while blasting to the carwash.

I swerve across the lot to find our van parked in the last bay. Dr. Bob keeps cool in a world intent on provoking him. Wearing blue surgical gloves, hair in a ponytail, and customary puka shell necklace, he blows the pressure hose over floor carpets hanging on the wall.

"This guy is huge." Dr. Bob quits the wand to give me the what's-what. "He promised not to blow so I put him up front. I was pulling over to let him puke when he inexplicably maneuvered into the rear of the cabin."

"Dying in the fire fumbling for an exit."

"Something like that." He itches under his shell necklace with a gloved finger. "More like the guy's exploded."

He drags aside the portside door like revealing a crime scene.

Funniest puke story I have took place in wintertime, a woman called me to halt and I did on a dime at the crest of a slick hilltop. She scrambled out and hit the ice on all fours, rotating through my headlights and blowing chow as the slope of the hill carried her away.

This puke story isn't nearly as fun. The drunk dude is bigger than Leon Bath and wedged between the front seats and rear bench, an island of shining flesh in a sea of predigested beer and barbeque sauce.

"The plan is to clean him up and get him home."

I suggest involving the proper authorities.

"Or is he a friend of the company, or what?"

"Friend of a friend. I told him it's this or jail and he put cash in my hand. There's $50 in it for you. Want gloves?"

We get to work and I ask him if he's talked to the new guy.

"Colby Cheese, the new rookie?"

"Naw that other new guy. Looks like a hobo."

"Billy Kinross? Billy's cool. You don't remember him?"

"I wouldn't forget."

"But you never drove together? He used to drive like 10 years ago. Maybe it was 15."

We climb inside Dr. Bob's van and drag the moose out by his shoulders, propping him against the wall of the carwash. Dr. Bob wands the van interior then wipes and scrubs and vacuums the carpet, the chair backs, portside door, window, handle and floor runnels while I go after our friend with the pressure washer. I drive him over until his shirt blows off and he's batting around like a roach in a commercial. As the quarters run out, I feel great.

"I really got something out of that," I tell Dr. Bob. "Just give me $20."

He orders the shirtless moose to get in the van and the moose does as ordered. Dr. Bob then forks over $40 and says he's not writing it on his tripsheet anyway.

"We haven't crossed paths since your inglorious return," he adds, shaking my hand with his blue gloved one. "Welcome back to the jungle, my friend."

Next, dispatch sends me to Maxie's to pick up Catfish, called so on account of his two-piece mustache. He lives in the crappiest part of town and throws $10 on his $5 fare. I roar back downtown and get flagged by a bartender buddy and his boss, the owner of the bar. Also friendly and always tipping, even when the night's shit all over them. In this jungle, we have fares that look out for us as we do them. Our friends of the company. They alleviate the load of the work, both in a fiscal sense and an emotional one. And it prepares me for the next two hours of bar rush and its madhouse non-stop speed trial as I rip from one end of the city to the other, always passing through the center of downtown and always landing at a different angle so that if you were to soft connect the points on a graph my journey would look like a daisy, or a mandala, until at last I snatch old Gunner Grulke off a corner. We loop on the One Ways from north to south and back, twenty minutes listening to Toots and the Maytals while shit falls apart downtown. "This's where the real party's at!" Gunner hollers as I sing with the chorus.

Run a taxi for 10,000 hours and the act of driving becomes

second nature. At night: Look for the flare of other headlights. By day: For the glint of sun off chrome. White line in fog and sun; yellow in rain; else, surface wear. Know where your wheels meet road. Top-pedal out of stops to keep from flooring it. Look to the horizon. Always be able to see the rear wheels of the car ahead. Know your D=RT. Know the traffic lights and speed tolerance. Know if the taxi needs oil, or anything else. Because you're meanwhile exchanging money; and/or smoking, eating sloppy food; defusing a fistfight; driving alone to or from a call; talking on the radio; witnessing a break-up, a cheating scandal, or love birds realizing what everyone else's been talking about; etc., ad nauseam.

Forty minutes later, dispatch has sent me way east of town where the smatter of rain has become a deluge as I hammer across country gravels for a dozen miles. But for the giant pines and high outer walls of the estate, I hardly spot the driveway until I'm on it and slew on wet gravel to make the turn. Then for the blinding rain I about smash the archway gate so I leave my brights burning all the way to the door.

I call for a punch over the radio and wonder if dispatch has copied me. Calls way out in the country during bad weather have a way of falling apart. I expect some rich asshole to stumble out the oaken front door, apologizing: "Our friend decided to drive! Sarry!" It's been an easy night and I'm due for trouble.

Our radios rash and squelch and I give him a verbose check to increase chances he's heard me: "Do you copy #22 is still not seeing anyone way out here in the country?"

But finally the door cracks open with a narrow band of light from which flees a young woman who I realize, once she's in the back, is actually still a girl. She's maybe fifteen.

I leave the domelight burning and look over the seat.

"Where're we going, young miss?"

She bursts crying and I shut down the domelight to wheel from the rotunda and back across the property, through the archway, and out to the county road. I ask if we're going into

town. She sobs and tells me to bring her to the Highlander Hotel.
"Is there anything I can do? I got a phone if you need to call your mom. Or the cops."
She promises she's okay. When we reach the hotel, the girl directs me around back. Mortified and apologizing, she hands me a hundred bucks.
"Hey," I call out. "This is too much."
"That's from the people I was babysitting for."
She hurries to the rear entrance and disappears inside.
Taxi drivers see a lot. More than most anybody. But I drive away stunned that the taxi gods are ever able to serve up new and wretched mysteries.

WHEN THE ACTION breaks and the radios shut up and the early drivers get cut, everybody else finds places to park and nap. A bunch of us hang around the old bus depot where Taxi Gold used to have its dispatch shack. We all worked here back in the truly badass days of just 20 taxis and thousands begging at bar rush. My best night ever, I made $60 an hour excluding the boss' cut. Since then, 60 more cabs have flooded the streets and it broke the action. Most quit Taxi Gold or came to work for Emerald like I did, or at one of the other startups. We flutter about the old depot like it's still our home. A busted place with plywood windows that looks somehow smaller than we remember.

#31 cruises up to greet me. Never mind that we're into cash tonight like we're printing it, he looks whipped.

"This shit was fun when it was fun but now it's fucked up. Always, 'I'm too drunk,' or 'I can't do it.'" He shakes his head, cold-stoking his humor. "'I can't pay you. I got to buy my junk!'"

We laugh to give our backbones ease.

"These motherfuckers going to make you quit?"

We can hear hordes still screaming downtown, 4:12 a.m.

"I can't do this anymore. This is my last season and I'm

done. I'm no lifer."

I want to agree but I'm already not as good as my word.

As each shift is called to close, we race for fuel then down to the taxi shack to count the take, and to fork over the boss's 60 percent, and to figure tips against expenses. Meanwhile we tell tales of the night. War stories, like herpes, want to be exchanged as soon and often as possible.

"And I watch her shit over her heels into the gutter like a bird."

"Tonight's the last fucking night I haul that nutjob out of Boston Way. Fuck that lady-bitch."

"And boyfriend's like, 'I'll bust the window and climb in then you lift her up.'"

"Boston Way's a little weird but she always holds her shit together around me."

"You know Redneck Homo? Goes casino? He tipped me $50. Even after I said no to a blowjob."

Over and again I'm asked: "Afterhours at your crib?"

On these last warm nights I drag open the big roll-up door and turn on the factory overheads like we've come to make the donuts. The garage is a hundred feet deep with an 18-foot ceiling. There's room enough to park my wood chipper, a skid loader, and the 'Yota, and with built-in storage racks and workbenches there's still room for an office and a short hall that leads to the rear exit. I've put together a makeshift stereo using a Discman harnessed to a 500-watt PA and Black Sabbath sounds killer in here. Me and Quiet Chuck and Jonah Lake and Dr. Bob drink beers on the couch and others trickle in as their shifts close out. Zina Schram and Joe Vega then Leon Bath who squeezes into my dad's ancient skid loader, shutting himself inside as if we don't know he's shooting up.

That creeper Billy Kinross has tagged along with one of them. He browses my stuff with hands driven into pockets as if he's afraid to steal something. And he'd better be.

I offer the tour to anybody who wants it, showing them where to piss and how I've rigged my shower. Breezing past the fake mantle of real firearms, I walk them into the rear office that I've turned into a bedroom, thumbing on the trouble lamps to show the room dressed like the cabin of a ship with bunk beds and a narrow captain's desk and two aquariums I put in the window cut-outs to keep with the seafaring theme. Then I explain how the previous tenant left enough teak paneling for a yacht. "And what the hell else was I going to do with it?"

Quiet Chuck asks: "You getting any fish?"

Zina and I have been warming to another at work but this is the first she's come to Freedom Cove. She's impressed with the firearms I bought out in Colorado.

"The Liberty Collection," I announce while passing her the .45 Ruger. There's also a Brazilian .357 and the classic Remington .870 pump-action shotgun. Their corresponding ammunitions are rowed along the mantle edge neat as soldiers.

Dr. Bob lifts a hand out of crossed arms to fiddle with his puka shells. "You know what they say about guns on mantles, brother. You'll end up using that shit."

I argue it out with him. "Maybe I'm a fucking jerk but how else do you want to guarantee my liberties? Are you gonna ward the wolves from my door with your ponytail, or what?"

I've rediscovered a white Culpeper flag and the red-striped Navy Jack. DONT TREAD ON ME. The Navy flag files over at the wash sink next to the bison head and the other floats above the sitting area of yard chairs and an ugly couch salvaged from the roadside. This is where we gravitate.

Vega casually tosses a crack bindle onto the plastic yard table and gives me a look. "It's cool?"

"This is Freedom Cove so be my guest."

I drag down the roll-up doors and Leon hustles out of the skid loader like a dog on scraps. He and Vega are the only two fools that mix with that shit and they smoke themselves laughing green on the couch, the fat man tap-tap-taps his foot, bends his elbow, makes round observations. "It evens them out, man. It evens them out."

I've meanwhile found the Wahl clippers and lean over a

garbage drum while Dr. Bob shaves my head. Vega yanks the drum toward him and flashes puke.

Billy Kinross pokes at the colorful bindles.

"Where'd you get this?"

"Why, bro? You a cop?"

"Naw, my old boy was slinging that shit a while back is all. That striped paper. It's proprietary, you know."

Dr. Bob complains: "That shit smells like plastic melting on a light bulb."

"Tastes like raspberries." Joe Vega waves the pipe at him. "Want a baby-taste?"

Vega was born for sales. Slick and intrusive while wearing a wormy thin mustache. Even his billboard name feels like a wanting handshake. I'm also surprised to hear Zina's dating him. I ask her: "Is it his sales pitch or his product?"

"Meh." She shrugs but tips her chin as if thinking about it honestly. "I'm bored."

Jonah Lake points at the game heads mounted randomly across the walls wherever I found a hanger.

"Did you hunt all those?"

"My dad hunted them in online auctions."

After Dad came off the road he wanted his home to reflect the sportsman's life he hadn't lived. He invested in game trophies and pinball machines and a Brunswick pool table he never bothered putting on legs. I liquidated the pinball machines long ago but the full lion and bears stand high in the storage racks. Dad bought four panoramas of wolf versus coyote over a deer kill and these stand at lower points. They watch our morning party out of dusty gloom as if drawn to the modern campfire.

Vega takes the shotgun off the mantle and attempts to blow smoke through the ejection port and down the barrel. Zina frowns and pushes the barrel out of her face.

Billy Kinross snatches the shotgun. "Shit's not a toy."

He carefully returns the shotgun to its place on the mantle. But his outburst has busted up the party and everyone stands to

hike up their trousers. It's getting on 9:00 a.m. anyway.
 Kinross still strikes me weird though his verve and respect for firearms is appreciated. I'm usually the one accused of being tightly wound. I even shake his hand as he goes, telling him to come back again. "We should do something sometime."
 Taxi driving builds camaraderie with the enthusiasm of cancer. And I wonder if I've meant what I told him, or if I'm drunk.

ONE NIGHT OFF, six back on, and payday is my first next night off of three.
 I got up early to prowl the student ghettos until I find a disused Trek. It's chained to a rack not far from where Geronimo Motherfucker leapt out. My lucky quarter I guess. Somebody has driven over the bike's wheels and skoached the seat but I have spares in the garage. I clip the chain and shove the carcass in the trunk and spend the afternoon bringing the bike to life.
 Then I buy a sixer of Pabst, stick it in a backpack, and booze-pedal to the shack to collect my pay. Except by the time I reach the taxi yard I need fresh sixer.
 From out in the lot I can hear dispatch hollering in his little box of an office. I make a quiet entrance through the garage and slip my check off the desk before he even realizes I'm there.
 Paulie Floyd is our dispatcher four overnights a week. He reminds me of Lady DJ from *The Warriors* due to their mutually unseen godlike oversight. But he's definitely not as cool. In fact, Paulie is volcanically hot and stamps feet like he's going to stroke out. A phone rings unanswered because already Paulie has two phones pressed to either side of his head, and this as drivers pile on the radio. He slaps the desk mic, barking: "Go #31; go #24; coming out for #18; punching for #96, who else checked?" The sideline rings and Paulie pounces on it as the main lines blow up again.

If Captain Jerry had to deal with this level of mayhem, he'd go back to drinking.

"Look," he barks in the phone, "These aren't helicopters. And you keep calling back like your trick is to speed up the taxi."

Slamming down the phone, Paulie hollers, "D-equals-RT, can't they get that!" He eyeballs my beer. "Can you drive? Or do you need a ride someplace too?"

I wag my last tallboy at him. "I came to collect my pay and bask in your tranquil vibes."

"Kumbaya, motherfucker." He glares unhappily. "Another driver got robbed. Marty over at Capitol."

Marty's robbery makes four in two weeks, including Wong Fen at Taxi Gold who got hit during the last football game. All the robberies have been committed by African American teens brandishing an automatic pistol and all occurred in the same neighborhood south of the highway.

The phone rings anew and I leave Paulie to his circus. Wheeling my bike out into the yard, I balance it on my hip so I can light a smoke. From out here you can see where the office took on water during the flood, the high mark pegged at three feet around the skin of the building.

Hearing feet in the gravel, I turn and from out of the dark walks the creeper, Billy Kinross.

"Hey bubba. What you up to?"

"Got my check. I'm cutting out."

"Getting my check too. Then how bout let's you go buy me a drink."

"And tell me what the fuck for."

"For calling me a hobo."

"What! Fuck off."

He presses me to join him, taking from his pocket an electronic cigarette. He offers the e-cig and I wave him off.

"That's as bad as offering me a Virginia Slim, bro."

"Suit yourself."

As he puffs on the thing the tip glows blue and he blows out

hash smoke. I've never seen anything like this and I clutch my head. "That's for real?"
"You buy me a drink then I'll buy you a drink," he says.
"And we do that til we forget you stepped on my toes."
Billy grins but his big doe-like eyes are fixed and sad. His face transmits a quiet blankness as dark breezes rile the high grass to rustling.
"Come on, bubba. It's our duty to get drunk downtown just like they do."
"Ah I'm pretty drunk as is."
"I got this here electronic hash pipe."
"Alright," I say, because I'm pretty drunk. "Let's go."

THE RAILROAD HOUSE is in a forgotten south town block, a lowdown joint set between legs of weeded-over track. When bikers come to town, they drink here and fight in the lot.
  I order beers and guide us to window seats from where I can watch my unchained bike. I've left it tipped next to four Harleys parked on the door. Billy brings peanuts from the bar.
  I ask: "So when'd you drive cab here? I mean before now."
  "Way back in the '90s. What about you?"
  "My mom moved us here in '96. It's weird we never met."
  "I was gone by then. And I'd remember a cranky bitch like you. But I don't." Billy munches a handful of peanuts. "How long you been driving taxis?"
  "Nearly half a million miles. Almost a decade."
  "Christ of God. I should ask what keeps you at it. I'm surprised you're not a bad drunk. Or shooting morphine in the neck, for example."
  "It doesn't hurt like that. And it's better than running a goddamned seed wagon."
  "What's one of those?"
  "Trucking," I tell him. "Soon as I was old enough, my dad

had me driving his daycab, running seed from here to Missouri. Seed, dead pigs, fallen down barns, you name it."

"You traded driving big rigs for driving cabs, huh?"

"Ah it sucked."

"Cab driving sucks. And I'd be dead if I was doing this for this rest of my life. I'd wedge my head under the table and fucking end that shit."

I must be giving a slanted look because Billy props up. "Don't get me wrong, bubba. Labor's labor. And it's got to be meaningful or else you wouldn't do it. Know what I'm saying?"

Something else has caught his eye. He's mad-dogging someone behind me but I don't turn to look. The bikers at the pool table are the only other patrons in here.

"You know those guys?"

Billy strokes the side of his neck. "Dude's got a tattoo. SS."

His eyes flick to my empty bottle then back to the game. I casually snap a blind pic with my phone. It looks like shit. Four hunks of dude in road leathers.

Billy rolls his eyes back to me. "Old Jerry says y'all were talking about me."

An awkward turn but an expected one and I roll with it. "He says he got you the job and I should play nice. Also says you went to prison but tells me to ask you what for."

Billy gets a bang out of that. "He didn't want to tell you I was robbing drug dealers."

I think about that a sec. "For real?"

"I got pinched in Texas and did seven real years for real." He tips his chin at the pool table. "Skins, white power Nazi brotherhood motherfucks. They're my lover boy."

His fingers wheel around the empty bottle the way a spider might its prey. Then he calls two more beers out of the bargirl.

"Did the old man tell how my brother got raped and killed?"

This curveball I'm not expecting. He dumps a handful of peanuts in his mouth and chews like a cow.

"That's how the old man introduces me to people. Like it'd

be awkward for it to come out later. Or like just in case you'd make a joke about killing a child."

"When it comes to murder I never kid around."

"I didn't specifically mean you. I meant like anybody he'd introduce me too."

I let our table fall quiet and listen to the racket of the pool balls.

"I got to be honest," I say at last. "I think all of that would've fucked me up for good."

"All of what?"

"Your whole life. All what happened to your brother. Then having to shack up with Preacher Jerry and Drunk Frank."

Billy shakes his head and scratches his beard, leaving peanut skins in the curls.

"I grew up in Chicago fucked up from the start. Not afraid of nothing. Not Mama yelling or Daddy peeling off his belt. The bullies was even scared of me. They'd talk shit but they'd go on cross the street to see me coming.

"First time I got kicked out of school was in third grade. It got to be this dare to run on me with a marker or this nail-polish wand. We was poor folks and I only got this one jacket, a white Members' Only nylon. It was St. Vincent's but I really liked it. Now these two kiddos ran up on me, front and back, and boom-boom. They came out with that nail polish and the marker. I felt one slash the back of my jacket and the other swabbed the nail-polish wand right here," slapping his left breast. "I thought it was a knife and grabbed the kiddo's hand but I was moving too slow. If it'd been a knife I'd've gotten cut.

"Busted that kiddo's arm though and that's what got me the boot. Next school was laughing at me too but not after they heard why my jacket was all marked up. I wore it that year and next with it shrinking up my arms."

Billy goes on telling about picking fights with skinheads and baiting cops with stolen cars and the first time he was shot. Hearing him run his highlights reel, I can see why old Jerry Nicodemus mistakes Billy for a misunderstood kid. But Billy's not a kid. I think he's a man right broken.

I catch him mad-dogging the biker dudes again and ask if he wants to split before he kills somebody.

"I don't want to see them die. I want to see them suffer."

"Want to split before you go to jail then?"

"Hell naw." He brings his eyes to mine, asks, "You ever think about the drug game?"

"What about it?"

"About getting in it."

"Slinging? That shit's for punks."

"Labor's labor, bubba. Lots of money on that table. Lots to be raked in the cab with it too."

This provokes me to tell my story about Colorado.

"Day after the bank took my house, I got a call from an old friend I knew on a landscape crew. Cheyenne Buck. And Cheyenne had a job for me on his Colorado farm. All I'd be doing is curing and cleaning medical weed and he was talking about pulling 30 g's. Monthly."

Billy likes where this story is going. But I don't.

"The money was good and we had legit investment. And the grow room looked like a future lab. He even had some cat from *High Times* out to shoot pictures. My busted truck was holding up and I lived in this old-school teardrop trailer. Things were good until we got trespassers shooting at the grow barn and slashing tires. Then we had a falling out over pay, me and my old friend. Cheyenne sent me off with half a pound, 'Have a good life, asshole.'"

"Bring any back?" he asks. "I could move a big enough pile."

I shake my head. "That pile moved itself on Federal Boulevard. Or most of it did."

"That's when I got a complaint from the neighbor. He's slo-pitch but a nice kid and I'd sold him a Z one eighth at a time. His brother said I'd ripped him selling it to him that way. But that's how the kid was buying it and I'd even thrown him some dimes. Next thing, his brother tells this other dude and this other dude runs with these Hondurans that don't like gringo

fuckhead in their playground."
This is the first I've told anyone this story and I hate it. I take down a long pull of beer.
"I was at Appleby's for lunch. Splurging while Rome's on fire, right? I'd tallied my funds and counted I could hang in Denver five more days. But when I get back to the mobile court, I see my camper burning down to its frame. Tiny little camper and she went fast. The bottom of my stash was in there too, the motherfuckers."
"When was all this?"
"Couple weeks back. Same day that I drove back to town." I tell him the truck I had wouldn't have made the trip so I traded it for the 'Yota. "'My Summer Vacation.'"
Billy nods. "You got bad luck with houses, bubba."
"That's what they tell me."
"So you out of the drug game because these Hondurans are gunning for you."
"They just wanted me to leave. So I left. And it's not them. It's me and dealing dope. That ain't my kind of work."
I tip my empty bottle and show that I'm ready to cash out.
"So you still think I'm a hobo?"
"Why do you care I even said that? Was your dad a hobo, or something?"
"It'd be kind of you to apologize."
"I was wrong," I tell him.
Good enough, I guess. Billy Kinross rises to see me out the door. He throws me a hug and his arms swallow me in his funk. "Be careful getting home in this dark rain, bubba."
Then I leave him to ogle the bikers and I roll along the tracks south to my garage. Riding in this rain doesn't feel dark or dangerous. In fact, I feel a lightness to be free of him as I'd be with any strange fare that was finally out of my cab.

3

MY EYES START and I buck up on the ugly couch to a pounding hangover. The garage is dark and cold and my waking cough rings like one man clapping in an enormous room.

Three in the afternoon, my second day off of two. I wake and light a cigarette. I stand and light another. I find 7/8's of a cold gas station pizza under a couch pillow and unthinkingly throw my toothbrush in the toilet. I fumble into Carhartts, boots and shirt and feel a hundred times readier. Janitorial chic is my single blessing.

Last night after shoving a wood burner into place and cutting a hole in the roof, I fell off on a liquid dinner. And now I'm fucking starved. So I pedal my bike toward downtown on a food hunt, my third cigarette burning between my knuckles. Wind rips at my hair and sand blows in my face. The stink basin isn't as strong anymore. Normal life is slithering back after the Great Flood just as the leaves are starting to turn.

Downtown sits atop a great hill overlooking the river. I keep off the steeper routes and ride in the floodplain. I sweep past the county jail and wave at the block windows. Next, I cut between student apartments and come out on the easiest slope to the hillcrest.

My assault of the crest is slow going nevertheless. Awake 20 minutes and I'm out of shape and need fuel, STAT. I cross the road pedaling toward the parking garage on the mall. I hear emergency trucks gathering nearby. Like something downtown is on fire.

A flutter on my left, and I look.

A deer has jumped out of the side of the parking garage. Not off the top but high enough that I can see her turn against the blue of the sky between buildings. A doe with a lime green splotch on the hind. She turns over end and crashes on her back.

Afterward I tip into the Mill for a Reuben and whiskeys, and never mind hot coffee.

ALL NIGHT LONG I won't shut up about the deer.

"I expect them to charge out from the underbrush. Not leap off the fucking mall."

I've freaked out the bargirls with this talk. Zina Schram has thicker skin and snarls her lips wanting to hear more.

"Did it burst open?"

"Imagine a banana big as a deer then throw it off the roof. It was horrible. Like a bad omen."

"Only for the deer."

Relationships can be difficult navigations for cab drivers. Circumstances have to fit the schedule so it's easy for us to pal up and put up with mountains of each others' shit. When Zina called saying she wanted it to be like old times, I told her to pick me up downtown. I'd only drunk enough to take the sting out of my afternoon and the Reuben didn't fill me.

Under a full moon, we eat carryout sushi and drink PBRs on the hood of her car parked on Forbidden Road. The last night of the weekend for both of us. The 5 o'clock news had a report on the deer and I relay the facts. The cops got tips of the deer wandering in the northside neighborhoods and next thing she was in the Ped Mall. With a straight face the reporter said the deer had been flushed into the parking garage where the cops said they intended to corner it.

"As if that was part of any fucking plan," I rail on. "And they think the deer was diseased as evidenced by that lime green splotch on its hind? You know what that was? Some asshole had shot the deer with a fucking paintball. You believe that? Who does shit like that but the same class of assholes that do shit like this?" I wave my hand at the cleared ground all around us. "Look what they do with their hundred million dollars. More investments for ignorant fucks like themselves."

It's my request that we've come to Forbidden Road. I want to honor the deer.

"I used to hunt morels out here and all through here was run with them. Then the developers come blow down the native elmwood and where else're the deer supposed to go? Do you know how many accidents they've caused just this year?"

"The elms or the developers?"

"The deer, goddammit."

Moonlight breaks through the clouds and glistens on the unpainted blacktop that bends across the clearing. One day it will connect the southside with the west and complete a ring of roads that encircle our city. The drivable portion of Forbidden Road is blocked with Jersey walls until the far end is complete. But we know the back ways and share a mutual desire for driving first on virgin roads. Zina loves it out here for the quiet state of things, and that it won't remain forever. She says it's like a park that doesn't exist. She says it's like Brahman.

We're parked not on the road itself but in one of its undeveloped cul-de-sacs budded off the main drag. The new hood is a field of gas taps and driveway pads glowing in the orange midnight of the construction lamps. Fat tongues of asphalt clump in the weeds where gutters await curbs. A billboard depicts a super-friendly white family fawning before three styles of home, captioned: THE FUTURE BROUGHT TO US BY DEVGRO.

"Those're the same fucks that collected my FEMA check."

"The white people?"

"The funding company. And not just this DevGRO. I mean anybody promising the future for a cut of your dollar. I mean the myriad predatory lenders," ticking them off on my fingers, "Banksters and hedge funders, the price fixers in the oil cartels."
"Who's approached you about a hedge fund?"
"Point is: They're the ones funding all this shit. Building the infrastructure and arterial roads and anchor corners. We should piss on every one of these driveways. If they wanted to kill all the deer, they ought to round them up and gas them like the fucking Germans."
"I think you're drawing your picture a little too far."
"I mean the German Germans. Fucking Nazis is what I mean."
"You're getting yourself riled up. And it's riling me up. So knock it off."
I apologize and take a re-up on beer, tobacco and weed. I crush my empty and throw it at the sign. "Fuck these clowns and their Forbidden Neighborhood."
"I hear you've been hanging around Billy Kinross."
She says this with a suspect tone. Like she's trying to tie me to something.
"We had a couple beers. He intrigues me. So what?"
"So what he's a scary guy. Scary like a hollow tree. Look in his eyes and tell me he's not empty in there, Vic."
"Why do you care anyway?"
"You can quiz why I'm fucking Joe Vega but I can't ask why you're hanging around a creep? Our road runs both ways, dude. You're like this when I mention you living in the garage too. You jump my case every time."
"Because you make it sound like I'm a homeless person."
"Because you are a homeless person."
"Then because it's nobody's fucking business."
That shuts us up and for a while the only sounds are the crickets and me cracking beers. I ask at last, "So how's Joe?"
"I can't believe you came back to this shit. You had the glint before you left and you're acting like you already got it back."
The glint. When a cab driver has pushed too many wheels

and seen so many faces that they spin into a single bloated monstrosity, his only use for other people will become their money. Every driver falls apart differently but the glint is always the same. It shows in the lift of the undersides of eyelids as you describe with menace breaking the will of a fare and how you reduced them to tears, cackling as you tell about it.

"You didn't have to do this again. You could go drive truck like your old man."

"I tried that already and no fucking way. Nobody's making me piss in a cup so I can run seed up the highway."

"At least you'd be homeless on wheels."

That drags a hard laugh out of me and we puff tobacco and blow smoke while the wind scours across the cleared ground. Feels like storms rolling in and the cold along with it.

NEXT NIGHT SHIFT is a slow Hell, even for a Wednesday. The suffering taverns are cheerfully lit but empty like the box left behind when the shoes go out dancing. The heart of downtown chokes with dozens of unneeded cabs and every company represents like corner gangs squared against the other cliques.

When I started out there were only two cab companies, Taxi Gold and Emerald Cab. Nine years later, the city clerk posts a count of 87 stickered taxicabs working for 16 companies, and the drivers come from as far as Rockford. It's the football money and weekend crowds that draw them like ants to bacon fat. I loop the loop unable to find standing anywhere and realize each of those little operations is squeezing us out. I feel like a foreigner in my own town.

I roll to the boarded-up bus depot and find Cowboy on the slab parked next to Harry Paines.

Cowboy's been knitting on about the robberies and rolls off soon after I walk up. We don't get along. Then Harry and I rap about the suicidal deer before I get to the matter at hand.

"You remember Billy Kinross? Folks say I ought to know him but I don't."
He thinks on that a minute. "Jerry didn't quit driving until June of '96. Kinross would've started the year before. I remember because I trained him." Harry trained me too when my illustrious career began at Taxi Gold. He's the most veteran driver in our town. Or he was once Jerry became a house cat.
"I see he's back working for y'all," says Harry.
"Jerry got him the job."
"Jerry got him the job then too. And he must've pulled strings with the insurance because Kinross was the youngest driver ever allowed in town. Of course he only lasted six months."
"How'd he strike you?"
"Weird guy."
"I don't know if he's a bad guy in a scuzzy coat," I say. "Or a good guy playing a bad guy in a scuzzy coat. Suffice to say, I find him interesting."
"Must be he is," says Harry. "You bored with most of us."

THE NEWSPAPER RUNS an infographic. It shows how the deer made its way through town based on calls to police and eyewitness reports. I cut it from the paper and pin it to the bulletin board in the shack, telling the old man, "You can figure out how tall's the parking garage by how long it took the deer to fall. And it's because all these new goddamned roads."
"Mind your blaspheming, son."
After 9/11, I became a news addict and I sincerely appreciate the infographic's artistic effort. It shows a local map with the deer's movements marked along a dotted line. At 12:07 p.m., she was first spotted dodging cars in front of the Catholic school. Based on a video that has surfaced on YouTube, the same deer was spotted in the Goosetown neighborhood two

hours later. Yelling jagoffs taunt the deer in their yard and one shoots her with a green paintball. The boys hoot and howl. The deer looks sick and skittish and rears against them as the video cuts to black. Police and DNR are said to be investigating. At 3:15 p.m., police arrived at the Student Union and cornered the deer in the adjacent park, which she escaped by leaping the fence. She ran up the hill and was next seen in the Ped Mall. She attempted to enter a ladies' boutique and a few minutes later leapt at another window. Police requested Fire to close the roads. At 3:25 p.m., she was seen bolting toward the parking garage with officers clapping behind her.

"The deer don't have anywhere to go but to come the fuck downtown. Everywhere we goddamn go is downtown anymore."

"I says mind your blaspheming."

To pin the infographic to the bulletin board, I've had to remove another official notice: YOUR A CAB DRIVER. HAVE A MAP AT ALL TIMES DUH! THX, *THE OWNERS*.

With his back to me, Jerry Nicodemus sits at the desk as if bent to an organ. At his left, two main phone lines plus ashtray and smokes. At his right, the radio and desk mic plus a sideline in reserve. His Levi's hang like drapes and nicotine has tarred his fingers orange, his eyes hardened as if from combat the glow of which has faded. Such is the veneer of Captain Jerry's three decades in the chair. He describes himself as 'ruggedly handsome' as if quoting somebody else. And though faith has elevated him to sobriety, it hasn't spared Jerry his health. Unwilling to trust his diagnoses of COPD and "the emph," he keeps smoking as if trying for cancer too.

He lets me smoke in the office and I draw a chair to his desk as the radio lets out a squelch then a long burst of static. Through the chopped signals, I can hear the greenhorn and Leon stomping on each other's traffic. Jerry says the radios have been this way all night.

"Been this way two years," I put in. "Thx the Owners promised to have that shit fixed."

On the desk beside his smokes, Jerry has a tall Mason jar filled with what looks like volcanic ash. "That all from you smoking?"

"This here's the remains of old Tex Feely."

"Fucking gross. And it's about time that creep died."

"He been gone one year today."

Tex Feely had been a giant with pink arms sprouting down to hands fat as crab pincers. The kind of asshole that would pull the tie from your shoe and grin in your face. He'd also been a girl toucher and spent eighteen months at Atascadero before finding Jesus and changing his name and moving here. He'd been Jerry's final roommate and they shared a double-wide as they did a religion, and he died in hospice with his feet turning as rotten as Nature made him.

"We got this pact to have our ashes buried all together up in Oakland Cemetery. Me and Tex and Tex's wife, Shelly."

I point at the jar. "Is she in there too?"

"Naw. She's on the mantle at home. We wasn't too close."

The old man shivers at a thought and I push him on it. He says, "I just dislike the notion that my ashes might be kept on the shelf forever is all. A man's got to be buried when he's dead."

Captain Jerry looks exhausted in his chair, the fight seeped of him like a slow leak in a tire. He leans on the desk, cigarette hand on his knee and the other wrapped around the Mason jar like he's about to take a big gulp.

He asks me: "You been kind to our friend Billy?"

"He's dented but we get on all right."

Tonight I've discovered another dent on Billy Kinross.

He'll check on the radio that he's stepping out at D-5 to fuel, or Kum & Go, wherever like that. I've gone by those places but haven't seen a cab out front. Didn't think much at first. But he's one of those cats that will step out 15 or 20 minutes at a stretch. Tonight, I found his taxi parked half a mile away in the student ghetto. The neighborhood is perforated with joined lots and driveways reaching to the alleys. I sharked around and soon enough spied a red Jeep draw up behind the empty cab. Billy hustled out carrying a black book bag that he dumped in the trunk of his taxi. Then he climbed inside the taxi and fired her up. Her emerald bubble light shone plain and true.

I waited for him to clear the end of the block then I crept behind the Wrangler and parked the cab. He'd left the doors unlatched and I peeped inside with my Maglite. Nothing in back. Nothing squeezed under the seats. No evidence in the ashtray or tucked in the visors. The Jeep was empty save for a Gideon's Bible stuffed in the glove box, which must be Billy's idea of a joke. Or maybe he lives in his Jeep.

Jerry Nicodemus taps his chest and implores me. "Billy had it rough but he means well in his heart."

"I think Billy's a bad dude."

The old man throws his eyebrows and brings his voice down. "Did he talk about prison?"

"A bit. He got on about other shit too."

Jerry doesn't want to hear any of it.

A taxi peels into the parking yard. And speak of the devil. I can tell it's Billy by the way he drives. He comes in the office to shake Jerry's paw and to give me a two-lump hug.

"What're we all talking about?"

"Fucking gypsies," I reply. "What else!"

Billy looks at Captain Jerry and they both look at me, confused. Jerry blows my cover, asks, "What gypsies?"

"The gypsy cabs," I rail back. "The dirty bitches. The guys sipping cash out of our wallets. Ten years ago there was a quarter of the cabs than are on the road today."

Billy replies, "Somebody should've slashed their tires when they showed up."

"It didn't work for Mohamet," says Jerry.

"Who's Mohamet?"

"He's the prick driver of UniCab #15," I fill in the details. "He sugared four of our tanks and a bunch at every other company except UniCab."

"How you know it was him?"

"I saw him come out of our yard throwing empty sugar boxes in the road and Wayne Linder watched him get on two cars at Capital Cab."

"Y'all probably called the cops."

"They didn't lift any prints off the boxes. So it was our word against his."

"And nobody kicked his ass? I might knife a son of a bitch doing that. That's livelihood he's taking from us all."

"Amen," Jerry and I say in chorus.

The phone rings twice and Jerry takes the calls. Me and Billy step outside to smoke.

Billy asks, "You know where this dude stay?"

"Sure I do."

He points at the Gerber tool on my belt. "That thing got a knife on it?"

"Sure it does."

"Then I think we ought to go over there and find his cab."

"We're at work, Billy."

He yells back into the office, asks the old man if we're clear to handle a special mission.

"Ain't a damn thing going on," Jerry hollers back. "Don't do nothing I wouldn't do."

THIS IS NO job for a company car so we sneak the 'Yota from the yard on its bum wheel.

"Did you hear about this deer jumped off the parking garage? I saw that shit."

"You hear I run over a squirrel? I did that shit but I ain't bragging. And I think you're car's been drinking, bubba. That front wheel's bobbing like a mug."

We don't talk after that.

Ten minutes later, we turn off the westside boulevard into a complex of two-stories. They stand along a flowing drive that runs up the hillcrest and back down in a loop. The university built them for athletes but students quit renting when it opened to Section 8.

I push us lumping around the loop until I see the purple and cream UniCab parked in the rows like an ice cream cone among the regular cars.

Billy asks, "You sure that's his van?"

"The rear's marked #15 like I said."

"Then douse them headlights and give me that knife."

I hand him the Gerber tool. Billy snaps it open and bends out its blade.

My lousy brakes wince and I blush. This is the wrong vehicle for any operation and I needlessly remark that I need to get the brakes fixed.

"This bitch needs junked." Now he's sharpening his eyes on me. "So maybe you want to do this thing, bubba. Since you hadn't taken the chance before."

Billy stares at me as I consider the dare he's slipped in like a pork rider on a farm bill. Then my hand slides the gearshift to park.

"Give me the knife."

He curses the brash domelight when I open the door and I'm fast to press it closed. Coming around the back of the 'Yota, I give a look.

Nobody around.

Crouching at the rear of the UniCab van, I stab the passenger side tire and twist my knife, letting air rush over my hand. It feels cool and smells like rubber.

Then I creep forward and stab the front tire. I twist out the knife and let the air rush over my hand. It's kind of relaxing.

Billy has gotten behind the wheel and eases off the brakes, grinding ahead to meet me on the other side of the van.

I'm coming around the front of the taxi when its driver unexpectedly climbs out.

"Ay! What you do on my taxi?"

Scrambling back the way I've come, I jump into the 'Yota's rear. The car hasn't any spunk yet Billy gets us out of the lot fast, popping on headlights as we bang over the curb, wobbling dangerous and barely making the curve of the road.

"Shimmy-she-wobble, you feel that? Junk this bitch."

Looking out the back window, I see the dude chasing us across the parking lot. My heart thumps like a drum and I fold my knife so I don't stab myself with it.

"Fucking Christ of God." I straddle the armrest and climb in front. "I was just about to get on that tire when he popped out. What the fuck was that guy doing there?"

Billy wheels hard through a wide turn and that's the last I see of the dude. He's chased us all the way to the boulevard.

"So," says Billy. "That was the pirate that sugared our tanks."

"Hell no." I feel like I've been punched in the gut. "That was some Turkish dude. Right taxi, wrong guy."

"Wrong guy, right company," Billy laughs like hell. "If you lie down with dogs, bubba, you're going to get up with fleas."

4

MY NEXT NIGHT off, I bike out to the taxi shack and find everybody freaking the fuck out. Paulie Floyd's in the parking yard smoking grass and he's got three cigarettes burning, two wedged in the downspout outside the office door. Our greenhorn, #12, also wears the long face like he's going to bust out crying.

"Fuck's matter with you two cows?"

"Leon got robbed," says Paulie.

I point at the greenhorn. "So what's wrong with him?"

"I almost got robbed," he says. "But then I screwed up and Leon took the call instead."

"I'm confused," I tell Paulie. "So did Leon get robbed?"

"Yes," he says, "Apparently."

We all know the trouble with Leon Bath.

Leon swears he and the old lady have kicked the dope but life's too long for his short lies. He brings in the low book most nights yet high-flags and cheats his tripsheets. Then he and his old lady shoot it all, even with a bunch of kids at home.

"So did Leon really get robbed?"

I don't feel so bad saying it when I see in Paulie's face that he's wondering the same.

"What do you mean?" The rookie's eyes boil with tears. "What do you mean?"

Paulie hustles back to his desk to chase a ringing phone and I give #12 a cigarette.

"What's your name—Corey?"

"Colby, sir."

"What's your play in all this?"

The rookie reports he was dispatched to the southside mall and that the guy was acting funny. The fare had him run across the river to a westside crib then to an apartment block up north then back to the southside.

"So how was he acting funny?"

"This whole time the guy's laughing and talking shit about me and pretending to be on the phone but he wasn't. I even saw his phone was shut off but he went on talking in it."

"Then what?"

"He made me go through the taco drive-thru and order a ton of food and then made me check the receipt before we could leave and he wasn't happy so he dug in the bags looking for what's wrong and finally they gave him the free stuff he kept asking for and we rolled across the street to those apartments."

"The Coronets."

"Whatever they are."

"Learn the names of things, it helps. What'd he look like?"

"The guy? He was just some black dude."

"Other black dudes disagree. Was he light-skinned or dark? What was his hair like?"

"He wore a hat and hoodie so I couldn't really tell."

"So what happened after the tacos?"

#12 presses wearily on. "He said he needed to run inside to get money for the fare. But I told him if he needed to do that then he needed to leave his food in the cab."

Kudos to the rookie. Always hold collateral whenever a fare leaves the cab. Take shoes or a jacket. Take their child. Even if they come back unable to pay, folks will almost always come back for a kid.

"What'd he do when you asked for collateral?"

"He got in my face and was yelling. Then he got out of the

cab and took his food and these neighborhood kids started rocking the cab so I left. I was so mad I came right down here to tell Mister Floyd about it."

"I've never heard Paulie called "Mister Floyd.""

"So then how did Leon fall in the jackpot? And for the love of fuck, don't call him 'Mister Bath.'"

"After I left, the guy called back and said he owed me money. Mister Floyd told me this over the radio but he also was giving another address and I mixed it up. I should've known better because that address was on the other side of town. But I drove there anyway and just when I'm pulling up I see our other cab and Mister Floyd's on the radio asking where was I because the guy at the Coronets was calling back."

"So Paulie called you clear and instead sent Leon after the dude at the Coronets."

"How do you all know that?"

Paulie comes out of his office and asks if #12 is ready to go.

"I'll go wherever you need me, sir."

I tell him to knock that shit off and Paulie sends him out to Hy-Vee East on a grocery run. The three of us hold-to a moment and catch a breath. They both look wrecked, each tasting his flavor of guilt. The greenhorn should've gotten robbed but didn't and Paulie put two drivers on the same bad call.

After #12 leaves the yard I ask again: "How do we know if Leon really got robbed?"

Paulie frowns. "He's talking to the cops so let's hope he did."

WE ALL WAIT for Leon Bath to show but Dr. Bob arrives first. He's curious to hear what's gone down.

"Me and the rook pulled up to the same address. I knew he was supposed to be at the Coronets so I just waved, 'Hi, little buddy!'"

Dr. Bob then announces he's knocking off for a nap and to wake him up should anything interesting happen.

Next the greenhorn returns and blows out of his taxi.

"Now what?"

"This guy messed with Mister Bath and now I want to go mess him up."

I tell the greenhorn it's a rough night and offer him another cigarette. "Hey, Dr. Bob. Wake up and tell him the one about the helicopter."

Dr. Bob, wearing his sunglasses for the moonlight, is stretched across the hood of his sedan like Moses reclining on Mount Nebo. "I'd met the Greyhound at the bus depot but nobody wanted a ride. After it pulled out, I remained there waiting."

His voice falls silent until we creep nearer. He remains reclined and only moves his hands to tell his story.

"Two sports suddenly hop in back. This Latino dude and a white boy freaking that they missed their bus. I'd seen them come off the bus and slip around back of the depot. Figuring they were doping, I hadn't any sympathy for their plight.

"Except the Latino threw cash at me so we chased their bus east toward Davenport – the city thereof, not our local road. When we didn't see their bus ahead, they insisted I drive faster. I told them getting pulled over wasn't going to help. So the Latino jabbed the back of my seat and white boy said, 'Pedal to the floor or he'll blow a hole in you, bitch. He's got a gun.'

"I wasn't convinced these fools had a gun but I wasn't going to ask to see it. I played along instead, picking up speed to placate my carjackers and moving erratic to gain the notice of fellow travelers. I hammered around trucks and tailgated. I flashed high beams and hit the horn. I squeezed onto the shoulder. Somebody was bound to phone me in.

"Fifteen minutes later we were already blowing through Walcott and finally passed a westbound state patrol car. If the trooper clocked me or had any other indication of my bad driving, they'd be flipping around. I didn't announce the cruiser but reminded the boys that state patrol would stop us sooner or later. This news caused them to argue. They'd screwed up bad and were looking at losing pinkies, or worse.

"I kept driving and my hope the cops would stop us was going unmet. In fact as we came to the Davenport exits I saw no vehicles to either side of the interstate.

"Then in the rearview I spied a patrol car rushing up behind us. The cruiser posted on my bumper. Then we passed a second patrol car and it pulled out to join the first. No cherries yet but I brought my foot off the pedal and told the boys we were getting pinched. If I was going to get shot, I figured this was it. Instead, they reduced to slapping each other mean as preschoolers.

"I saw a third cruiser up ahead, its trooper in the median deploying stop-sticks and now cherries burst in the rearview so I pulled right over. The interstate was quiet and I could hear the cops over the loudspeaker ordering me to exit the taxi. I got out hands up and walked backward like they wanted. This was when I heard the helicopter rounding overhead. The cops hadn't drawn their weapons but the helicopter was flattering.

"A trooper stuffed me in his cruiser to run my license and to hear my story. Then he got out to conference with his buddies searching the cab. He came back after a bit. 'The bus driver didn't like those two and radioed ahead. We stopped and searched the bus at Walcott and discovered contraband among their belongings.'

"The trooper then explained law enforcement would very much appreciate if I drove these boys to Davenport where they could be casually reunited with said belongings. Waving my license under my nose, he reminded me I could lose it all.

"We were close to the depot. Eight minutes at posted speeds. The trooper confirmed my riders in fact hadn't any weapons and they had already fronted me enough cash to cover the fare plus a tip. But I wasn't sure how my thugs would swallow our catch and release.

"Yet when I returned to the taxi they were giggly and didn't think it at all strange we were allowed to drive out of there. Even seeing the D-port cops parked at every light watching us along the route, the white boy merely said, 'They're really hawking to see if you drive right.'

"When I got to the station, the boys panicked that their bus wasn't there and I assured them it was right behind us. And it surely was."

Dr. Bob falls quiet and I blow smoke at the yellow lamps hanging along the garage. A whippoorwill cries and loops over the riverfront and the yonder fires of the hobo camp.

The rookie frowns dissatisfied, still needing to be told what happened. I jump at the chance to stick my fork in him. "Those guys were junkies and who gives a shit? The point is to out-do big with bigger. Out-bad bad with badder."

Whereas I tend to escalate, Dr. Bob brings it down and he's kinder with his parting comment.

"The point is I'd already been paid and had enough BS on the dime of those clowns. It was time to get back to work."

I FETCH BEER for me and Paulie and a regular party breaks out in the shack. Quiet Chuck comes down after clearing his call and we're joined by sleazy Joe Vega and Zina Schram. Dr. Bob sips herbal tea and smokes Paulie's grass. He lets his hair out of its ponytail and we all give him shit for his ladylike appearance. Even Zina rags on him.

I've also sent Billy a text that we're down here. He shows up on foot and out of the dark, always creeping. I can tell it's him by the throbbing blue glow of his electronic cigarette.

"What's the story, bitches?"

We're giving him the what's-what when Leon Bath's taxi rattles over the gravel into the yard. Leon used to weigh 300 pounds but the heroin and meth diet keeps him under two these days. His former self hangs around him loose as a bag.

He tumbles clumsy from the taxi. All of us want to know how he's doing but we make room like he's just had a heart attack on a beach.

"I'm all right, you guys."

Now that our boy's home safe, the party returns to the office where there isn't any real business save for the rookie bouncing after every $4 bullshit hop. Leon remains outside to smoke the cigarettes Paulie has left stuck in the downspout.

Billy eyeballs the tallboy in my hand.

"If we aim to do something about this, you best disco that."

"It's only my second."

"Dump it or stay on the bench," he says. "I don't give a shit."

Next he moves through the room like a cat and nobody else sees him slip out, not even watchful Quiet Chuck. Billy wants to have a tête-à-tête with Leon.

I follow him on the same idea but cut out through the garage to dump my beer in the trash. When I get outside I see Leon's eyes shine from crying and his hand quakes to lift the cig to his mouth. I might be a notorious unfeeling hard-ass but I pat the big man on his shoulder.

"Anybody smoke menthol?"

Hell no, nobody else does and he knows that. He settles for one of mine and sucks it deep like he might find menthol in there anyhow.

Billy says, "Tell me what he did."

Leon foots around like he could use a shot of dope. "Punk ass turned me into a driveway then stuck a gun in my ear. That's what he did. They're having kids rob us. That's what's going on."

"Whoa whoa whoa," says Billy, telling Leon to slow down and start over.

"I been using again, me and the old lady. It's like the devil, you guys. I've tried so hard—"

Billy smacks him in the chest. "Just tell me what the fuck."

"When I'm holding off or can't find crank or if I need a kick-up, I go to the Coronets and get a little white. I been going over there a bit now and those guys got to talking about their business. And they told me they're getting hit."

"Hit?"

"Somebody's been robbing them. And they told me they needed to rob somebody else. That this is how America works. They said, 'Hey you a cab driver. How much money you got on you?' I wasn't going to tell them. But they bought it out of me. And they told me they'd be sending shorties out to rob some cabs. And now they done it to me."

"Did you tell the cops any of this?"

Leon shakes his head and moans through the tears.

"Go home," Billy says. "Take a shower and get some rest."

"Get something to eat," I add. "And stay away from the dope."

We linger on the yard watching the fat man shuffle to the office until Billy says, "Let's go."

Once again, we sneak the 'Yota out of the yard and creep away beneath the yellow lamps through the industrial park. Leon may be a lost cause but we have to avenge this. Not for him but for all of us cab drivers. The robberies have to stop.

"This wobbledy-ass rig," Billy gripes. He points me onto the highway frontage. "My Jeep's parked down here."

I turn left and go where he says until I see the red Jeep.

"I've seen that red Jeep before."

"Lots of red Jeeps in this town."

"Nah. That's the same Wrangler."

Billy tosses me the keys and tells me the doors are open.

"Where to?"

"Your crib."

"So what's our plan?"

"We're still working on that."

I drive us north into town with Billy bitching all the way how I'm mashing his clutch when I'm not. "Seven years," he goes on, and I think he's talking about his car. "Where were you seven years ago today?"

He reminds me that it's 9/11.

"I was camping in the Black Hills, North Dakota," I tell him. "I woke up at noon and knew something was wrong because the sky was clear of any air traffic. You never see that out there."

"Not for a long time anyway," says Billy. "I was eating

breakfast with my sister at this outdoor café in Manhattan. I'd just gotten out of the pen and we hadn't talked in a long time. She got to yelling about how I am and I watched that first plane zoom right over her head."

I curse brightly and press him for details. But Billy feigns like he doesn't want to talk about it. Instead he wants to talk about how I'm mashing his clutch. And he's used 9/11 to distract me from my primary line of questioning. So I pounce.

"What you do in this Jeep?"

"What're you asking me?"

"You step out for 20 minutes at a time. But you're never parked where you say you're at. Because you're ripping around town in this red Jeep. You want to tell me about that?"

Billy runs a hand on his face and won't look at me. He points at the road. "Just let's get to your crib and I'll tell you my bit."

At the garage, Billy lifts the roll-up door. I back the Jeep inside and Billy chains the door shut. From the rear of the Jeep he removes a maroon bomber jacket, a folded plastic contraption, and the same black gear bag I saw him dump in the trunk of his taxi.

"What's in the bag?"

"I'm using this," he says as he takes over my workbench.

From inside the bag he pulls out a license plate which he replaces with the one on the Jeep. Billy shows how the registration sticker is stuck on a magnet which he pries from the old plate and plunks on the new.

"It's just like Leon said. These guys have been getting robbed. And I'm the one robbing them."

Billy lets that sink in.

"I now have a burning need to do something right about that. I am personally responsible, you feel me? And I could use your help."

My words come out dry and quiet.

"So what the fuck're we gonna do?"

"We're getting our shit back."

Billy yanks off his sweatshirt and unfolds the plastic

contraption which I now see is body armor. He straps it around his chest and zips the maroon bomber over the top. He takes black gloves from the gear bag then shows me a balaclava and a ski-mask.

I point at the ski-mask. "Go menacing."

He stuffs gloves and mask in his bomber pocket and tugs at the neck of his armor. Then he gives a big empty look like Zina called it.

"There's something else," he says. "I need a piece."

"No way."

"I'm a felon, bubba. I get caught with guns and that's a one-way to the pen."

"So how do you rob these dudes without a pistol?"

"I got a sling billy and a good sap. A knife if I have to. But I usually hit dudes one at a time. Could be a lot more tonight."

Incredible.

"Go ahead," I relent. "Make somebody's day."

Billy consults the Liberty Collection and lifts the shotgun off the mantle.

"I won't shoot nobody because I'm not even going to load it. This is worst case scenario, you feel me?"

"So what if you have to shoot somebody?"

Billy scoops a handful of buck shells into his jacket pockets. "It's just in case. And if I have to shoot, I'll make sure nobody's left breathing to sue you for letting me shoot them. All right? I've done this a whole lot and I ain't ever shot nobody when doing it."

"You got collared."

"I got collared because being in jail was better than being dead. Trust me on this."

TWO MINUTES LATER we're in the Jeep with the fake plates rolling up Hwy 6 across the southeast side. Now Billy feeds shells into the shotgun until its belly is full. "No way can I go in there unloaded. They could have ten dudes up in there."

"No shit."

I feel like I'm at work, managing a routine task that is at once odd and dangerous, stupid and unlawful.

All the drivers got robbed south of the highway where the city has congregated its poor folks black and white to gather apart in gloomy blocks reserved for Section-8 and prefabs with sagging porches. The streets need asphalt and the curbs need done. Billy points out a car blocked on smashed plastic crates which had served their purpose until the jacks were taken out. "Two months that car's been there."

We come up the back road past squat and joyless three-rise condos with big grassy plazas. The next driveway is long and winding and ties into parking bays outside the Coronet Apartments. Kids hang out in the lots on bikes and throw bones for dollars. Others holler that they're selling.

"You notice how nobody ever gets killed around here?"

"People get killed plenty enough."

"What I'm saying is that there's no gangland murders," says Billy. "There're no kids getting killed in our streets. Now look at all the cities around us and each one's got even a few. What's that tell you?"

"What do you want it to tell me?"

"This is Partytown U.S.A., bubba. Either these are the only cops in America capable of dealing with the drug trade. Or deals have been struck with some big bad wolves."

We roll out the Coronets and back past the condos. Billy's keyed up and stares out the window at the apartment blocks.

"You know the name Chemo Phipps?"

I let it ring in my ear. "Nope."

"You remember the dude during the flood high on PCP? Yelling 'Admiral Akbar!' and chopping on a cop car with a sword?"

"That kid with orange cornrows?" I'd read about this out in Colorado. It stuck out because I recognized the kid. "I've almost run that asshole down. He's fucking nuts."

"That asshole runs the show around here. Stay careful if

you see him."

We draw around the block to where the backside of the Coronets looms over the neighborhood like a dark crown.

"I need ten minutes." Billy reaches in the back and snatches a light wool blanket that he wraps around my shotgun. "Look at the clock. In ten minutes exactly, cruise up through the Coronets. Then go buy a pack of smokes at that corner store. I'll get at you less than five minutes after that. Then pick me up right back here. Easy as a cake."

Billy pries the cover off the domelight and yanks its bulb, putting it in the pocket of his bomber. "Slow up but don't stop."

Then he leaps out of the Jeep running, cuts between cars, disappears among the houses. The door swings shut as I drive off.

I cruise the neighborhood sweating and smoking my last two cigarettes. I've brought my Maglite along like a good luck charm and it rides under my left leg in its usual spot. Driving a soft 25, I pass a tenth of a mile every 18 seconds and 600 seconds at that rate is roughly a three-mile curlicue around the quarter. My D=RT is perfect and I turn into the Coronets driveway at exactly the ten minute mark.

The window's cracked an inch and I peer out. Wheeling on my flanks, kids stunt bike with the handlebars kicked forward and seats jacked high. One shouts if I'm looking.

I keep driving, both hands on the wheel.

Back on the public road I turn toward the highway and pull in the lot for the tobacco shack.

I park the Jeep and see a group has tailed me from across the road. I shove through the shop door as one shouts at me.

I keep moving forward and my eyes search for a weapon. Glass bottles. Sticker gun. The broom handle leaning on the coolers.

The glass door bangs open and orange-headed Chemo Phipps rides into the shop on a BMX trailed by two of his dudes. "What you doing up in here?"

"I'm buying smokes and PBR because I'm broke as fuck and it's cheap here. What're you doing in here?"

"That ain't why you here. Why I see you cruising like you

casing the spot? That's what it look to me, motherfucker."
  Chemo Phipps is pushy and sure of himself. And he's instinct is dead on.
  So I tell him like Leon Bath told me and Billy.
  "I'm fighting the devil."
  "What you mean by that?"
  It's all theater from here. Ten years of driving taxi and I'm addicted to scenes like this.
  "You know what I mean by that. Even this scared-ass lady behind the counter knows what I mean. That's why they're selling paper roses in decorative glass sleeves."
  The orange head twists up his mouth, says, "You had another dude with you."
  "He split," I fire back. "And why am I even talking to you?"
  I pull a twelver out of the cooler then go to the counter. I can see the lady's hands are trembling and then realize I know her. Meth has sucked the shape from her face but sure enough it's Bonnie Reding. She used to drive cab until an OWI wiped her out.
  I tell Bonnie: "It's gonna be all right."
  "No it ain't gonna be all right." Chemo throws his bike on the floor. "Do you know who I am?"
  Just then my phone chirps with a new text. Of course it can only be from Billy. My mouth tastes like salt.
  Chemo too has gotten a text. He looks at his phone and asks one of his dudes, "Why your sister getting at me with this?"
  A new message comes through and the orange head looks like he's been hit with a brick. "What the fuck!"
  Whipping up the bike by its handlebars, he rides out of the shop knees pumping high while his dudes hold the doors.
  I leave the beer at the counter and hustle for the Jeep. I can see Chemo's knees pumping hard under the lot lights. He's riding toward the Coronets. His whole entourage runs after him.
  Turning out of the parking lot, I shoot past the Coronets and then the condos.
  I get a second text and it reminds me to look at the first. Both are from Billy.

COME AHEAD EASY NO CRAZY TAXI.
The second says: HURRY UP.
I punch around both corners and hustle to our rendezvous, careening the Jeep around the potholes. Ahead I see Billy jog out of the tree shadows. He comes onto the road wearing the ski mask and bearing the shotgun, and seeing that makes me want to keep driving.

He leaps inside and yanks the mask off, throws it with his blanket in the rear. Sliding the shotgun to his feet, Billy holds up a pink school bag. His cheeks are red and he's puffing.

"Let's go," he says. "You won't believe what's in here."

5

WE RETURN TO Freedom Cove and Billy opens the roll-up door. I pull in and Billy chains the door shut. I leave off the factory overheads because they glow along the door bottoms.

I drop the pink school bag on the workbench and thumb on the trouble lamps. Billy slings off his bomber and the armor. Then he goes into a zippered pouch on his black bag to come out with a sleeve of blue surgical gloves. He takes out a pair and stretches them over his hands. "Suit up," he says.

Billy yawns open the bag and stacks its contents on the desk.

First out is a swap-meet survival knife with a compass in its butt. Then six cellphones, some banged up and taped, others brand new. Billy pulled the batteries as we drove and he piles these beside the phones. Next we have four handguns, three .9s and a revolver. I inspect the pistols, pulling clips and winding the revolver's loose cylinder. All the serials are filed off.

"Aw man you snatched a dude's nunchucks?"

I dip in the pink school bag to pick them out. That's when I spy the rubber-banded stack of cash among the cocaine. Both rock and powder parceled for sale.

"Lot of heroin too," says Billy, poking at the largest bundle.

He waves a hand over the loot. "I know a guy that'll take the guns and the other contraband. And I want the phones to comb through for evidence."

I lift the school bag and it weighs like a basket of Halloween candy. Freedom Cove may be a paradise of wanton liberty but I got to play within minimum guidelines to keep it that way.

"Take it all," I tell him. "I can't have this shit in here."

Billy plucks out the stack of cash and counts a hundred and fifty Ben Franklins. Both of us whistle and he says, "These dudes are dressed better than a bank teller."

He stuffs the cash in my gloved hands so I can hold it. The bills are stiff and the ink smells fresh. Not a filthy one in the stack.

"This isn't junkie cash. Where're the small bills?"

"They're drug dealers." He shrugs and takes back the cash. "Probably had it changed up because they think it looks dope. And don't it though?"

Billy fans our score in the glow of the trouble lights and lifts it under his nose.

I tell him: "We need to figure out what everybody's owed."

"So how's that break out?"

I count the victims on my fingers. "Cowboy and Fen over at Taxi Gold. Marty at Capitol, Habib or whatever over at UniCab, plus two other UniCabs that didn't report. And then Leon."

"How much they peel off Leon?"

"Leon says a buck-fifty but other drivers were around $80."

Billy pulls a laptop from his gear bag and wakes it. Meanwhile, peeping in his bag, I find it full of tricks. Flashlights, zip ties, Ziplocs, lock picks, tools. I take out a headset and night vision goggles but can't figure the dovetail clamp.

"Are these for fucking real NVGs?"

"Come look at this."

He digs into a desktop folder where he's stored four police reports. Cycling through them, he checks the amounts each cab driver reported stolen. Cowboy lost $150, plus tips; Marty at Capitol lost $180, plus tips; Habib Marwan at UniCab was taken for $200, plus tips; Wong Fen for $725 and tips.

Billy thumbs bills out of the stack into separate counts and decides to call $200 for everybody but Fen who gets $800. "We still have to figure what to give Leon."

I ask, "Where'd you get those cop reports?"

"You pay for wi-fi here?"

"I pillage the neighbor's broadcast."

"Good deal."

Billy brings up a notepad file and the police department's public website. Then he pastes a string of code into the address bar which takes him to a login. From the same notepad file, he pastes the name and password into the login field.

Next, we arrive to the live police database.

"You're in the cop servers?"

"This is a regular fishing hole," he says. "Too early yet for Leon's report to be swimming here. Let's give him a hundred."

I eyeball the counts of cash and the remaining fat stack. "What about the other UniCab dudes that didn't report?"

Billy nods and lets out a wry grin. "Wouldn't it be a bitch if it's that Turk with the flat tires?"

He rocks on his feet, a man relishing a mess he's made. And I delight to pop his bubble.

"We've got to pay that dude for his tires. I'll walk it to him if I have to."

"I hear that."

"And a little scrub for punking him too."

"Aye." Billy throws down five bills. "Why the fuck not?"

We sit on the ugly couch. I bounce a knee and tie my arms in knots while Billy puffs his electric hash pipe and yanks SIM cards from the cellphones. He puts the cards in mini-Ziplocs and markers each with a number.

"I waited those ten minutes watching their stash house," he tells me. "It's in the back, three floors up. And exactly when you made your pass through the lot, I dropped that ski mask over my chin and came out of the trees. I watched you roll through and the kids following on bikes. Nobody saw me cross the back lot. And nobody saw me going up those stairs.

"There was a guard on the landing but dude was watching the kids follow you. I threw that blanket over his head and butted him down with the shotgun. I took one pistol off him and two phones. Then I zipped his hands out front and took his belt off, right? I ran the tongue in the buckle and made a loop what I hugged around old boy's neck. Then I knocked out the overhead light and stood him to his feet and we rapped on the stash house door.

"I got inside pushing through with that guard on my leash and the shotgun pressed to his neck. That got everybody's attention. I had them bring it in the kitchen. Five altogether with the guard. One of the other dude's was orange-head Chemo's older brother, Damen Phipps. You know him?"

I shake my head.

"It was funny, bubba. He's kite-high and got his shirt off about to fuck this white bitch lying on the couch. Did I mention the white bitch? She was a weird deal, yo."

He puffs on his electric pipe.

"These dudes is mostly some punk ass kids and she's more like our age. And a junky too. I seen her around. She got spry and dangerous eyes."

"Sounds like a dozen women I know."

He lifts the bills under his nose again. "Girl kept peeping me while I'm working."

Billy says he made them give up the guns, the knife and nunchuks, and their other phones. He also threw in a handful of plastic ties and ordered they zip each other up, hands out front. The guard didn't know where the drugs were hidden so Billy dropped the belt over Damen's head and forced him into the bedroom where the stash was kept. Billy made him put the loot in the pink school bag then shoved him back to the kitchen and had him tie in with the others.

Then he left the apartment.

"I was getting out at just the right time too because shoes were pounding up the stairs with loud talking. I had to go over the railing and hang between the floors until they came up and when they did I swung onto the landing below and ran down the stairs and was out."

Billy's face glows darkly. "And I've changed my mind, bubba. We're going to dump the drugs."

"In the river? I thought you knew a dude."

"But what if I didn't want these drugs to be sold? What if I'm playing the same move from a different angle?"

"I don't understand."

We wear fresh gloves and breathers as we scissor the bindles and tap the junk out over the drain. Among the packaged drugs Billy also finds a sack of cocaine bigger than a baby fist. He offers me a sniff but powders aren't my thing.

"Lots of money to be feeding to the fish," he groans.

"How much you think all this is? Like, what percentage?"

He weighs the block of coke in his hand. "Less than a half a key." Then he slits the bag with the scissors and powders it over the drain. "I don't know about supply percentages or what not."

"What about the heroin?"

I mean the big brick sealed in thick brown plastic with garish party colors pressed in the seam.

"The coke and the little shit," he shrugs. "Somebody'll be mad. But a kilogram of wherever this came from might push folks into a killing mood. Might be wise to stow this just in case."

"If you know what you're doing," I tell him.

Then I crank the hose of my makeshift shower and we watch the powder mountain sift and crumble and swirl through the drain. I expect to feel immediately better, and don't.

BILLY DRIVES US over the civil war bridge and parks where we can reach the riverside. We march down through the brush until the highway lights shine above us.

We hurl the phones and batteries in the water. Same for the Rambo knife and nunchucks. Billy has stripped the guns and throws them in too figuring they aren't worth their price to shift.

Downtown we find Cowboy parked by the hotel and give

him two bills. We find Marty in the Groove and give him two more. They take the money and ask where it comes from. Billy says we've collected donations.

Habib at UniCab is parked by the West Bank. We give him $600 and tell him to divide it with his fellow drivers that didn't report. Billy warns that he'll find out if the money isn't shared right. "I'll take it all back and break your fingers."

Habib shakes hands profusely and thanks us, assuring the money will be shared. He's the only one to swear nobody will talk.

We give eight bills to Wong Fen at the gas pumps and he stuffs the cash in his shirt. "Thanks, I guess."

Wong Fen looks like his name but his voice sounds like Oklahoma City where he's from. He's always been a jerk.

"Have a good night, Fen."

"Yeah, I'm going to try."

Finally we cruise until I see the purple and white UniCab #15 and I tell Billy to let me out.

I meet the driver at the window and he shoots before I get a word in. "Where you going?"

"Hey man, you don't know me. But something fucked up happened to your tires. Your vehicle was mistaken for somebody else's. Somebody had bad information."

"What information?"

"Bad information," I tell him. "My friends want to pay you back for the tires and there's a gratuity for your understanding."

The driver freaks and threatens to call the cops. "And how about I call my lawyer then and I tell him your name?"

"They went after the wrong guy and they're sorry."

"Or how bout I send my boy over to stab out your tires?"

"Then I'll break his hands with a tire iron."

I hold up the bills and the Turk snatches it out of my fingers. Like Wong Fen, he stuffs the cash in his shirt. "You bitches is not seen the rest of me."

His taxi burps away from the curb, cutting off traffic and causing horns to blow.

* * *

BILLY COUNTS OUR cut in the parking lot at D-5. I scan around to watch for anybody creeping on us.
"You got change for a hundred?"
We both laugh, hearing that as often as we do. And we've both got the change once the wallets come out. He thumbs out 50 bills and gives me $40 more. I count it all twice once I get it in hand. $5,040. I do the math in my head and figure it at 40 percent. Same cut offered by the taxi shack.
"You unhappy about your cut?"
"You're the one doing the G.I. Joe shit."
"Then what is it?"
I want to tell Billy it's like a hand tugging on me from behind. Yet I can't name what it is. Part of me feels good about what we've done. Like knights slaying dragons, or some other bullshit. But I've crossed a line, personally. I can feel it like a magnetic tug. I don't think Billy has any moral compass so I just stare back into the abyss of his eyes.
"You can give it to me if'n you want. But you're my partner in this and I prefer we split the take. That all right with you?"
I try jamming the stack in my billfold then settle for stuffing the wad in my jeans and finally I tell him, "All right."

NEXT TWO MORNINGS I wake up chilled and aching like I'm coming down with Shanghai Flu. And consulting the mantle of firearms, I notice Billy hasn't returned my shotgun.
In my dreams, dozens of men played chance around a massive table on a ship, or in a windowless building with tilting rooms. The players wagered heaps in the pot and the game grew so elaborate that when the floor tilted the heaps of coin slid to one edge of the table then another and the men seated at those places were able to keep whatever chips they caught while

the chips that weren't caught got snatched by other men crawling on the barroom floor, always hoping for a place at the table but only ever returning the chips so that play might continue.

I let the shower run cold to wake me out of that.

After I dress and go outside, I see the 'Yota parked on the apron and it reminds me about the bike.

Last night I left my reclaimed Trek parked against the 'Yota while I swept off the garage floor. I pulled the big door down to puff a little weed while I did my chores so I didn't see who took the bike but it's rolled off. I should've left the keys in the 'Yota.

Friday night in Partytown is likewise a raw deal.

"I know drivers who'd totally give me a discount for showing him these."

"The fare is seven bucks. Cough it up."

Says she to her gal pal: "I'm showing my tits and he won't give us a break?"

Time for an extra-strength application of the #22. "You want to pay with your mams? Then lop one off and pass it on up cuz my stomach's growling."

"O.M.G.," clucks the gal pal and the other snaps bra over breasts like snatching two bucks back from a thief. She glares at me in the rearview. "You're a asshole!"

Our football team's won and there's a raunchy fête at one of the clubs. Ladies too young wander the streets looking as if they've emerged from a boudoir. Wolf packs of skinny bitches high on cocaine. Meanwhile, some UFC fight is broadcast at Buffalo Wild Wings. From corner to corner ginned-up boys slug it out and drool at coeds peeled of their outerwear.

Grinding away from the Sheraton, I see a happy couple making out on the corner. They stumble into the road forcing me to a sliding halt. Like it's all part of the show, dude lifts her butt onto my hood and they go on mashing face. Blasting my horn gets their attention and the young lady swings a lazy arm overhead. "Hey taxi!"

They climb in and he tells me they're going to the Sevilles.

"Take a right right here."

"I know where the Sevilles are at so keep your shirt on. And hers too."

I bang over the curb making the turn.

"Touch this," I hear her say to him, and then to me she says, "Touch this."

We're stopped at a red light so I take a look. A gleaming and enormous white breast has been rested on the shoulder of my seat.

"This ride is cash only."

"Feel it. It's totally fake. Both of them. Feel my fake titty."

I take the moral risk in the name of science. "Feels real. But the ride's cash only."

"You're a asshole!"

I drop them at the Sevilles and dude ponies up the fare as the girl reminds him to tip me, remarkably.

"Here's a tip," he says. "Eat these."

Dude passes me a dime bag that I hold to the domelight. Two plain white pills.

"Where'd you get these?"

"Just eat up. Alice-style, nigga-bruh."

On that note, I recall the young lady to my window. She wobbles over and I give her a card with my cell number on it. "In case things get hinky in there."

She's all laughs and charm, drunk and blushless.

"Things're getting hinky, all right. He's going to fuck me in the butt!"

I SHOULD HAVE caught it by the death stare and green breath. I should have heard it in his throat. I do, however, see the arms wheel in my rearview and my foot comes off the gas. Jamming the brakes soft as I can stomp, I drift to curbside as he brings it up for a vote, slapping his hand over mouth to fire auxiliary gouts from out of his nostrils.

I throw on the lights and have a look. Save for a bench shot, dude seems to have kept most of it on himself. I even pay him a compliment. "I thought you might've blown full out."

Next he bends and sends everything from asshole forward roaring onto the carpet in three good heaves, what on later inspection proves to be a muddle of dark beer happy hour nachos two kinds of red sauce white liquor hot wings bite-shaped bits of dough and margarita mix all of which he has fanned onto the back of the passenger seat and into the door pocket and over the window crank as I'm hollering, "Fucking take it outside the cab."

His girl laughs like she doesn't know much else. She yells out to where he's tumbled in the grass. "Negative chug, whisky-dick!"

I want to ask what she finds so funny. Instead, I grunt, "That's a lousy way to spend a hundred bucks."

"It's a hundred dollars to puke in here? Nuh-uh!"

"Uh-huh—it's right there on my rate sheet."

"Right there on the where? What's on a rate sheet?"

I pluck the rate sheet off the dash. "See under BODILY FLUIDS? It's a hundred bucks to hork in the cab. Two hundred if you hork on me."

"I did not *hork* on you."

"That I am not disputing, ma'am. But likewise you cannot dispute that your companion has horked in the taxicab."

"And that's a hundred bucks," we say together like a refrain.

Her dude flops against the window like a zombie. Next he bumbles the door open and falls against the girl whose eyes are burning at me like coal cinders.

I ask him: "You all cleaned out, dude?"

She says, "You're a asshole."

"Sing it to the beef whistler, honey. I need a hundred bucks or we're not moving."

"I'm not *talking* to you," she snaps, still pushing her eyes on me. "I'm talking to *you*." She slugs her man. "This is a hundred bucks and you have to pay him right now!"

Shoved over to have his wallet extracted, he lets rip a great fart and causes himself to laugh. The woman sighs exaggeratedly and climbs over the seat to get up front with me. She hands me his credit card and returns to railing on the dude. "Three hours ago I told you to quit drinking. Tonight was a date."

We get to his place and I run his card for the meter plus a hundred, plus a few bucks more to take the girl her separate way. We leave him in the street hollering fuck yous but not before I tell him to throw out his clothes.

Next stop, I pound over the curb rolling into girl's driveway and immediately gear into R, ready to back out and haul ass for the car wash. My cab stinks of rotten ginko and cheese and liquor, and my jaw hurts from mouth-breathing. I want to shower and brush my teeth.

But the girl's looking at me with intense eyes. "So how much do you charge for other bodily fluids?"

I'm obtuse with chicks so I ask her to spell it out.

"I'm getting laid one way or another," she says. "You could plug in if you want."

I look at the young woman and tell her, "One time I had a guy's colostomy bag burst right where you're sitting. It burst like a dam. Washed over the entire surface of the seat."

She slams the door with terrific force and yells at the sky. "Why are all guys such assholes!"

ANOTHER HOUR LATER I've shampooed and vacuumed my cab in time for bar rush. I hit up D-5 for fresh smokes and find Billy fueling at the pumps.

"You look all crapped out. Was your puker that bad?"

"It's that money," I tell him.

Billy shrugs. "I told you I'd take it if you don't want it."

"It's not that."

Talking about the money puts pressure on my chest and swells my eyes. The money's been burning a hole in my gut.

"You think it's dirty? That it's not yours or that it belongs in some other fool's purse? That you didn't earn it right and proper like? Do you even know who we robbed?"

"Just some drug dealers."

"The Phipps Bros. That's *Bros*, not *Brothers*, and this due to their previous affiliation with the Chi Fam."

"What's the shy fam?"

"Chi as in Chicago. Fam like Family. The Phipps Bros for a long time got supplied by the Chi Fam. Their mother, Levelva Phipps, used to courier dope out of Chicago until she got nabbed with three keys crack-cocaine in her trunk."

"How do you know all that?"

Billy shows me each of his hands. "I follow the news and play in the fields, fool."

Levelva's name sounds familiar once I sound it out in my mouth. If I recall, the drugs were wrapped in Christmas paper tagged FOR MOM. Her lawyer claimed the drugs obviously belonged to one of her children.

"What kind of mother throws her kids under the bus?"

"Same kind that sets them up to push drugs I'd guess. And there you go feeling sorry again. We hit them because they hit us. So don't feel nothing for those dudes."

Billy softens on me, drops his head the other way. "I see this hurting you, bubba. Let me think what we can do on that."

"Sure, *bubba*. You do that."

I roar out of the parking lane and bounce the curb on my exit at the same time I crush my cigarette against the unopened window trying to throw it out. "Fuck!"

I want to feel anything other than what I feel right now. And by this point I'm willing to find out what the little white pills do. They disappear as suggested, Alice-style.

"22–CATFISH–OTEL."

Rough night of raw deals and the radios are shit. After grabbing him out of the Sheraton, he asks for the Coronets and my guts lock up.

But then he wants to hit the club for a night cap and

laughs all the way about some young thug-ass bitches getting hit for all their drugs and money.

"You all right, silky?"

"Just real sleepy I guess. I had to take a pill for my back."

"All right, bro. Here's some money and you be safe."

He gives me $5 on a $4.75 fare.

A while later I find myself parked in an uptown driveway that I do not know. Why am I here? Did I drop somebody off? My cellphone sounds like it's underwater. It rings and stops, rings and stops three or four times before I pick up the radio mic and say, "Hullo?"

But that's not my phone. So I flip the phone open and lift it to my ear and now the radio cracks, "WHO CHECKED?"

The voice on the phone sounds like a record played slow. It's a bawling woman and I've given her my personal number, apparently. But I never do that. This must be serious.

I straighten in my seat and wide my eyes.

I can't hear much with her crying though I make out the Sevilles so I loop over there. Every turn is monumental and I keep on task by chanting *Seville Seville Seville*....Streetlights burn soft and time creeps with the taxi.

Then I am in a different part of town.

Seville Apartments.

What am I doing here?

I see a girl crying on the curb. Ah! This is the girl with the fakes. And it's her boyfriend who gave me the little white pills. But what's with the tears?

"Did you and your beau get into it?"

"He's not my beau. My beau's downtown!"

She cries like a spring storm and I drive ahead. The roadway sways and streetlights buzz.

I ask, "What was in those pills?"

She has no idea about any pills.

"I shouldn't have done it," she says. "He's going to kill me. They're best friends!"

"Been there, done that. Nobody killed anybody."

"These are his! He paid for them! We haven't been married a whole year!"
In the rearview I see her clutching hands over her chest. I don't know who paid for what but I feel awful. And I don't know why but I'm crying too.
In the rearview, I also see her smelling her hand.
"Oh my God and I'm sitting in puke!"
The girl shrieks like an elephant squeezed in a clamp truck and my hands turn the cauliflower wheel as we bawl together and the road beneath us feels made of glass the light fantastic and shining air bright as gongs shimmer between my ears.

ZINA SCHRAM SAYS I look like hell and that I still have the glint. So I explain how I roofied myself.
"I have no idea how my shift ended but I woke in my bunk wearing clothes and purse. My taxi was tucked in the garage bay. I'm lucky I got home alive and with any cash at all. If a son bitch slipped one of those in my drink, I'd want to cut the bastard's throat as he took his last sip of whiskey."
I'm splurging on us at Oyama, ordering edamame and hot sakes, a Dragon Roll, two Spicy Tunas, Black Sea Bass, and weird Ika.
"You on drugs? Besides weed and alcohol, I mean."
"Those aren't drugs."
Zina throws an eyebrow. I shrug it off and she keeps zeroing in on a problem.
"Billy seems like a druggie."
"'Druggie,' as a term, is *trés passé*."
I want her to laugh but Zina pouts. She excuses herself for the restroom and I watch her go. She looks back at me before disappearing behind the door.
My pocket buzzes and I find a text from Billy. BET $2

CASINO WILL FIX U. I pocket the phone and make a plan of drinking tonight until I can't remember anything. I wonder if I can find any more of those pills. There's a nurse I could call.

When Zina returns to the table, I'm already handing cash to our server and ready for the door.

She invites me over to her place. "Let's get high and watch *Practical Magic.*"

She looks at me with warm eyes but all I can see is the puker's date asking if I want to plug in. I tell her I need to go home.

I SEND BILLY a text as soon as Zina drops me off. A torrent of rain drums on the garage roof. They keep saying the river won't flood again this year.

Billy calls right back.

"I'm outside," he says creepily enough.

I tell him I'm taking a dump and need a few. Instead I sit on the couch watching rain fall through the hole I've cut for a chimney. I remove the cash from hiding in my tool chest and count my take onto the yard table as the rain drums overhead.

The roar of it stays with me as we blast through country dark, drinking, smoking electric hash, Billy driving, me howling. And when we get to the casino I hear the roar of rain over the song and chatter of the slots. Every machine brightly boasts twenty ways to win when all I want is to lose.

Billy's plan is simple. I'll buy us steaks and lobster. I'll get us drunk on top shelf scotch. I'll tip the shit out of everybody and we'll play the tables until I've blown my cut of the score.

"It's like puking, bubba. You'll feel better to be rid of it."

Dinner lasts three hours and costs $700. I touch none of my plates and drink scotch as prescribed. I blow the remainder in 20 minutes on craps.

"Snake eyes!"

I thought he was right. I thought I'd feel better once the money was gone. But I don't. I even yell at the lobby guards. "Fucking dumb busted. But we're too drunk to leave now!" Billy tells them: "I'm getting us a taxi."

Then he guides me outside where the rain crashes down and drowns out my hollering.

//

TOURS OF THE OUTER DARK

6

TEXAS IS WHERE our storms are born. When they sprawl furious, you can smell seawater blown here from the Gulf. Roughly 850 air-miles. People don't believe a storm could carry seawater so far but the smell of salt and oil and dead fish is unmistakable. I've rolled late out of bed to consider this as I lump in the 'Yota toward thunderheads all the way to the shack.

Paulie Floyd is scheduled to dispatch but I see him on the garage roof fiddling with our radio antenna, which looks dramatic against the boiling clouds and flares of lightning. He hollers down at me, "I know why the radio's fucked, yo."

"The lightning's fucked, yo. Get off that roof."

Paulie is our little shit geek of a brother. After driving out his license, he resigned to become a dispatcher and has gone on to build our website and repair vehicles, clean the office and toilet, handle scheduling and payroll distro. He's in charge of hiring/firing, posting the notes from Thx the Owners, and still he hasn't a desk that he doesn't share. Unless he buys a cab shack, Paulie has climbed as high as his career will go.

Thunder shudders out of the southlands and he monkeys with the antenna.

"Bad news," he shouts. "Wayne Linder's got your cab."

"What's wrong with Wayne's van?"

"Alternator crapped out."

Like their drivers, each taxicab is enumerated and comes with its special perks and quirks. My cab #90 is a '99 Crown Vic police package with a badly placed fuel tank prone to explode in rear-end collisions. But she takes off at chase speeds and steers nimble. I hide the extra keys from a wire nail under the dispatch desk and realize Paulie must've sold me out.

Three taxis are left in the yard and none worth the tires keeping them off the ground.

"So what am I driving?"

"Don't worry. I had Wayne pick up a new alternator but—"

Cue the thunder as more antenna busts loose. Paulie lifts the bundle of copper yarn at the sky and shouts a blue streak like he really wants his ticket punched.

"So then where's this alternator at? I'll put it in myself."

"It's up here with me."

It takes a moment to grasp but I've heard him right.

"Is Wayne's van up there too?"

Paulie wants to explain as the rain blows down in silver dollars. I hustle for the garage and find Wayne's van in the bay, hood up. The garage stinks like an electrical fire. I open the big door to air the room and fire up a cigarette under the NO SMOKING sign.

Business has run thin all season with too many taxis on the road. We drivers blame the gypsy cabs because that's who we find camped in our spots. But Thx the Owners can't blame gypsies to the out-of-house mechanic with whom they've run up a four-month tab. It would be cheaper, of course, to have an in-house mechanic. We drivers have instead been told that the money for paying off the bill is waiting to be collected from the street so let's get to it. If any taxis blow up this week, we have to fix them ourselves. And this is exactly why I'm pissed. Wayne swapped into my cab after his died, and that's acceptable. But why'd he bother picking up a replacement part and leaving the repair to somebody else?

Here comes Paulie climbing off the roof, sopping wet, new alternator stuffed under the arm like a rescued baby, the first day of the rest of my life unfolding as if I've joined a highwire act.

I have to ask: "So who's dispatching?"

"I got to finish that antenna. And city says no smoking in here."

I make him hand over the new part and send him back up the ladder into the lightning.

The alternator is a small generator that changes the engine's mechanical energy into electricity used to power onboard electronics and charge the battery. Meters and radios suck the life out of them but it's an easy repair and quick enough.

I'm tying down the last bolt when Wayne Linder rolls my sedan onto the apron.

"So's the van fixed yet?"

I show him my dirty hands. "I patched her into service so I'm driving her tonight."

"But that's my cab."

"Then you might've come put the alternator in her."

Wayne Linder's face grows a red beard lazy as volunteer tomatoes and I can smell the rural on his boots. He lives down in Washington County and strives to be a man of his own principles. Instead of feeding his farm to predatory lenders, Wayne quit the agribusiness, kept most of his land, and has taken work driving taxi to keep out of the bottle.

"Look," I tell him. "You can drive the van but I need my labor."

Wayne scratches his messy beard when I call my labor $40. But I know he sees my angle because he digs his purse from the bib of his overalls.

"I only took your cab because I didn't think none of it," he says, forking over a crisp pair of $20s. "We didn't get no blood in it, or nothing."

"What's that supposed to mean?"

"Paulie didn't tell you? My personal's still down so it's my girl that dropped me off. Paulie sends me right out for that part and the only cab I got's yours. And when I come back, here she is, 'Daddy, I'm having my baby!' So we shot off to the hospital."

"Hallelujah and congratulations. But why didn't you stay with your daughter?"

"I needed to get here and fix my cab."
I stuff the cash back in Wayne's hands.
"You don't want to get paid?"
"I'm fucking with you, gramps. Paulie fixed that shit before he climbed on the roof."
Wayne Linder puzzles up his eyes and the crashing rain sprays our faces with flecks of salt and oil and things that once lived in the sea.
"What's that dummy doing up there in this storm?"

FIFTEEN MINUTES LATER I pull up for my first fare and assault rifles swarm the taxi. The upside here is that it's always fun to explain what "SFP" means to a cop.
For example: "Dispatch said she was going SFP."
The cop turns his ear on it. "Where the heck's that?"
"Some fucking place."
"Ah."
The Coronet Apartments tonight are the scene of a big bad disco show. Colored lights chase on the apartment faces and the mishmash of poor folk and men with guns crowd the walks, the main drive jammed with squad cars, a fire truck, and the county hoodoo wagon. Cops press back those who've come to gawk despite the rain.
The wipers work the glass and tick like a clock.
When I came up the road and first saw the lights, I wheeled into the tobacco shack to ask Bonnie if she knew the score. But Bonnie wasn't working. It's been a week since we hit the Phipps Bros and I haven't been to this side of town since. Tonight's my bad luck, I guess.
Though bad luck has not unfurled its black flags for me alone. From where I'm parked at the pickup curb, I can see on the far sidewalk, up among the obscuring pines, a yellow plastic tarp from under which sticks a pair of black-on-black

Jordans. No evidence markers staked out. Maybe dude got stabbed to death. More than one bad dude lives up in the Coronets and it could be anybody under that tarp.

"Big trouble tonight?"

The cop bends at my window: "So then you don't know who you're picking up?"

"It's like I says. Dispatch sent me here and he says the fare's going SFP."

On this cue my fare emerges from the apartments and I spy a feathered bouffant that can only belong to Dorothy, last name unknown. The officers are quick to decide Dorothy isn't the man they're looking for and escort her to my taxi, handsome gents in tactical helmets with rifles slung at ready, plus two detectives in Kevlar who have at either elbow Dorothy with her big beautiful hair, wearing a flashy pastel blouse over a conservative knee-skirt. She has popped above all their heads a pink country club umbrella.

"I need to get out here," she tells me. "Po-lice give me the heebie-jeebies."

"You and me both, sister. Where're we going?"

"Your dispatcher didn't tell you? I'm looking at a new apartment and don't know the address!"

The radios are shot for the bad antenna so I call Paulie on my cell to sort it out while Dorothy moans and I slow roll around the police cars parked catawampus in the roadway.

Dorothy doesn't care to drive, or walk, so she rides with us enough to impact Emerald's annual gross revs. She'd been living in Saint Bernard Parish during Katrina and fled north after escaping the Terrordome. She was living across from the art campus when the Great Flood hit. It's like water's got something against her.

I listen to Paulie in my phone then relay the what's-what.

"Dispatch says he didn't understand the address and that he asked you write it down for me."

Despite having written it down, Dorothy forgot to bring the note and cannot recall even the name of the street. She'd also

phoned the landlord from her landline.
I offer to turn back.
"Nuh-uh am I going back there tonight. Let's just go downtown and get me a hotel. They shot a boy to death because he was standing in front of a gun. These people is crazy-nuts."

THE MIDNIGHT LULL is a regular occurrence in our work. The phones quit and nobody takes cabs into town. Nor do they take them anywhere. This is the brief stand of the tide before everybody turns outbound for home.

I head to the shack to smoke cigarettes and cherry-pick calls off Paulie's desk. When I arrive a bunch of drivers are in the yard standing at the puddle edges. Their voices ring jubilant. Everybody says the dead kid is Chemo Phipps.

Joe Vega sticks up both his arms and howls at the busted-up clouds. "The punk ass bitch that robbed us has gotten his!"

Leon has been telling everybody who'd been robbing us and he needs to shut the fuck up.

"That's the little fuck who stuck a pistol in my fucking ear," Leon retells his tale for the umpteenth time. How the kid told him to pull in a driveway of a house that was dark. How the neighbors were dark too. How even the street lamp died when Leon rolled under it. "It's just like God set it up for this punk."

"Was it the dead guy that robbed you?"

"Naw but he was sending out those punk kids to do it. Bitch deserves what he got."

I leave to join Paulie in the office. He's slipped the No-Haul list out from under the Plexiglas desk mat and strikes Leon's robber from its illustrious rolls.

I also spot a new missive from our overseers. AFFECTIVE IMEDIATELY WE NOW CHARGEING A $.50 CENTS FUEL SURCHARGE ON <u>EVERY FARES AND ALL CHARGE ACCOUNTS</u>. DO NOT INCLUDE RAILROAD ACCOUNT. COLLCET $.50 CENTS

AND MARK IT ON TRIPSHEETS. THX, *THE OWNERS*
"Why do we slave for those that write like monkeys?"
"So was it the dead kid that was robbing us?"
"I don't know nothing about it, Paulie."
I drag the mouse and keyboard out of his way and wake up the office computer. Paulie's got a bunch of national news tabs open, every headline screaming, 'WE MAY NOT HAVE AN ECONOMY ON MONDAY.' What happened to me and my dad's house is starting to happen everywhere.

I close the tabs and jump to local news where the shooting at the Coronets trumps the global economy. The outlets all report a shooting death but none are releasing names. Just a blurb about a black male gunned down in a suspiciously poor neighborhood. MORE AFTER THE JUMP, I'm promised. But the overnight desk is not delivering.

Googling his name brings up last year's news about Admiral Akbar, later identified as 23-year-old Chemo Phipps, high on PCP and brandishing a samurai sword. Police tased him multiple times and Mr. Phipps was offered probation with court-ordered treatment. His lawyer, Stanislau Bakuyan, made a blank statement in the bottom of the article. A search for the lawyer sends me to website parking. But the avatar omehCP420 appears on Worldstarhiphop, rapbasement, and metrolyrics, and these direct me to an outdated MySpace page in promotion of Chemo's beats and raps.

Letting the music play, I go to the cop site and look for Chemo there. I wish I had Billy's special code so I could buzz reports from the scene. A check of the online courts brings up a dozen years of lawful complaints against Chemo Aton Phipps, with references to juvenile courts before a list of aggravated misdemeanors; simple assault; multiple serious assaults; felony assault; going armed with intent. The serious charges all occurred in the last four years. Lots of violence but no drug arrests. The dead kid's MySpace page raps, "I got to think fast and I got to think big/Y'all got to wear snowshoes round my crib."

So a dopeman on dope gets court-ordered treatment and

probation. After beating hell out of that cop car with a sword. But Chemo has no arrests for possession. No intent to deliver. No tax stamp violations. Not even a paraphernalia charge. So how does a dude like him travel his circles without a drug collar? And what does that have to do with him dying young?

Strange math like that gets me thinking afield. I find a bunch of stories on the mom, Levelva Phipps, currently paying 30 years in Mitchellville. Police received an anonymous tip and she was busted on the Iowa side of the Illinois border with three kilos of crack-cocaine in her trunk. I pay special attention to the article where her lawyer claimed Levelva had been set her up by one of her sons though declined to name which brother was responsible. I also note that the Phipps retained different high dollar lawyers. Justice for all who can afford it, indeed.

Next I search for the brother, 28-year-old Damen Phipps, who's a saint by the logs of the state judiciary. My record search shows he's been twice sued by landlords and pinched on three marijuana charges plus a cocaine bid, all dismissed with no code given. I google for him in more lawful places and find he attended the community college. Links to a PowerPoint. Pics with his peers in business school. His dates span two years with no mention of graduation.

Damen is a sharp dresser by the photos. I find a pic of a delighted blonde with his head tipped to her shoulder. Is this the woman Billy saw in the stash house?

Paulie has been taking calls but hasn't bothered me with any work. I ask him: "Would it be killing you if I cut out? My guts are like worms on fire."

He thumbs through the morning appointments.

"Go knock off. I'll have Big Mike come in early."

* * *

I RIP OVER to Maxie's in hopes of catching Catfish before last call. He's known me almost the whole time I've driven cab. He lives up in the condos next to the Coronets and I bet he can talk about the shooting.

Since the Outer Limits closed, Maxie's is the only bar south of the highway and that makes it the only bar in poortown. Regular brawls inside, or so they tell me. Walking through the door, I slide my palm over the tool on my belt. It's tucked in the sheath with the Gerber stamp against my hip so I can get the knife out fast without having to fish.

The lighting is low and moody, the reception cold. R&B melts out of the juke and the bartender won't serve until Catfish sees it's me. He calls manners and tells the bartender to pour a drink. Bartender won't take my order though. He pours a Crown Royal on the rocks and delivers it to Catfish and Catfish slides it over to me.

I slide over to him a box of American Spirits in return. "I brought you that tobacco you like."

Taking a whiff of the high-power weed, Catfish pats my shoulder and disappears the box into his shirt.

"That's real special, baby." He orders me a second drink. "Make this'n a double."

"How about that shooting tonight."

"Yeah, I seen that shit."

My skin prickles all over.

"Hopheads all got turned on to see this car show up. This old oxblood Caddy. And they all rushed out thinking it was the dopeman. I thought the same, why not? But it was a white dude was driving and he stayed with the brougham. He didn't park up in a slot neither. Other dude got out to arbitrate with the young man. He was calling truce. 'I want to settle out, let's talk. Folks's starving, bruh.' Like that.

"I was out walking the dog and wasn't paying mind, you see. Not until I notice that old oxblood Caddy creeping toward the street. Those taillights, boy. Daddy had that Caddy ready to roll out.

"Now I look over at them boys walking the walk and: BLAM–BLAM BLAM BLAM!"

Catfish pounds each shot on the bar. The barman stares like he's heard this story one too many and I make a show of dropping dollars in front of us.

"Boy goes down and don't get up," Catfish says. "Shooter ran to the Caddy and that big car roared out and was gone."

"Who got shot?"

"Son of that bitch Levy Phipps. The orange-headed fool."

Now that I know for sure, I can imagine the scene. Chemo Phipps breathing hard. Shaking legs and pissing trousers. Leaned in a girl's lap like a modern pieta.

"You talk to the cops?"

"Hell no. They had plenty talking to them."

"What about plates on the Caddy?"

"Local tags."

"And it was a white dude driving?"

"And black dude shooting. How about them apples?"

Catfish tells me the plate number and I write it down on the back of my hand. Maybe Billy can do something with it.

Blasting out the door, I can hear Catfish holler after me.

"Don't let your meat loaf."

I SEND BILLY a text that we need to talk. He wants to meet down at the arts campus parking lot on the river.

The lot is huge and once served the university auditorium, alumni center, and the arts campus, defunct in their entirety, plus Dorothy's old apartment building all boarded up. Flood rot is thick down here as cleanup goes on around the clock. Lighting plants powered by roaring generators throw orange midnight on everything. Industrial blowers hook into an array of huge blue ductwork that snakes across the lot and on through loading docks and lobby doors. South parking is horsed off and crowded with FEMA vans. Mold remediation and new carpets won't salvage anything down here and I wonder when they'll surrender with the wrecking ball.

I smoke outside the 'Yota and wait, trying not to think about the sixer I've brought and left to sweat in the car. I want a clear head for this.

Billy takes forever to show up and I bitch about it.

"I had personal business." He sucks on his electric pipe. "Why you so edgy?"

"Did you hear who got fucking killed tonight? Do you know our robbery turned into a killing? That kid's the one that jumped me in the tobacco shack. And he's dead."

"Ah don't be an asshole."

"As assholes go I'm a regular champ. I'm a magnet for bullshit and weird jams. But knowing this guy got killed after the shit we pulled is not part of my day-to-day, Billy."

"Is today." He shrugs. "And for dudes like Chemo Phipps, it's been day-to-day every day for every day. Know what I'm saying?"

"There's a dead kid taking his last poop in a bag up the road and I need to know that's not on us."

"Ain't on me." Shakes his head, more shrugging. "And he could've died worse."

I tell him he's talking shit and Billy presses me. Our argument feels like explaining argyle to the blind.

"You ever wonder why I went after those dudes?" he asks. "You ever wonder who gave them the drugs to sell? It started with their mother. But who now?"

"So you're teasing out their distribution? First with little hits and then with the great big one."

"All I care about is finding my way inside their distro network," he says, nodding big and slow. "Not some two-bit that walked hisself in front of bullets."

Billy Kinross stares and I swear the lighting plants flicker on the cleanup site. Zina is right about his eyes. His look is hollow and his eyes are a vacuum. Like he no longer generates electricity in the right parts of his brain, or heart. The kind of eyes that look at you and see dinner.

"Whatever Jerry told you about me is wrong. And about my brother. About him getting snatched and killed. What all'd he tell you anyway?"

"I don't even remember."

"I remember November 11, 1985," says Billy, announcing like it's the start of a show. "Veterans' Day with all them little red poppies. Forget-Me-Nots. It was a Monday."

"What's this got to do with dead Chemo Phipps?"

"My brother Ethan was a weird kid," he soldiers on. "Ethan'd go down alleys collecting junk. And I'm not kidding. He'd drag back with busted lamps, phonebooks, a rollerskate and a bag of socks. A refrigerator door. All sorts of useless shit somebody was right to throw away and he'd organize it on the sidewalk right out in front of the house.

"I was raking the lawn and Ethan comes back with this globe that had been busted out of its stand so it was just like this tin ball. It had this hole punched in the South Pacific and I told him the whole thing would go like that. Someday the bottom would open up and the world'd get sucked down like in a drain. Also told him those alleys was dangerous because there's great big holes in them where monsters took little boys. Little shit didn't believe that neither."

Billy sucks on his glowing blue hash pipe and I really want a beer. I tell him that after all this we're talking about Chemo Phipps and I am ignored.

"I made fun of his globe and Ethan grabbed my rake and hit me with it. Boy I was mad as hell. I ran to the backyard and found a just right rock. The rock was perfect and I come back front wanting to bash Ethan's face with it. But he must've gone back to hunting alley junk. So I hid in the bushes and waited to jump his ass.

"While I'm in the bushes, this car kept cruising the house. A dark blue Grand Marquis with flop lamps and four doors. At one point, I heard the driver talking. But nobody was in the car with him and I thought he was talking to me.

"That's when I saw Ethan toddling out front in his library of junk. And that creep at the wheel was talking to my kid brother. And I'm just in the bush holding that rock."

Billy lifts his hand like he's trying to show me.

"The driver of the Marquis. He wore a mustache and what looked like a wig. Curly dirty blond. Maybe fake glasses. Weighed on the fat side. He kept inching the car and made Ethan walk along to keep talking. And fool kid did just like that.

"I watched the backdoor swing open over the curb. Some other dude was lying on the floor in back. His arms closed around Ethan and pulled him into that big blue car and it squealed off and the door shut and I ran from the bushes and finally threw that goddamned rock."

"Smart," I say out of instinct. "Mark the fucking car."

"I was just mad. Missed it wide and hit a parked van. And then he was gone.

"A couple months after Ethan got snatched, Chicago cops found two dead boys in this dude's basement and PD said they got their man. He went to prison where he confessed to a bunch more killing, including killing my brother. Some freelance bitch wrote a book about him, *Fred Austin Frohn: Boy Killer*. Like that's some name we ought to remember. That was before they learned Fred was a liar and had made up his stories. By then he'd been bled out in a shower.

"For the record I never believed he had anything to do with Ethan. He didn't own or drive a Marquis for one. And he didn't look like the driver, or the dude in back. But what if it'd been a gang that was snatching kids, and I mean a bunch of people working together. Organized. Dedicated. But that'd be totally crazy, right?"

Like he's daring me to disagree.

"Then one day Ethan came home," he says. "Twelve years after he disappeared. Everybody thought he was dead and I did too. But there he was standing in Ma's living room. Told them he'd been kidnapped by two dudes that sold to another group.

And he wasn't the only one. He said these people had a whole lot of kids. Girls and boys. They was herding them like in *Pinocchio*. Living in motels and traveling by van. Selling them to men and women all over the country.

"Ethan said they worked him to snatch other kids as he got to being a man. That's what made him bust out. He'd never tried escaping because escapees were murdered in front of the others.

"And can you imagine that? My folks listening to this? Ethan said people would do him up in airplanes. Now you tell me what they think of when they look to their god."

I ask him: "You were in prison for all this?"

"Solitary," admits Billy. "Heard it all over a payphone once I got that freedom restored. And I didn't believe it. Not for a long time. Even after I believed it, I didn't really. Not until I saw one of their abuse videos."

"Jesus H. Christ," as I lean in the 'Yota to grab two bottles.

"This beer's warm," he complains. Then: "Do you know when we're conceived in our ma's belly, our cells divide and build and divide until this little ring of cells builds to make a tube. What they call the Alimentary Canal. One end of the tube is your mouth and the other's your asshole. And bubba that is all we really are. Just a mouth and a asshole. Birth to death, eating and shitting then maybe making more asshole-mouths that eat and shit and fuck. We're just big worms, man."

"You're fucking weird."

"It was fucking weird for Ethan too. I seen the note he left Ma. She didn't give it to the cops because she believed Ethan was right to keep his mouth shut. He'd admitted to bad things in that letter. Things that made him more than a kidnapper. Then after writing it, he hanged himself in the closet of the bedroom where he didn't grow up."

Billy sharpens his eyes on me.

"Getting shot on a street corner doesn't seem so bad now does it? It seems petty, you know? So next time you feel the nuts to come at me, think about Ethan."

"Fuck off. And thanks for your tragic bout of intimacy but

we still got a dead kid problem."
"You're a bigger asshole than I thought."
"I'm glad somebody finally noticed. Ay, where're you going?"
Billy climbs into his Jeep. "I got a bigger fish to catch." He cranks it to life. "But you go on ahead with your dead kid problem. Before you go snitch to the cops, know that I got ways and means, asshole. They'll be on hands and knees looking for splinters of your bones. Don't get in my way."
In a single turn, I've been called a snitch and threatened with my life. It makes me yell with my rarest fury and as the Jeep peels out of the lot around me, I throw my bottle at it.
The bottle smashes in the road. I've been left aside among the roaring generators. The rain starts back up and I rub from the back of my hand the plate number Catfish had given me.

7

I CALL OFF sick to work Friday and again on Saturday. I hide out in Freedom Cove with lights off and wait for trouble to come knocking. As of Sunday afternoon, nobody's knocked so I go back to work.

Sundays blow gentle breezes around the taxi shack, the pace slow and steady, our money for easy labor. People don't fuck around on Sundays like it's a rule.

Jerry Nicodemus works every Sunday due to celebrating Friday Sabbath with his temple, a triple offshoot from the Church of God Int'l. They observe O.T. law and speak in tongues, craft rationales for burning the Quran and believe the Earth's age to be 6,000 years. Me and the old man get along fine because we don't talk Jesus or we don't talk at all.

Yet here I am asking him for worldly advice. Not for his Christian perspective but because he's survived to become an old man.

"Let's say somebody steals from you. What do you do?"
"I call the police."
"All right let's say we want to avoid the cops."
Jerry lifts a brow.
"You're talking about these taxi robberies."
"I maybe might be."

The mainline rings and he answers. "Where are you? . . . Going where? . . . How many passengers? . . ."

Between the telephones is a tilted wooden cubby like two ice-cube trays slapped to sides. Dispatch uses this box to sort the call tickets. As Jerry takes calls off the phone and dispatches them to his drivers, he writes a ticket and puts it in the proper driver's slot. It reads like an easy juggle, but it's not.

"Sounds like you don't need a taxi, ma'am." He frowns into the phone. "We'll carry packages for you but we don't have those kinds of escorts." Shaking his head as he rings off, Jerry asks, "Did you get Billy tied into this?"

"Billy got me tied into this."

"Ah Vic."

"You told me to play nice."

Jerry rubs a weathered paw on his chin.

"Billy's not exactly a right man."

"Which is why I'm coming to you with this."

"So what all happened?"

I make Jerry promise to keep the story between us and not go to the cops.

"We found out who was robbing us. So Billy robbed them back. I did the driving. And I have reason to believe our actions have had a terminally negative impact on a local drug dealer."

Jerry Nicodemus considers what I've said until he tips his head and drops his toothless jaw.

"This kid getting killed?"

"Let me be clear we didn't shoot nobody. It was somebody else that shot him. But I think we may be a precipitating factor."

The mainline rings and he lets the call die on the vine, his eyes hurt and disturbed.

"I was doing what I thought was right," I admit. "The robberies needed to stop. But I take it to Billy that this guy's dead and he doesn't give a shit."

Jerry's laugh is hard and incredulous.

"You two don't know shit from apple butter. You was bringing a thief to justice, is that it? You was rousting him out

and mobbing him to the jail house? Damn, Victor. It might feel good but there's no justice in stealing back from a thief."
"Yeah, roger that."
"Yeah, you know that now." Still incredulous. "See what I mean about them two ways to go through life? You got to know which road's underfoot, Vic. And always know your turnoff."

Jerry shakes his chin, disgusted, and thumbs a short pile of blank call tickets cornered under the clasp of his clipboard. "Proverbs 28:24," he announces. "'Anybody stealing who asks, "What's wrong with that?" ain't no better than a murderer.'"

"I can see the wrong in it, hey. I'm not coming to you because I can't see what's wrong. I don't need spiritual advice."

"What other advice you expect? I can comfort you with the Scripture. But it ain't my task to make you feel better about your bad decisions."

"Ah fuck this noise." I stand up to check the money in my hip-sack and to get a cigarette.

"If you can't go to the police," he says, "where do you go?"
"I don't know."

"From who're you going to seek forgiveness, Vic Pasternak? Maybe you ought to be asking that. Honor your pledges and follow the general rules for living and steer from evil. You'll be fine. Return what's stolen. You'll be finer still. That is the message of Ezekiel's watchman."

"I'm going the fuck back to work."

The mainline rings and Jerry runs his mantra. When he rings off, he holds out the call ticket. It shows the address of our local massage parlor.

"You're out of rotation but go to D-5 and buy a packet of snack crackers. Then bring them there."

"Snack crackers?"

"Snack crackers. 'Orange with the cheese,' she said." He plays at a shiver and grins toothless. "Hookers get munchies too, kiddo. But she's also got a live call so move your butt."

So I go to D-5 and buy the crackers then drive over to the red house. I get out to pound on the door. KNOCK HARD somebody has Sharpied over the knob.

"You my taxi?"

I'm startled by a dude coming out from the bushes. He wears a sour puss and puts out his hands to show no harm. This must be my other call.

"Hang on, buddy. I got snack crackers for the lady."

The waiting room is dressed like a dental lobby on low lighting. The air smells like cotton candy. An overstuffed black couch sits alone among the unadorned walls. Potted peacock feathers in the corner, men's magazines spilled on the coffee table. There's a counter at front for the till and a menu card that describes the variety of massage treatments. The short hallway leads to numbered exam rooms shut with unpainted Luan doors. A fifth door hangs open on the john at the end and its toilet hisses.

The lady of the house appears from Door #3 with two brassy guys in tow. She's a farm girl in city girl makeup and wears a belly shirt that shows the black hairs on her navel. It takes a moment but I realize she's Letty Fetch, local party girl. We'd messed around a dozen years ago before I figured her to be a psychic vampire.

"You next in line or are you the cab?" asks one of the brassy guys. Both wear wedding bands and their hairlines look enriched.

"And where's my snack crackers, Vicky?"

Letty has always called me that. But she hasn't always talked in a wispy Minnie Mouse voice. She pays me ten, telling me to keep the change. Her clients fork over three c-notes and tell her the same.

Back at my taxi, I see the sour dude that came out of the bushes has occupied the front seat.

The midlife crisis team isn't having it.

"This is bullshit," one gripes, keeping the door open and his foot on the curb. "We had her specifically call for this taxi. This is our taxi, do you speak English?"

I get the guy in the front to tell me where he's going then flatten the waves with practiced ease. "You shut the fuck up or

I'll send you back inside to the herpes queen. Now look. We're all going the same direction. You two guys to the hotel past the interstate and this guy to a farm out past that. So this is easy. If you want a ride, pull your leg inside, and shut the fucking door."

It's a weird trip and not only because I've forced it into a corner. The two men in back brag about motorcycling cross-country. They're enthusiasts wearing Eddie Bauer leathers and puffing Cohibas. The kind of rich assholes that confuse Eric Clapton for a legendary bluesman.

The fare sitting shotgun doesn't like them either. He chews on a lip and grinds his boot heels in the mat, his eyes popping like his head wants to explode. I also spy him twisting the gold band on his ring finger like he can't pull it off.

The two in back roll on laughing.

"When she peeled off that negligee, or whatever—fuck me."

The other blows a fart before they both burst laughing.

"I can smell her ass on my hand."

"Your hand smells like my balls."

I draw into the Highlander where they pay and tell me to keep the change. Then they walk off leaving the doors open so I scream wheels and shut the doors that way.

My remaining fare asks, "Can I smoke here?"

We both light up as I hit the Herbert Hoover Highway, a.k.a. the Triple H, and drive out toward Cedar Bluff, rolling over and through valleys patched with fog. I turn up the pleasure radio though it's just more bad news about global economic disaster. My sour passenger could give a fuck less. He stares hard out the window as if hoping to burn a hole in the sky.

His farm has its barn built against the road and I roll into the yard cluttered with haycarts, beater cars, and a skidsteer. The house is dark enough to look abandoned.

But here come the dogs barking. Their master hollers at them to quit and climbs out to pay his fare. He tips a fin then bends to look at me in the domelight.

"She ain't coming home tonight."

"Who ain't?"

"That bitch what used to live here."

He points back toward town and his few words suck the wind out of me.

"It's tonight I find out how she's filling the fridge. Told me she was working at a all-night dry cleaner. Now how about that?"

He yanks his wedding band off and hurls it across the road.

"You might regret that."

"And fuck you too."

SHIFT IS HALF done when I hit a drive-thru for grub. I eat it while cruising the downtown loop. I approach my job as would a shark: Don't stop moving until you find a fare, or die.

I get called over the radio by Zina and she asks that we meet at the old bus depot. When I roll up behind her van, she's out smoking and talking with Helene. And they go on talking a minute before Zina finally climbs in my taxi.

"I need to know what's going on with you. Something's eating you and it's why you were green all last week and tonight too."

"It's that killing on the southside," I let out. "That kid? His gang? Those were the dudes robbing us."

She scoffs. "Short sighted, dumb ass kids. I'm just glad he wasn't killed by one of us going vigilante."

"It didn't unfold quite like that."

That grabs Zina's toes. "What! You shot him?"

"Hell naw. Look. Billy and me, we figured out these dudes were robbing us and he wanted to rob them back. I was his driver."

"So Billy the Creep shot him?"

"Jesus, fuck, no. Absolutely not. Look. Neither of us shot him. That killing was gang-related. Not Vic-related. We did, however, rob those guys. Billy robbed those guys. But I only drove him there and back. I'm merely an accessory."

"So how did robbing them get somebody killed?"

Zina's reaction is more severe than old Jerry's and it's

scaring me off. I want to coax her back to my side but my lie sounds weak. "I don't really know how he got shot."

"Because you idiots robbed a bunch of drug dealers. People join that trade and die, Vic."

"I'm not in the drug trade. I was briefly in the stick-up trade but that's all over."

"All right," says Zina. "If you can tell me this dead young man isn't haunting you then we're in the clear. But if you're still looking for a way out, I can't help you. And I don't even want to hear about it."

I can feel her staring me down.

"So which is it?"

"There's still something I got to set right."

Zina pushes the door open and puts one foot on the curb.

I try and stop her. "Look."

"You're in a dark way, Vic. And that can't be my problem."

"Then I won't say any more save that I didn't kill anybody. And I won't be killing anybody. But I got to make this thing right or it's going to stick with me."

"That sounds serious," she says before slamming the door. "Feel free to call me again after you get your shit wired right."

Then she storms off beautiful as a bygone day.

ONE GOOD TRICK I've learned from taxi driving is that it's best to meet adversity with ever-greater adversity. Do this until you've survived. Anything else is cut and run.

Zina's right. Time to get my shit wired tight. Time to confront the truth and come what may. I'm going to end the trouble Billy and I started.

For two more grams of high-power weed, Catfish has traded me two addresses where Damen Phipps hangs out. Both are south of the highway.

I've also told Jerry I need to go see somebody and he

knows I'm cruising in my taxi with the bubble light off. Catfish said the place on Miami Road is where Damen's girl lives. I've twice wheeled by and see dudes sitting on the stoop as if guarding it. I'm a cab and they pay me no mind.

I don't see anybody guarding Damen's house though. The address I have is in Indigo Court, a cul-de-sac planted with modest ranches. There's a FOR SALE sign in the neighbor's yard and I pull over beside it. I can't tell if Damen Phipps is home or if the address Catfish gave me is any good. I look at the front door of the place and see mail sticking out of the box. Huh.

I kill the engine. In my heart and mind, I want this to be a friendly call so I leave the Maglite. Then I get out and press the door closed and listen to the wind. Hearing nothing, I cross up the driveway and keep my eyes peeled for watchers. But no one watches me. It's after midnight and Indigo Court is sleeping.

To the left of the door is a bay window covered with venetians. I soft-shoe onto the porch and reach for the mail. Too late I hear small barking from inside. Lights flare on and a hand rattles the shades. I retreat out of the glare but stay on the porch, catching sight of a vehicle parked in the driveway of the house for sale. A red Jeep Wrangler tucked back by the garage.

Front door sucks on storm. I turn to the man coming to greet me and recognize Damen from his business school snapshots. He shoves the storm door wide so we can talk.

"Ah you don't not know me but—"

The pipe of a pump shotgun lifts under my nose. I sidestep into the angle of the storm door until I can see that it's Billy at the deciding end of the weapon.

"Don't ever point a gun at me." I walk him backward into the entryway. "Especially my own fucking gun."

I haven't heard him rack the slide but I don't expect he'll shoot me, no matter his recent threat. He lowers the muzzle and grins like a kid shitting his pants.

We crowd at the door as the little pug dashes across the living room yapping and wagging her nip of tail. She bolts around like we're all here to play.

I don't feel comfortable to enter a stranger's home. It always comes with liabilities.

Billy asks: "What're you doing here?"

"I was going to ask you the same thing."

"You came here to rat me out," he says, raising the shotgun, and I charge, pushing the gun straight up and away as Billy crabs backward. I eat the pocket in two brisk strides and send the barrel over my shoulder as I slide hands down the stock to pinch the webs of his hands, stomping my foot on his foot, smacking my forehead into his. Billy curses as the shotgun comes up in my grip. I butt him hard in his thigh and he goes to the floor like dirty clothes.

I turn the gun on him as that pug comes yapping at my shoes and my heart is pounding. "Now how's this feel?"

Billy moans with his face in the white shag rug. "Like I wasn't expecting it."

Slipping my finger around the trigger guard and pressing the release, I pump the slide and eject a live shell. My risk paid out but Billy could've shot me.

Everything moves fast. While I'm patting Billy for other weapons, our host displays a silver pistol that he carefully places on the coffee table. I boot the pug away and she angrily clamps to the leg of my jeans.

Damen asks, "Can't we all just calm down, please?"

He seems like the kind of a man who'd get real shook if shooting broke out in his living room. He's taller and thinner than his brother and shows none of the family wild stripes. Dressed more like a tech from IT and not at all the kingpin I've envisioned. His home is rent-to-own refined with an overblown white leather couch and thick white carpeting. The widescreen shows muted coverage of the money crisis. He keeps an ashtray on his coffee table though the air smells like a plug-in, which almost covers Billy's weird stink.

I lift the barrel at the ceiling and finger the release to eject another shell. "Unload your piece too, bro. And get your bitch off my leg."

All of our hands are quaking. Damen fumbles his pistol to unseat its clip and shows he hadn't even one in the chamber. Then he pulls his pug off my jeans and closes her in a room off the kitchen. I wait until he comes back empty-handed before dumping my remaining shells.

Billy, growling, lifts up off the floor and wavers on the bad leg like he might lunge. I casually bring the shotgun to slope arms. "Come at me and I'll beat your other one."

"You selfish fuck. Tell him what you came to tell him. Tell him you're here to rat me out."

Damen asks: "What are you ratting him out about?"

I bring the shotgun off my shoulder and lean it against the wall. "It was all y'all that robbed the taxis. Wasn't it?"

"I didn't rob anybody," Damen implores. "But our street crews were getting robbed every week. We had to make up that balance." He glances at Billy. "But it was my brother's idea to rob the drivers. It was his idea to recruit those kids to carry it out and I had nothing to do with that. I hope you aren't taking all this personally."

"Maybe I am."

"Chemo did too." His eyes widen at mention of the name. "Chemo wanted to cut off your hands and keep them in a box. I don't even know where he came up with that." He points at Billy. "We've come to more rational terms."

Damen blinks at me, unnerved and playing at fear. But he's none too afraid of me, or Billy. And I realize he already knows that we robbed him. Billy has beaten me to the punch. He's come here as I have and already confronted Damen with the truth.

"What new terms?"

"He's going to repay what you did by helping make this right."

I wave at Billy and shake my chin. "Your brother's dead. How's he going help that?"

"Fuck you, Pasternak. Damen, don't tell him anything."

Damen lets out a sigh and collapses on his great white couch, leaning deliberately for a silver case of cigs. I don't dare reach for my own. I won't share in his weakness.

I ask him, "Why'd they murder Chemo?"

"Keep your mouth shut, Damen."

"Our suppliers pay a monthly fee to operate," he says. "The stolen money belongs to them. So do the drugs. And they didn't just kill my brother. They held us both to account. I got cut out of their supply chain. And that's where Billy's going to help. He's going to help me take my business back."

Billy presses him to shut up but Damen can't help himself. I consider his mother, Levelva, in prison 30 years on drug possession and her lawyer blaming her sons for setting her up and I begin to understand Damen is the snitch.

"Who held you to account, Damen?"

"A guy named Don Salukus."

"Goddammit, Damen."

"Sounds like mafia."

Damen shakes his head. "They're more corporate than that. At least from what I've seen."

"So Salukus is the boss?"

"He just secures product delivery and the cash flows. The boss is Old Henry."

"How'd you start dealing for Old Henry?"

"We didn't deal for anybody. We'd taken on his product line for distribution. That was the relationship. To answer your question, I first met Don Salukus about a year ago. He came to my door at night like you did and showed me a photo of Chemo beat up and in a cage.

"So I let him drive me out to meet his boss, Old Henry. He lives in a castle-like place with tall brick walls and turrets and iron work, you know? He's got a private zoo in the back, which is where they had Chemo. Locked inside the cage with him was a bear.

"Old Henry said he'd reached an agreement with our suppliers at that time. The Chi Fam. So now we'd be distributing for him and that's why the operating fee. Payable to the Chi. The problem was Chemo. They wouldn't stand for him acting badly. Old Henry said it was my job to do whatever was necessary to keep our business on the narrow."

For the brother of the dead, he doesn't seem too busted up.

"They must've been impressed when he attacked the cops." Damen hangs his head. "That was Chemo for you. Always unruly. But we had a knack. Working with the new product lines, my book exploded until I was feeding dealers in the towns around us. Chemo was a madman though. He had two or three cliques in every neighborhood and got us in with those motel pimps out on the Strip. For a minute, we had it pretty good."

At last he looks at Billy who leans on the fireplace mantle in favor of the bad leg, his face bunched in disgust. "You let every other goddamned cat out so just tell him already. Go ahead. Tell him about the fucking warehouse."

The pain in his face is real but Billy's sparring with Damen feels like an act. Like they've worked out walking me through this conversation.

"There's this warehouse," Damen says.

I start breaking the script immediately. "First tell me about this 15 grand. Why would you pay your suppliers an operating fee?"

"The fee is paid to Chi Fam for staying out of town. Old Henry bought out our network."

I hear a clang in the universe. "Are the cops in with this?"

"Just tell him about the warehouse, Damen."

"They're corporate like I said. They run a truck terminal."

I flatten a hand in Damen's face. "Not from you. I want hear it from him."

Billy puts his eyes to mine and shakes his head.

"I hardly know any more than you."

"You're lying, Billy. Damen, where's this warehouse?"

"I've never been there but it's supposed to be out in the country. I heard it's a big red barn. Or something."

"You're a bad liar too, my friend. I bet Billy knows exactly where it's at."

"We don't know exactly anything yet," Billy clarifies. "But we're going to have to put our three heads together and find it. If we can find this warehouse, we can take back Damen's business. There's a whole lot of money on the table."

Damen smiles genuinely. He says to me, "We'll catch ourselves a big old fish!"

Un-fucking-believable. I bristle to hear Billy's words in Damen's mouth. They're both angling for that bigger fish. And they want my help landing it.

"What in the fuck for? You think I'd actually work with you on anything like this ever again? I'd rather parachute into Tehran. Besides: These third party motherfuckers ain't got shit on me."

Billy shakes his head.

"Salukus pulled the camera footage from the tobacco shack." He means the video of me and Chemo on the night of the robbery. "Salukus knows your face."

"Bullshit."

"It's true," Damen says, sweeping in for support. "Salukus showed me the tape to ask if I knew who you were. Tonight I knew you at my door right off. But not when he showed me the tape. Billy didn't ever want us to meet face to face."

Damen's eyelids drop like sandbags.

Another big clang in the universe.

I ask Billy: "He knew about the robbery?"

Damen looks at Billy who is gazes at his shoes.

I ask Damen: "You were in on this? Did he even tie anybody up or did you just hand over the pink bag?"

He looks out at me with his plainest face.

"Motherfucker," I call Billy out. "It was your idea to rob the cabs. Wasn't it?"

"Don't take it that far, man. Leon's already claimed that shit."

"Bullshit. Dressing up like a fucking commando and sneaking in yards. Taking off with my shotgun. And all that was a fucking show? For me? So why me?"

Damen's mouth makes the shape of words that won't come. From the mantle, Billy stares at me with blood in his face. They need me in their game but neither will tell me the truth. I feel the room coming unglued around me.

Time to cut and run.

"Where're you going?"

"It's time to get back to work."

Billy keeps up the argument. "So we rob this dude and his brother gets killed and you won't help make that right? This is our chance like you wanted, Vic."

I almost argue it out with the manipulative fuck but instead bang out the storm door. I've taken my shotgun and swing it down along my leg. I don't look back and I don't slow my step.

They stare from the porch as I roar off. Damen Phipps is going to end up dead as his brother, and Billy Kinross with him.

"#22, back in and ready to go."

"FEEL BETTER, 22? ALL QUIET. BRING IT DOWNTOWN."

8

I LIFT THE flap on the peephole and regard the world outside my door. The rear of Kum & Go, our big shared apronway, the cage for the LP tanks. Nobody running or screaming, nothing on fire. I smoke at the peephole, watching.

I haven't heard from either Billy or Damen. Billy's no-called/no-showed all week too. Fuck him. I almost deleted him from my cell but I want a heads up if it's ever him calling.

I don't believe there's any drug warehouse out in the country. Some big red barn, or whatever. My belly caved-in to hear that the stolen money belonged to an unforgiving third party. But no enforcers have rapped on my door and that makes me doubt I'm on any videotape. I haven't made it that hard to find me.

Or maybe precautions are paying off. I've stayed low. No afterhours, no drinking. I've stored the 'Yota inside the garage to keep it off the street. I stay out of public unless I'm working. I haven't slept for shit and not drinking has me on pins and I'm worn out and fucking cranky. I stay up until noon thinking about Denver. The Hondurans of Federal Blvd and my trailer wreathed in flame. I won't let that happen to me again.

The peephole flares with setting sun. Time to go to work.

I exit through the rear. The door lets out to a narrow lane

shared with the neighbors. From back here I can cut out from a dozen ways between buildings. I stay off the roads and walk to work on the riverside bike trail and across the river on the train bridge. No one follows.

I'm on infinitely higher alert in the cab. Always in gear, always ready to jump off the brake. I park in the street with full clearance front, back, and to at least one side. I leave the window open only a crack and won't unlock the doors until motherfuckers tell me where they're going. I'm enduring swells of paranoia as I wait out a retribution that has no-called/no-showed on me too.

I remember being a healthful sport with an eye on a bright future. This job has ruined the fuck out of all that. "*I meet a lot of people from every walk, race, and creed / From the poor and healthy, to the sick and wealthy, to every angel-devil in between.*" I wrote that my first year pushing the wheel. It's shit, but accurate. We see a broad cross-section of everybody and my work reveals to me routines that would otherwise go unnoticed. I give 40 rides a night and every ride opens a glimpse into a stranger's life. It's like I'm looking down a kaleidoscope to see how we're all swimming together. Peep too long though and get black-eyed by the trick tube. For example, I see people only one way anymore. Before they've opened their mouths, I'm already zeroing in on their worst stereotype and working outward. *What kind of devil are you?* I used to worry I treaded a moral danger with that. After Billy, not anymore.

I see a shivery black dude flagging me to the curb in front of SpoCo and the Deadwood. He wags $20s overhead, international sign for "Keep on driving." More to the point, I know the guy. We call him Hustler and I've got no interest in hauling him anywhere ever again.

Further along the curb I see a white dipshit wearing suit pants but no coat with shirttails flying and his tie out of knot. He likewise wags a flag of $20s overhead. I should heed both signs and keep driving around the corner. But since I've already ruled out picking up the shivery black dude, I slide fast past him and take a gamble on the devil I don't know.

"Party Down!" he crows, and then to his unseen companion, "This is Party Down, dude! He's the baddest ass driver in this town." He's confused me for another. But the dipshit keeps squeezing my shoulder, and he cheers, "Party Down! How you been, bro?"

Hustler hustles to the cab and slides in next to the white kid.

"Ho ho ho—this is his cab," I tell Hustler as the white kid talks over me: "It's cool, bro. He's with me. We're one big family. Peace. So let's go."

What the fuck?

"So where're we all going?"

"Pull around the corner. We got another bro to get."

I round the corner and park, showing good form in waiting to punch the extra on my meter.

The dipshit says to Hustler: "This is Party Down, dude. I've seen him do rails off a clipboard while busting through traffic. I bet he knows where to get the good white."

"Oh yeah?" says Hustler, smooth as duck shit.

"The fuck I can," I bark through my teeth and the hand returns to my shoulder. "Quit squeezing the fucking Charmin."

The dipshit snaps his fingers back like I might bite them.

We call the other guy Hustler due to his lifestyle. He's an old hand from the way back still wearing kid shoes and eking out runs. Last time he was in my cab, I ditched him in Cedar Rapids just as the cops swarmed him.

The dipshit says to him: "Dude, you have no idea, bro. We've been fishing to get more but everybody's totally out."

"Mebbe we should ask this cab driver what he knows, haw!"

"Fuck it. Let's steal his cab and drive to Chicago."

In the rearview, I see an exchange of cash. Now a handshake. "Thanks, bruh. We'll see you around." The dipshit just can't keep his hands off my shoulders. "And thank you, Party Down! Keep it real."

Then he opens the door and exits into the road.

I turn in my seat and give Hustler maddog eyes. "You

flagged me down to run a dope deal? That's a $40 flat fee."

"Hold up a minute, I need a ride too. Just hold up."

Hustler gets out of the back to climb up front beside me. His age is tough to peg, 40 or 60. He has trouble spitting out words while grinding his teeth.

"I need a ride and can pay you, see?" He shows me big bills cuffed in his fist like they were face cards. "Take me out to Coralville. I got a nut to make."

I drive us across the river and follow the highway west until we reach the Strip. When Hwy 6 was the big cross-country road, the Strip sprouted from swamp to advertise GAS FOOD LODGING. Today you can also get Indian cuisine, tattoos, shisha for your hookah, and saltwater fish. Or you could. The Great Flood fucked the highway up to 10th Ave. A lot of shops are still boarded over and some won't be coming back.

The fleabag motels were first to reopen and Hustler wants to hit them all. This is how he makes his nut. He makes house calls with a little black purse worn looped around his wrist. He'll disappear ten minutes inside a room, or a few. Every motel door shows worn and battered, every lot parked with cars that look lived in. The motel turf belongs to the Phipps Bros, or so claimed Damen Phipps. If that's true, Hustler must sell for them. Or sold.

For the standby service, Hustler pays me a $100 retainer and will fork over another if that runs out. I always have to warn him against getting high with his clients. "You get high? You get to stay here and I get the high bill. Got it?"

"You don't got to tell me twice, brother-man."

"I got to tell you every time we stop the cab."

This is Hustler's routine and I'm in it. This is what I'd hoped to avoid by blowing past him on the curb. This is what we call a vision quest, a journey of rushing recklessly ahead possessed by a moment already forgotten. The truest American pastime. The goal never deters, sick bastards seeking relief from the midnight pain of being alive, and its usual foil is hard drugs. "I got to pick up my keys," or, "I left my baby's binky."

Except Hustler's vision quest is reversed. He's the one with the vision looking for a seeker among a legion of unreliable customers. Sometimes they can't be located. Or they show up but don't have money. Or the money they have isn't enough. Or they have money but it's in a different place and everybody piles in my cab to go there. Maybe he's lousy at business, maybe this is all he's got to work with. I don't give a shit. I blow through half my cigarettes waiting on him and at 75¢ a minute wait-time, Hustler's paying for a week of tobacco.

I've parked in the office rotunda at the Iowa Lodge. The spot has good sightlines and nobody can approach except in the open. Hustler, for example, running to the cab in my rearview. He claws through the door and falls in beside me.

"No getting high I told you. This ride's over."

He peers through the back window, watching and waiting. "They're after me," he says, desperate. "Last two places we been they say they just been around."

I make my own scan of the lot and lock the doors.

"How serious is it?"

"Ah it only money." Hustler busily twists his head and scans for bogeys. "It's like this, man. These's lean days. Time was we got our supply out of Chicago. Now I get it from these local cats and they spotty."

"Sounds like time to find a new supplier."

"That's what I did. But I wasn't sposed to. I ain't sposed to cross no lines to do bidness with the Chi. They got a rule, dig? And now these dudes is after me."

"If they've already been here maybe you should stick around."

Hustler shakes his head. "No point running. I got to learn one way or another. Take me on home to Capri."

The Capri is across the highway and a long block west. Hustler wants #9, around back. Coming out of the turn I see two men standing in the lot outside his door. One big black dude and a dumpy white guy wearing a crappy mustache.

"Ah keep driving!"

Too late. The crappy mustache steps fast in front of the cab with hands out. Now both crowd either side of the taxi. The big guy yanks Hustler out through the window by his collar, slapping him repeatedly without saying a word. The other comes to my window, peels his jacket to show a badge on his belt. He won't show his face and the badge looks fake.

I take my window half down and he asks, "What's he owe?"

"The meter says $45."

The crappy mustache flips $20s in my window and walks off.

"Hey," I call him. "I thought cops were the good guys."

"Fuck off outta here."

As I roll away, I see the big guy shove Hustler through door #9 and the mustache saunters in behind them. I got $40 plus the $100 retainer plus the $40 asshole tax for the drug deal and that's a good rake.

DEJA-VU ALL OVER again, three hours to the minute later. Same corner and same dipshit dude now with red sauce dribbled onto his shirt. This time around he's been stuffed back in his jacket and he's still mistaking me for that other driver.

"Party Down! Bro, you're alive!"

Once again, he's with companion, another suit but less drunk and better put together. I recognize him as one of the meat market bartenders.

The dipshit goes, "We partay at the countray club, bitchez!"

"Sit down and shut up. This guy's fucking cool. So be cool." Then he says to me, "Hey bro, sorry about him. But we're going to the country club like he says."

. The dipshit looks amazed. "You know this dude too? Shit, everybody knows Party Down!"

I jump the stoplight and blaze for the interstate route. Meanwhile, the dipshit comes out of his suit coat with that mini-Ziploc of yellow coke I'd seen him buy off Hustler.

"Partay-partay-partaaay!"

The bartender scolds him and in the rearview I see him

snatch the bad coke and give it to the open window.

"You fucker!"

"Ruh-lax. We got a boat coming in."

"You tossed all my goody, fucker. You got to cover that. You sure we gonna be covered?"

"Bro's at the party, bro. And maybe I got a little bit."

The bartender tells me to drive steady and grinds from the bottom of a coke mill his last bit of marching powder onto the end of a house key. "You want a sniff?"

I wave it off. "I've got court in the morning."

When we get to the country club, the dipshit pushes me to step out and join the party.

"You got to come in with us, bro. Nobody gives a shit about court dates!"

The bartender says: "I got an extra jacket in my chick's car."

"I need a jacket?"

"It's a benefit dinner. There'll be hot chicks and there'll be blow. C'mon inside."

"I'm at work," I tell them, shaking my head. "I got a retainer of $100 per hour, upfront."

This provokes the dipshit to fork over twenties. "I will totally pay that, you're awesome! Haha! You see that? Party Down is the man, bro!"

The entrance is centered on a glamorous lighted fountain flanked by slick rides parked in rows. I slip the cab next to the chick's Mercedes so the bartender can get me that jacket. It's tight through the shoulders and short at the wrists yet looks stylishly West Coast over my black t-shirt and Carhartt ducks.

I follow my wards into a foyer stuffed with gilded trophy cases. A dark Indonesian dude in safari getup greets everybody amid a floor decorated with huge placard photos. Dead bucks and other game and the same old white hunter in different hats. Suddenly, a photograph of a young man in a coma. The benefit must be for him.

"Enjoy your stay," says the little safari man.

I note the exits and the way to the lockers if I need to slip off for a puff. My eyes then catch on a well-built guy in a black-on-black suit. He tips his head to the side as if to recognize me.

Hustling to keep with my wards, I slide past white-gloved ushers and through a huge walnut doorway into the ballroom where the ceiling disappears among bouquets of chandeliers. Two-story windows gaze onto the golf course lit up this evening to showcase the rear double-fountain. The dance floor glows and the stage is dressed in bunting. Plus more photo boards of larger-than-life elk and another of the coma guy.

My fares have ditched me so I make way for the bar to join the line of other bored dudes staring at the muted television. Ticker reads: LARGEST BANK FAILURE IN US HISTORY.

"No tie," the barman says, pointing at his throat.

"I'm the driver, pal. Give me a break and a cherry soda."

I crumple a fiver onto the bar and eyeball the exits while he fixes me up. The drink comes in actual glass with garnish. I toss the straw onto the gilded napkin.

The microphone whines and the deejay fades and we're welcomed to our charitable after-dinner. A hot young corn queen with shallow blue eyes comes around to give me an order form and a golf pencil. "For the silent auction," she whispers.

I try to give it back but she moves unstoppably onward.

The brochure is from Heritage Gaming Preserves and the map shows a place way out east of town. Apparently the real hubbub tonight is an exotic animal auction to raise funds for the coma guy. A great elk adorns the pamphlet standing picturesque on a hill framed with a promise of 100% GUARANTEED KILLS!

I take another look at that order form. Heritage Gaming is a private hunting preserve. The kind of hunting with ten-high fences and animals that trust humans. 100% guaranteed kills, indeed. The auction is for the purchase of your own "spirit animal." Among the stock are ram, elk, beef bulls, and Hogzillas, domestic whitetail, fallow deer from Persia, Sika and Père David from Asia, and the European Red Stag. All money goes to coma guy and the price list makes me whistle. The cost of shooting your spirit animal in a box is comparable to buying a used car.

This crowd is definitely not my tribe. I catch an inebriated woman fishing for a glance. She wears bottle-red hair and a half-million in diamonds. "Do you know your spirit animal?"

"I'm a fucking tiger, ma'am. Can we get tigers?"

"Why I don't know. Oh Roger—?"

She calls the elbow of her doddering old boy and puts the question to him. Next, I get an earful about how he's a lawyer and that it's against the law to transport such beasts for the purpose of killing them.

I bunch up my face. "What are you suggesting? I wouldn't want to kill the tiger, Matlock. I'd put that big son bitch in my parlor. Let him growl at the mailman."

The wife is delighted at my antics but not old boy.

"Transporting such animals across state lines for the purpose of companionship is also against the law."

I see my fare, the bartender, crossing the dance floor with an unknown man. The unknown is barrel-chested and swarthy, and carries a black backpack over the shoulder. They go together through the kitchen door. When they come out it's the bartender wearing the black bag.

They stop by my post at the bar.

"That jacket makes me look gay, bro. But you look sharp," says the bartender. "I got to go play Santa Claus. Make sure my dipshit pal gets home."

He stuffs more cash in the breast of my jacket and cut outs the side door.

The swarthy man remains and grins at me like a mule chewing garlic. "So. You are the great Party Down. My friends have told me all about you." He calls himself Stan and stinks of Tommy Hilfiger. "But you must call me the Kushite!"

"Sure thing, Stan."

"I have an idea for you, bro. But you must give me half of everything you make on it."

"Then I don't even want to hear it. Where's my leverage?"

"All right," he concedes at once. "But if you become a

millionaire on this idea, I want my share back. Are you ready?"
"I was born ready."
"I think you should run a getaway car service."
"I already run a getaway car."
"But I mean for criminals. You know, like bank robbers."
"I'm telling you I already do. Not to the scale of bank robbers but I carry people through the shade all day."
"So you market yourself as an escape service?"
"That would dissolve all use of said service. If we're talking about running a discreet operation. But thanks, Stan. I appreciate you trying to make me rich."
"Please, bro. Call me the Kushite."

The room bursts with applause as the emcee throws to our host, H. Thomas Houston II, who takes his time getting to the stage amid the gladhanders. I recognize him as the old white hunter from the billboard photos. Arrived to the microphone, he cuts right to extolling the valor and industry of his son, H. Thomas Houston III, who parked his car into a tree last winter. His son had founded an upstart financial firm and the old dad alleges many here tonight have invested in its products. When he utters its name, I realize I've thrown beer cans at its billboards.

"DevGRO has been allowed to grow with your investment." The crowd applauds itself. "Today DevGRO is underwriting the development of our southwest corridor which includes funding the construction of new arterial roads and three communities. DevGRO has also assisted this country club with recent renovations. Veritably, the future is brought to us by DevGRO." And another rash of applause.

"Lord, where's my rifle? If they'd let me have a tiger for a spirit animal, I'd sic it on this fucking guy."

My buddy Stan agrees, in a general sense.

"Tigers? Man, bro. Tigers'd be fucking great!"

"Protestant whiskey." I knock on the barman's table and point at the bottle. "Make it a double, neat."

In the mirror I spy a guy scanning those of us at the bar. It's the well-built suit from the lobby. I casually turn and take my own gander. Ushers bustle everywhere but this guard dog is different. He looks like private security. Understated in a black coat and black collarless shirt. We look like twins from the waist up. I get nothing but bad vibes from him.

He makes an approach as the barman delivers my whiskey.

"Might I buy you a drink after that?"

Looking him in the eye, I shoot the glass. "I'm the D.D. and that was my one gimme."

"Don't I know you from somewhere?"

Stan makes the introductions. "Ah Don—this is Party Down, getaway driver *par excellence*," giving me the wink and nudge. "Chris Paine hired him for the night."

As if summoned from the aether, my dipshit ward piles onto our shoulders. "Don! Omigod, Salukus knows him too! Everybody knows Party Down!"

Don Salukus. Ah shit.

The only way out is to go dumb.

I clutch Salukus at the shoulder. "Waitaminute! I do know you. Dave Salukus, right?"

"Don," he says instantly. Then his face hardens. "That's me."

"I remember you from my cab. You was with friends coming out this nice eastside house. You introduced yourself because my dad's name's Dave too. He's a plumber."

The hard face blanks a moment while the brain behind it tries the connections until he gives up. "I take a lot of cabs so that must be it."

Even my pal Stan vouches for me. "He's a good guy, Don."

Yeah, half-cop: I'm not the droid you're looking for. Maybe he did grab that video from the tobacco shack but he hasn't placed me. Or he's pretending not to.

Whichever, he bids us all a good night and wanders off, scanning the crowd as he goes.

Stan's eyes go are wide as he gives me a high five on the DL.

"You are a legend. Do you know who that was? He's a stone killer, bro. Did you know he was sniffing you out?"

"Why else would I've shut him down?"

"Of course! I've never seen anybody shut him down like that, haha! If you drive half as well as you think on your feet, you would be an exceptional asset."

"What can I say, pal? People live like they drive."

STAN THE KUSHITE lives on the close side of the county lake. I drive fast across the night watching for deer. Stan brags on about how good he has it. More pussy than I can possibly imagine. A hot wife, and wife's got a hot car, and he's got an Audi and a '72 Mustang Mach 1. He is a very important person, he assures me.

The Kushite household is in a subdivision on a fake pond where a three-stall garage comes with every house. We ditched the dipshit at the party. When I said the only way the deal could be broken was if Stan bought me out, he laid down four times the original retainer.

"You're my cab driver now," he said, and we cut out the side door just like the bartender.

As I'm turning into his driveway, he says to me: "Wait, let's go up more. You know that cemetery?"

"What's up there?"

"I want to show you, bro."

"Nuh-uh. Whatever you want to show me, you can show me in your driveway."

"Aw man. All right, look. Just come inside for a sec."

"I don't go inside homes, homie."

I'm ready to explain why but Stan doesn't want to hear it. "Then just in my garage, man. Just step inside, that's all. I'll leave the door open, bro."

"Why the fuck for, *bro*? I mean really."

"I want to give you some weed."

"Weed. For real?"

I'm ready to tell him to fuck off for being cagey. But it's

been a lucky night and he's not going to rob me. I've impressed Stan and now he wants to bring me into his private routine.

"All right. But I'm only stepping in the garage."

He goes through the house and from inside opens the first bay door and kicks on the fluorescents. I light a smoke and make sure Salukus isn't waiting in a corner. I shake off the twinge of liability then step inside.

His worktable is arranged with ashtrays and dozens of beer cans and half-spent roaches. We share garage habits. The second bay is occupied by a car tarped over. I can tell it's the Mustang by the tires. More mysterious is the gray 10-foot container stored deep in bay three.

Stan the Kushite enters the garage carrying a fancy blonde electric guitar, the body of which he bangs on the jamb coming through the door.

"Check it. 1964 Gibson ES-335 with the beefy neck. The last year they were worth a shit."

I can understand geek love. This is the same kind of object affection I have for Cab #90.

"But that don't look like weed."

"Right," he says, leading me to the 10-foot container. Stan spins into the Master lock and pulls the bolt then the door creaks open. "Welcome to my lair."

Before he turns on the light, part of me expects to see a metal chair unfolded on a plastic tarp.

Instead it's five microwave boxes stacked on the floor. My host peeps in the first box then punches his way through the top of the next.

"Yeah, this's the one!"

He pulls from the box a clear plastic shipping pillow of marijuana. Next, he bites off a corner and tears it open from there. Inside the air pillow is a string of heat-sealed pouches and he unfurls the whole batch and the pack job is profesh.

"A whole pound of fresh Afghan Kush. This is why I am called the Kushite!"

Next he rips a pouch off on its perforation and chews

doggedly at the plastic corner. I spot scissors on the workbench but his approach is entertaining to watch.

When he at last rips the sack open, Stan withdraws a bud the size of a Coulter pinecone. He holds it up to the container lamp. "I got three boxes of this and one from Colorado and another from Amsterdam. Do you know the value of everything in this container? Do you understand how much capital this represents, bro?"

He stuffs the bud in my hands.

"Ah that ain't enough," and so he tears another nugget off the branch in the pouch, until, "Fuck it," he hands over the whole ounce and the pouch to carry it. "Take it, bro. It belongs to you, you deserving son of a bitch!"

"Thanks, I guess. Where'd this all come from?"

"I can't tell you that," he says. "But I can tell you this is military grade. For real. Brought to you by soldiers in the field."

That gives me a picture and I ask him, "Did they scream up in a Humvee, or what?"

"Special logistics call for special market pricing and this shit goes for a c-note per three-point-five grams. Rate equals Distance divvied by Time, my friend. Five days from the drying shed to the American market. Plus whatever it takes to move in a truck.

"But that's what I can't talk about. Not exactly. But, dude: They truck in all the good shit. I got my hand in the cookie jar of the military-industrial complex, booyah!"

My job never ceases to amaze me for the scenes it conjures when the curtains pull open.

I peep inside the shipping box. Four more air pillows. Sticking from the lid of the box is a packing slip in its plastic sleeve. The sleeve isn't taped over and the bill hangs out like it wants me to snatch it.

"On paper, I'm a lawyer if you ever need one." He snatches a card out of his billfold and gives it over. STANISLAU BAKUYAN, ESQUIRE. "I'm a fucking lawyer, bitches. But now you know what I really do for a living."

He leads out of the container and I, with finger and thumb,

pluck the packing slip from its sleeve and fast stuff it in my hip-sack. Then I dope along out of the shipping can on a slow follow.

"And I can just tip inside this warehouse and buy a sack?"

"Oh hell naw," he says, laughing. "It's a strict program, bro. High dollar buy-ins and bulk sales only. And no walk-ins."

The Kushite finds on his bench a jar with a black resin top. Must be his personal supply.

"You like fine chicks? Young girls with no-hair pussies?"

"As long as they're at least barely legal."

He shows me his smartphone dialed to a video.

"This one's almost barely legal."

The video shows a nude young woman in a horse stall and a gang of cocks. An amateur sex film. But the woman doesn't look barely legal. In fact, I wouldn't put her at 17.

The Kushite whispers with his lips at my ear. "She's 15, bro. Maybe." Same time, he's placed a hand on the small of my back. "This kind of thing turns me on."

"Turn that shit off. And don't touch the cab driver."

He kills the video at once and the tile image returns to the girl's face. I've only caught a glimpse because I'm already marching out of the garage and down the creep's driveway, black-eyed once again by the trick kaleidoscope.

"I can get you Kush and I can get you push," he yells after me. "Know what I mean, baby? This place is wild. I can get you girls, bro. Girls like this."

I consider the girl in the video and the warehouse and what I've been told about the dead brother. And all at once Billy Kinross' bigger fish is no longer a mystery.

9

PAULIE CUTS ME loose at four in the morning for lack of biz. I tally my tripsheet and count my heavy rake and brag for fat tips. After tipping out Paulie, I drop my cash in the safe and walk out of the shop on a strut.

After leaving the Kushite's garage, I'd rolled back through the country club. In part to see if the dipshit was hanging around for his ride, and to see if I could catch sight of Salukus. I saw both in the lobby, laughing with friends, having a casual chat. Nobody wanted my cab or had me as a hot item on their to-do list. Even if Salukus had recognized me from that fucking surveillance tape.

My happy bubble pops soon as I get home. The front doorjamb shows pry marks and the lock is jimmied. The door around back is busted too.

Returning out front, I spy two early bird canners drinking down the apronway. I'd rousted them last week when my bike disappeared. They didn't know anything then and likewise have nothing to do with the current burglary. But they did see two guys pry through the front door.

"It's a Cadillac they drove," the lady says. "A old boxy one."

"What color was it?"

"It was like a red but dark," adds the man. "It was a dark red."

"Oxblood maybe?"
"Is arxblood dark red because I guess so."
"Y'all call the cops?"
"Oh hell no."

I check the busted door and run my hand over the welt pressed in the frame.

Much as I like to shoot and display guns, I don't like to publicly carry the extra weight and responsibility, and I'd never take one in the cab. That leaves me ill-equipped for a scene like this. So I call a couple drivers for backup. I also ring Billy and to my surprise he answers right off.

"I got something on that warehouse. Meet me at my place."

I kill the call before he replies and he doesn't call back.

Quiet Chuck blows across the lot causing the canners to yell. Wayne Linder is a minute behind and finds us buying smokes at the Kum & Go. I ask if they got flashlights and Wayne shows he's got a pistol. I tell him, "You're coming with me."

Chuck parks his van against the front door so it can't be escaped and I tell him to yell if anything rattles.

At the back door, Wayne and I crunch over the glass of the busted overhead lamp. The ground glitters under our flashlights.

Wayne keeps his voice low. "He pried through the front and this'ne too. Now what kind of drugged-up mental defective would do that?"

I run my hand over the gnarled metal and read the warning that I'm no longer safe in Freedom Cove.

I toe the door and Wayne moves ahead like a professional party breaker, knees bent and feet walking heel-toe, penlight stuck between his knuckles under the barrel. All tricks he's learned from YouTube.

A quick pass with our lights shows the place ransacked and I brick the door shut behind us. Moving forward, Wayne clears the sleeping cabin and bathroom while I turn on the factory overheads. Piles of broken shit everywhere. Boxes of books split open and janitor clothes scattered. Bunk beds toppled, aquariums smashed, freedom flags torn. The hydraulic hoses are slashed on the machines and the wheels of the 'Yota are stabbed out. My Liberty Collection is also missing.

Chuck has pulled from the door and joins us in the mess.

"At least you never got any fish."

I've confided in both of them the misadventure with UniCab #15 and seeing the 'Yota's tires Wayne asks, "Is this the Turk getting back at you?"

"I paid that dude off. This is something different."

The burglars even cut up the taxidermied animals. I drag a hand through my hair and curse.

We all smoke cigarettes and Wayne opens the mini-fridge.

"More bad news. They took all your beer, fella."

He offers to bribe the Kum & Go clerk for an afterhours sale and I tell him I'm not drinking. In fact, what I need is breathing room. "Thank you boys but I need to clean shit up."

After they bang out the front door, I have time enough to light a cigarette before hearing the brick scrape open in back. Billy Kinross stands in the breach. He must've been nearby.

"What happened here?"

I point my Maglite at him. "I'm gonna fuck somebody up. They took the time to cut the glass eyes out of all my animals."

Billy limps from me butting him with the shotgun.

"They took your heat," he waves at the empty mantle. "You got to report that."

"Ah I've had a wild-ass night."

"Was this Salukus?" His face has gone gray. "Did Salukus find you out?"

"It was either Salukus or it was you. But this time I'm sticking with the devil I know."

"And what's that supposed mean?"

I dig in my purse for the packing slip. "I snatched this off a box filled with high grade cannabis. Bona fide lawyer weed."

I show Billy the weed and the food-grade pouch it came in.

"Five boxes of the shit and dude called it military grade. The box he opened originally shipped from Afghanistan."

Impressed, Billy pulls the longest branch from the sleeve

and holds it in the overhead light, takes a whiff. "How many pounds per unit?"

"Five per box for twenty-five total. Dude bragged that he gets all kinds of grass. Stan the Kushite. He's a lawyer but said this was his real job."

My show-and-tell isn't garnering the kind of amazement I was expecting so I spell it out.

"We got an address, Billy. We got a location for that black market warehouse."

He looks at the bill and he looks at me.

"I'm curious why you suddenly give a shit."

"You don't know where it's at and whoomp there it is."

"That doesn't tell me why you care. Somebody trashes you're home and you want to roll out Rambo, I get it." He waves the bill at me. "But this don't add up."

"It's something else the guy showed me. He had a video on his cell phone of this too young a girl."

"They can make those barely legal girls look real young."

"He told me she was fifteen, Billy. He said he could get all these kinds of girls. Young girls. Just like he could get a mountain of Kush."

Billy shrugs unimpressed so I throw an ace.

"And what doesn't add up is anything you've told me. What you haven't told me about this warehouse. And why you're really robbing drug dealers. And what any of it's got to do with your dead brother."

He's cut by the last remark but disappears his feelings in the hollow of his eyes.

"That all's too long for tonight. Too many stories."

"It's been too many from the get with you, Billy. You crazy fuck. You were into big shit when we robbed those dudes. You should've warned me how big."

"Ever since I met you, you've been an asshole. Thinking I'm a hobo. Thinking I'm fucked up for good because of my whole bad life. Hitting me with that shotgun."

"Draw on me again and I'll be inclined to use the other end."

"And look how you jelloed after punk-ass got killed. And you wanted to what? Go tell everybody what we did? That's weak shit and so fuck you."

This argument isn't going where I want so I throw my bluff.

"If you don't tell me what's going on, I'm going to the cops with what I got on this dude Salukus and their drug warehouse. And the sex slaves too."

The last note grabs him by the short hairs. But he fights it.

"You won't go to the cops."

"Until I get Salukus and whoever else off my back, there's no Freedom Cove for me anywhere. Telling cops is one way of ending this bullshit."

"Telling the cops is a one way ticket to prison. And you know that. That's why you didn't go to the cops the other night."

That sets me off and I yell kicking trash around my garage until I see he's waving the packing slip at me.

"C'mon. Let's take a ride."

"I'm driving then. I'm all amped up on this shit."

He throws me the keys to the Jeep and I head for the toilet.

They haven't taken all my guns. I punch a hole in the drywall above the tank using its porcelain lid. From out of the hole I take a freezer bag. Inside the bag, a Glock 17 9mm with the numbers drilled off the receiver, plus two loaded clips.

Billy tells me, "You won't need that."

After strangers have broken into my home, I lament not having a concealed carry permit. But rolling with Billy Kinross, I'd be fool to go unarmed.

WE ROAR ACROSS the outer dark under clear skies and bright stars. The air is chill and I bring the window up. The route takes us seven miles south and a few more due east until we arrive at an untillable corner of our county. The glow of the place beyond the hills can be seen from three miles off. I cut my speed in half as we drive up on it.

"Your pal Damen's got bad info," I report right off. "It ain't a big red barn."

The warehouse is big but beige and set an easy hundred yards south from the road. A guard mans the gated turnabout and I can see scales behind the razor-top fence. Standard warning plaques are posted but there are no corporate banners on the warehouse.

A half mile on, Billy points me right onto a gravel leg that a mile further brings us to an unsigned crossroads. He puts me into another right so that we come along the first road south of the warehouse. A half mile on, he points me over a cattle bridge and we roll north on a creekside track that warns ENTER AT YOUR OWN RISK. Billy tells me to kill the lights.

We arrive to a stand of rotten pines and the shell of a farmhouse. He unpacks a black kitbag from the Jeep and turns on a red-lens flashlight. I keep my Maglite holstered in my hammer pocket and cover him with the Glock.

"Knock that shit off," he says.

The farmhouse had its north face blown off long ago and all furnishings picked soon thereafter. Only a rusty old clapbed in the corner remains. The floorboards have been kicked in and the cabinets yanked down. A roost for animals and birds.

"How do you know about this place?"

"Because you're right that I know about this place," he says. "That's my bed in the corner."

I look at the bed and I look at him.

"If you already knew this place, then my packing slip is shit."

"It's evidence, bubba," he disputes. "And evidence we need. It's proof of concept."

Billy unzips the kitbag and unpacks a spotting scope. When he kicks out the tripod, he gives me first view. The rangefinder tells me the fence is a little over 1000 yards away. Adjusting the glass, I see the two-story terminal building stands 200 yards beyond that. The yard is huge with a laydown for machinery and boom trucks lined up with diggers and cranes. I can hear the chirp of backup signals on forklifts. Twelve docks on the terminal's westside, three with interior bays. Two tall doors at the rear that must be the mechanics garage. Probably fewer docks on the eastside because that's where the office windows are footed. Cameras peep on every corner.

"Looks legit. Why do you think that's a black market?"

Billy tells me they call it National Dunnage & Barrow, doing business as ND&B.

"Our country imports more cocaine and heroin than any other kid on the block. Most of it ships through Mexico where smugglers move 900 tons of cocaine every year. Worldwide, they're moving 9000 tons heroin. That's a lot of tough logistics and transport. And that's what ND&B brings to the table.

"ND&B owns 11 freight hubs all over North America. They operate the docks and manage the yards. They own a fleet of trucks, which is how they move illegal goods alongside legal. They also operate a brokerage and it's somebody in the brokerage handling the black loads. That's what your packing slip tells me."

Lackluster moonlight glows on his face, making it float like a mask. I've noticed his shift in tone and depth. In his word choices at the atomic level. I feel for the first time I'm seeing the monster at its bony core. The real Billy Kinross. The mask of his face retreats into dark.

"I'm taking down ND&B because they buy and sell kids. Women and illegals too. But I'm here for the kids."

"So where do they shelve kids in a warehouse?"

"They move them cross-country between motels, safe houses, shop basements. Like that. Like with the drugs, ND&B brokers the deal and the transport."

"You've got proof of this?"

"That's why I'm watching them. Because I need evidence, Vic. Real evidence. Something with teeth."

"What're you going to do when you find these teeth?"

His face rushes glowing into the moonlight.

"'Whosoever should steal a man for the purpose of selling

him shall be put to death.'"

"Sounds like Captain Jerry."

"It's the only scripture I know."

If Billy isn't some kind of twisted fucked-up hero, he's a twisted fuck-up with a hero complex. Whichever, I'm not moved by his sense of duty. It's the plight of the girl in the video and Billy's brother, Ethan, who have me shivering out here.

"Why'd you lie to me about this place? Why'd you say you didn't know where it was?"

"That was theatrics for Damen Phipps. I got him looking for a red barn, remember?"

"So what about Phipps helping you rob his own gang?"

"What about it?"

"You lied, fuckface. You lied to me. That score was huge and you didn't tell me you were working with the lynchpin of the gang we robbed. What you did was spin bullshit about tying up those dudes." I point to the warehouse. "Now you got me spying on what looks like a legitimate crossdock but you say they're running dope out of there. So what's your real angle? Wait, don't tell me because it's just more bullshit."

Billy gives a long blank look.

"I don't care about the drugs. I never robbed the Phipps Bros for their drugs, or their money. I wanted a gate to the people behind them. To ND&B."

"So it doesn't matter that a young dude got killed?"

"I was onto ND&B when I went after the Phipps Bros. They're the weak link. And it's true that Damen told me about the score, and that I cut him in. But that scene played like I said. With the gun on that dude's neck and those bitches left tied up. And I didn't have shit to do with the cab drivers getting robbed. All that's on Leon and the dead brother."

"You still should've told me."

"If I'd told you I was using you as bait, you wouldn't have helped. So I apologize if a white lie has hurt your swollen feelings. Let's just call it even for you calling me a hobo."

"Are you fucking serious?"

Billy gives me his serious eyes.

"We ought to split before sun up," he says.

He breaks down the scope while I surrender a yawn and a big stretch, all the fight bled out of me.

I ask, "Can you talk and steer?"

"Sho nuff, bubba."

I hand him the keys. "Then you drive us home."

BILLY TAKES US out the Level B road and back to the gravel then west until we hit blacktop that could take us back to town. But he opts to take the long way home on Hwy 218. The freeway thickens with pickups and Subarus as dawn shines on storm clouds towering in the west. The Glock weighs heavy in my waistband so I dump it and the clips in the glove box with the motel Bible. Then I shut my eyes.

I come awake to Billy signaling off the interstate. We've blown past our exit and come 10 miles north of town. "What're we doing up here?"

"Going to my crib. I got a spare room and didn't think you'd want to go back home."

The Jeep booms over blacktop past county reserves and private communities north of the lake. Playing passenger is liberating when I'm so used to being the driver. I let my eyes roam to where an early orange glow prowls the waysides.

In and out of trees, we cross the hill country until Billy turns into a gated lane. He codes through and we enter on a white granite gravel driveway that runs half a mile through the woods.

The driveway ends at a rotunda drive and two-door garage belong to an über-modern home built on a bluff that overlooks the lake. On the whole, it resembles a spaceship. Or a modern art school with its glass walls and exaggerated peaks.

"I knew it! You hobos make bank on all those cans."

"Real fucking funny, asshole."

In the foyer, I detect a damp odor. Something warm and fungal. He throws on the globe lamps. We descend the stairs onto a big landing and see that everything else is built three stories down including an awesome great room with glass walls that offer wooded views of the lakefront.

"Watch this shit."

He thumbs a remote to darken the towering windows and I catch that odor again. Deeper and fouler as we descend into the home. This is the funk I've whiffed from Billy's clothes.

"Did this place flood?"

"We're thirty feet above the water."

"So what's that smell?"

"They tell me it's old pipes. Or a leak in the wall."

"Could be black mold."

"Relax. I'm only renting."

From the landing we come down a spiral staircase into a sitting area of modern square couches, orange cushions atop white casings. The floor is heated slate and the glass fireplace is big enough for a Yule log.

The blackout windows have returned the setting to a kind of nighttime darkness and I eyeball the bar. Ensconced lighting glows out of the ceiling above and behind is a wall full of mirrors and an aquarium swimming with saltwater fish. A waterfall rushes out of the wall into a bubbling pond.

"Is it the pond that stinks?"

"I hardly smell it," Billy says, cranking on the ceiling fans.

"Inhaling it all this time I bet you don't."

"The rental agent knows but I don't push the issue. Getting it cleaned means having people around. Plus he's cut two grand a month off the rent as is."

"Where the hell do you get the money to pay for all this?"

"Ask me about the money in the morning. Right now we got something else."

He pulls the handle of a slim refrigerator that rolls out of the wall, grabs us beers and limps ahead down more stairs.

We enter a closed-up portion of the house, a hall full of

doors. The door at the end leads to a windowless office with two big computer stations and six monitors hung on VESA mounts. The far wall is further decked with two huge LCD monitors and there's a walk-in server closet chilled with its own AC unit.

Billy keys into a database and the big wall of monitors render a flowchart covered in names and lines of relation and photographs. "This is what I want to show you."

The bottom of Billy's chart focuses on DAMEN PHIPPS.

"Far as I can tell, the Phipps Bros weren't very organized until they got on the ND&B supply. After that, they began resupplying sellers all over town."

The flow of lines places the Phipps Bros at the head of MAJOR LOCAL DEALERS, including a list of frats and clubs, and a listing for POSER BIKERS. All these groups are shown to receive supply from DON SALUKUS, the chart's central figure.

"Deliveries are made by Salukus and his associate, Charley. At least that's been my experience."

"I'm surprised you'd risk buying direct from them."

"I had to test the waters," he says.

Salukus has three lieutenants working for him and Billy enlarges their images on the main screen. The three faces are marked with radio call signs and I recognize two right off. AVERIL is a big round black dude and BUNKER is a dumpy white guy with a crappy mustache. The same team that roughed up Hustler for buying from another supplier. CHARLEY looks like Radar O'Reilly.

The head of the chart describes the buttoned-down end of the business. Supply comes from ND&B which is shown to have a relationship with a local investment firm, DEVGRO.

"Is this for fucking real? These are the same guys building the southwest corridor."

"ND&B supplies product but only with large local investment fronting the risk. In this case, DevGRO. In turn, ND&B handles sales and delivery to local buyers."

Billy brings up pictures of the firm's officers: H. THOMAS HOUSTON III, CHRISTIAN PAINE, STANISLAU BAKUYAN.

Fuck me. I recognize Christian Paine as my dipshit fare and

H. Thomas Houston III as the coma guy.

"And you got a picture of the Kushite? This dude Bakuyan."

Billy adds the nickname to his database.

"So is this guy Salukus red mafia or Albanian, or what?"

He shakes his head then shrugs.

"They're multinationals, maybe. A global corporate mafia. Maybe it's cartel business. Or CIA. Like you say, 'military.' But the paperwork all ties to a dead guy in Florida. Whoever runs it is sophisticated and avoids the law. Buyers issue anonymous orders through an encrypted website and pay for them via escrow."

"They offer escrow services?"

"Like I said: Sophisticated. ND&B holds the funds and provides facilities for the physical transfer of said goods. I might not know who's sitting at the head of their boardroom but I'm burning my way up the ladder to find out."

I'm worn out and the one beer is hitting me like a punch on the chin. Yet my skin prickles to talk.

"It's Salukus that sacked Freedom Cove," I finally tell him. "When I got home, these canners said the burglars drove an oxblood Caddy. Same car Catfish said was driving the killers of Chemo Phipps." I make my warning clear. "We need to exercise extreme caution around Salukus. And if this operation is a military grade, we might want to split for fucking Canada."

"He's a tough nut, no doubt," Billy says "He made quick work of you, anyway. How'd he find out where you stay?"

"Only ones that know are you, the drivers, a few friends, some canners, and my landlord." Now I'm staring at the floor thinking about it. "But isn't there another way of getting in there besides going through Salukus?"

"How do you mean?"

"Would they take us for suppliers? Like what if we had 50 pounds of fake weed, or pills? What about repacking that heroin you put aside?"

Billy shakes his head without thinking much about it. "First off, we stole that heroin from them, bubba."

"That's what's clever about the plan—*bubba*."

"Second: They wouldn't buy one key unless we had 50 more. And that's what wrong with the rest of it. None of that would work unless chumps like us had mad volume."

10

WE RIDE IN a great orange lifeboat, the bunch of us from the old crew at Taxi Gold. Jerry's there dispatching. Chuck and Wayne and Paulie are there, and Leon is stabbing a needle in his neck. Big Mike and Helene, and Big Jim and Geoff, Phi, #5, and Perry and Norbert who trained everybody Harry didn't, and there's Joe Vega and Billy and Zina and me. The raft is a huge orange wheel with all of us facing each other like it's an amusement park ride. The sky above is shocking azure blown with heroic clouds that wage against an endless sunset. We all scream as the sea heaves our craft across terrifying waves and the water's surface ruptures with the fins of mechanical sharks. No land in site.

"Man overboard!"

Billy flops in the green waves and chokes water, struggles to reach the craft, reaches his hand out to mine. As I grab hold of him, I draw from behind my back a curved blade that I run across his arm. Then I let him go to bleed out in the shark water. I retake my seat. The seas have calmed at once and only Leon complains. "But he knew where to score heroin!"

I wake to coffee grinding. I shuffle to the kitchen and take a stool at the marble kitchen island, sleepy eyed and jonesing for a cigarette. I can smell he doesn't smoke in the house.

"Morning."

I read the bag of coffee beans like I'll read anything. It tells me Billy likes local roast beans traded from Oaxaca, Mexico. "Bet you'd drink this stuff from Patagonia. These beans that a marmot shits out."

"They're from the Philippines and get passed through what's called a civet. Makes pretty decent juice. Pricey though."

Billy limps to a boiling water kettle and fills the coffee plunger. He's wearing his face clean shaven for the first since I've known him.

Despite the gagged-pipe stink, the digs are sweet. The kind of house in a Williams-Sonoma catalog. Afternoon sun plays through the high windows and every room is spectacular. A big flatscreen hangs over the kitchen island and shows HLN's up-to-the-minute coverage of global bullshit. A massive glass nook overlooks the side acreage. Its table is arranged with four place settings. The plates looks dusty but I have to ask: "We expecting two more?"

"Oh I don't ever eat over there. I just think it looks homey."

Billy halves blood oranges and juices them by hand, meantime frying eggs, ham steaks, and a pile of shoestring potatoes. The toast pops and he shoves the butter bell my way. Then he keeps up with oranges until he's like, "Fuck this baloney," and passes me a quarter glass. "Coffee will be right up. Marmalade for the toast?"

"Not my style, bro."

Sitting at the kitchen island, forking through breakfast at three in the afternoon, I handle the remote and dim the window shade just a bit. Then I dial it back up a little. The ham and eggs are delicious and the Mexican coffee is out of sight. "Pour me another cup of that God Almighty and tell me how we're getting inside this warehouse. We need evidence with teeth."

"You gave me the idea," he says. "They might bite if we had enough product to sell. And if we get in on the buying side, I can get the layout or a passcard and bust in later."

"So you know a killer weed farm we could rob? Or what?"

"Anhydrous ammonia."

"Ammonia?"

"All the farms around here use it. It also a lead ingredient in the production of crystal meth."

"I know what it is, dickweed. But how much do we need to steal? A nurse tank?"

"A whole big-ass tanker."

"I spose we just run farm to farm with our tanker nipping gallons at a time."

"I'm piecing it together, bubba, so let me. I had this biker a while back tell me about some shit." He grabs up his smokes. "Come on. I got to put a call in before I get into the rest of it."

I follow him out of the kitchen.

"You're just like Bruce Wayne up in here. You should have fire poles installed."

Billy puzzles up his face. "He's a fireman?"

"Naw, man. I mean, here you are in your mansion living off an unseen pile of cash and you got this secret basement from where you hack bad guys then go hunt them down. You already got a mask and you ought to wear a cape."

That gets Billy nodding.

"I was going to say that all sounds like Batman."

AFTERNOON IS COOL and we sit on the wraparound porch what overlooks the lake, Billy lounging in a sunbather and me in the hot tub, both of us wearing sunglasses and smoking tobacco and Kush. We also iron out the details for Plan B: Selling a Stolen Tanker of Anhydrous Ammonia to a Mobile Black Market in Effort to Gain Evidence of a Child Pornography Ring.

Billy asks: "You know Shake Reding?"

"He was driving when I got my start. His old lady Bonnie was working in the tobacco shack that night."

Just like with Bonnie, it was speed that put Shake Reding on the fade from taxi driving and eventually into prison.

"Shake can put us in touch with the ammonia," says Billy. "And once we can get it, we better be ready to move."

Next, he calls a meeting with Shake and Shake tells us to come over this afternoon.

We next call in sick to work using different excuses and flipping coins for who gets to call first. On Billy's losing turn, he hands the phone to me. "Somebody wanted to talk but you rushed through your bit too fast."

"Hullo?"

I can the hear radio chatter and noise of the taxi shack in the background but for a moment it's just dead air. Finally Captain Jerry gets on asking if it's me in the phone.

"The one and only."

"I got to tell you, buddy. I'm sorry."

"What do you got to be sorry for?"

"Those two fellas came by for Billy and I told them he might be over at your garage."

"When was this?"

"Late last night. Early this morning."

"So you sent them to my crib?"

"I realize it was the wrong thing to do. And I am so sorry."

"Jerry, goddammit. They wrecked all my shit, man. All my taxidermied animals. They carved up the felt on my Brunswick table and busted the stone."

I'll yell at anybody. And when he wants to go on apologizing, I hang up.

"Did you hear that shit?"

"You didn't ask what they look like. And I'd've done the same thing at his age. Go easy on an old man."

He opens the laptop and starts hunting for semis online.

"You're buying a truck?"

"It's not like Rent-a-Wreck lends them out," he says. "Besides all we need is a day cab. Find one at a good price and I can flip it on the backside."

"Can you drive one?"

"Hell no. Your idea, you're driving the truck."

He doesn't even ask if I can manage it.

"So where'd you get the money for all this?"

Billy looks off the edge of the deck as if still looking for a way to hold off the question. Then I see a shift in the lizard brain shrouded behind his eyes and he speaks.

"I was seventeen last time I got out of juvie. Uncle Frank was in a nine-month county bid so it was just me and Jerry in the house. Jerry had gone sober and to preaching Jesus. Telling how he was going to help me. Pushing me to attend his downstate church. It was a small congregation for real fuckups, mostly men. The preacher looked cool though. Mick Jagger with surfer hair. I asked what kid he'd fucked to be the head of Kid Fucker Church. Instead of punching me or leaving off like the others, the preacher laughed. Said he wasn't a toucher. Said he felt moved by the spirit to help these men. Etcetera. Also said he liked my spirit and my red mohawk too."

Since Jerry mentioned it, I've been trying to picture the mohawk on Billy but I just can't see it.

"The preacher owned land a couple hours down in Missoura," he goes on. "His sons threw thrash parties. All next week was a big jamboree in fact with bands and people from all over and wouldn't I like to party with badass dudes? But I wasn't there a minute before I realized the jamboree was all white power bros and Nazi skins and Klansmen."

"I hate Missouri Nazis."

"I hate them all," he says. "For a whole week I had to bolt my mouth shut and not think. And they kept us twisted, bubba. Riled on crank and shine til we puked and drank and snorted and smoked more. We were awake for days."

Billy lifts his t-shirt over his head but leaves his arms inside. The center of his chest is tattooed with a thick black swastika. It's tipped on one point and outlined so the icon really stamps on the eye.

Then he yanks the shirt back over his head.

"It's not what you think," he warns. "They got me while I was out of my mind."

"Lie down with Nazis, get up with tattoos."

"I'm only thankful the inkman kept a steady hand. I wanted to burn those motherfuckers to death. Instead I ran and hid in the trees. And I just kept running until I was hitchhiking north. I finally came down outside of Mexico, Missoura."

He falls quiet and I watch a bald eagle soar overhead as it follows the shoreline. The hot tub churns and I listen for birdsongs and hear Billy lighting a cigarette.

"That the end of your story?"

"That's the first that needed told," he says. "Because after they gave me their mark, I decided to use it."

"And how in the fuck?"

"I hit my first skins in the town of Mexico. I knocked on the clubhouse door and they let me right in when I showed them my sign. Then I worked my way down the Ozarks into Oklahoma and Texas. I'd drift into town to pal up with WP dudes. Peel off my shirt and play their game. Then I'd swoop in and snatch their shit and move on."

The big eagle has rounded overhead again. Billy spies it with a hand at his brow.

"About a year later I was in Waco when the Feds killed all those people. I met a dude that was gun crazy and talk crazy and hawking white books out his car. So I latched on tight. He was called Timmy Tuttle.

"Meeting him was important," says Billy. "Because a year after that I was worming into this Aryan militia in Oklahoma hill country and who shows up but everybody's buddy, Timmy Tuttle. He's got deep credit with these fools and he vouched for seeing me at Waco. Swore I was a true patriot and all that.

"Same time, the hill country gang got in a score. One night they rushed back to the farm and dumped a stolen Durango shoveled full of cash. Loot plucked off another hill country gang. They were putting it on me and Timmy until the heat died down.

"But they all died before the heat did. And in the thick of it, Timmy Tuttle kept his shit wired. He figured cops were coming, or worse. 'Better on us than them, right?' So we shoveled the cash into Timmy's car and drove up to Kansas where he had a friend with a backhoe and some backland. I spend the drive packing cash in double Ziplocs and we buried the money in a field. "Two years later we were both headed to prison. We'd split long before that. Timmy couldn't shut up about his revolution and I wasn't down. And even though we had a gentleman's agreement about the money, I figured he'd dug it up. Especially when I learned what he'd done."

"What'd he do?"

"The point is I didn't know yet what he'd done," he replies. "I was in prison that whole time and didn't keep with the outside. Didn't get calls from home except the one about Ethan. That single phone call was like getting bit by a power line. Knowing he'd been alive and what was happening to him while I played bad boy. Knowing he'd escaped just to kill himself. I knew then I'd spend the rest of my life hunting down that entire business.

"I got out of prison June 11, 2001. There I am at Huntsville bus station reading in the *Dallas Morning News* about my buddy, Timmy Tuttle. Scheduled to be executed by lethal injection that morning. It was already noon so I went to a bar and got drunk watching the television. That's when I learned everybody else knew him as Tim McVeigh."

That grabs my ears. "Say again?"

Billy says, "I'd heard about the bombing but didn't know none of it in prison. Didn't care to. I actually thought it was something from the Civil War. But fresh out in Huntsville, it was go-time. Timmy was dead and our agreement was to leave the money buried 20 years unless the other man died. And it being go-time, I had to try for that money. I stole a car and drove to Kansas and found the spot by GPS and dug by my headlights until the sun came up. That's when I found what we'd buried. Over $2-million in double-sealed Ziplocs."

He puffs on his hash pipe and I climb up on the lip of the hot tub and leave my feet dangling in the jets.

"So you just blow cash chasing kiddie peddlers and driving cabs, or what?"

"After I got out of the joint, I hooked up with this guy, Roberto Castillo. Called J-Bob. He'd been a federal agent and you might've read about him. Got the boot for killing the man who sold his daughter to the cartels."

"I dunno," I tell him.

"J-Bob brought me into his organization. They were ex-cops and military dads, and a few lean, pissed-off moms. Everybody had lost somebody to the sex trade and everybody wanted justice. We worked just like you saw in my basement but on a large scale. J-Bob taught me how to trade stocks too and we made my little chunk of cash into a big one."

"So what happened to you and them?"

"They didn't care for my methods." Billy shrugs. "Ah brother, I don't talk enough about this shit. My ma and daddy. And Ethan. They're all dead. And I don't talk to my sister. I don't have family. Through all this though you and me have become kind of like that. Family. I decided you're all right."

I shiver like somebody's walked over my grave. "When'd you decide that?"

"Back when I told you about Ethan. Now I've told you the rest of it. The milestones anyway. Feels good to talk about it."

Billy Kinross. He who would make lemonade from swastikas, and whose path is the creepiest that I've ever crossed.

SHAKE AND BONNIE Reding have been speeding since the '70s. They were both driving cab when I started and we were all pals, sharing war stories and blowing our minds on alcohol and pills at Sunday morning afterhours.

Shake went to prison for not recognizing that the poleman hanging on the wire tree outside his trailer was a state investigator taking pictures. His old lady, Bonnie, was left to spin out. She struggled while he was inside and eventually got slapped with an OWI and possession. I cut my ties and never wrote to Shake, even though I said I would, and wouldn't answer when Bonnie called.

Today they stay down in Washington County in a mobile court that hugs a bend in the river. We park the Jeep and Billy limps across the planks laid over the drain ditch. At the far end of the boards, Shake and Bonnie have put up a welcome trellis though it's bare of any roses. In the yard beyond, ornamental stone chicks and a gazing ball fallen off its pedestal. Nothing remains of the pink flamingos but their metal stakes.

The sagging trailer looks ready to be cubed and sent to China. But Shake has built a handsome tractor shed in the yard behind it. We bypass the trailer door and follow classic rock and work noises buzzing out of the shed. The door hangs open and shirtless Shake Redding is digging in the guts of a machine.

"Howdy, stranger!" He grips my hand and pulls me in for a bear hug. "How've you been?"

He gives Billy the same hearty treatment and shows us the clothes dryer he's dismantled to get the tumble drum out to use as a firepit. He's removed the drum but continues to reduce the dryer into its many hundreds of parts. Screws and bushings and cut copper hairs have been arranged on the floor in what must be a mandala until I see Shake is replicating the exploded diagram from the repair manual. I tell him he looks busy.

"Ah fuck this noise. Let's go smoke grass."

Shake pulls on his shirt and leads us to the trailer, jogging ahead and shoving the door wide.

"Look who it is!"

The trailer is dark and cool as a cave though the floor is like cardboard. The air stinks of ashtrays and cat piss. The walls are decorated with three-coyote banners, shag tapestries, pictures of dream catchers. Three dogs and four cats race from one end of the trailer to the other and the television is the size of a billboard.

Shake falls in his La-Z-Boy and reaches for a pair of forceps fitted with a roach. He digs into old times right away. "You remember when Bonnie gave you that ditchweed and you had a airport delivery and Dick Cheney was there and secret service searched your cab?"

"Like it happened yesterday," I tell him.

"What was the delivery again?"

"Eyeballs."

"That's it! Eyeballs."

The animals race to the other side of the trailer barking and bounding, and Billy and I grab couch space in view of the giant television, currently airing the cable index.

"Oh my God. Vic Pasternak!"

I can tell Bonnie's voice anywhere. Nasal, tinny, and rough. She puts out her arms wanting a big hug so I get off the couch and cross the spongy floor to give her one.

The bathroom is behind the kitchen and now its door half opens. I see a hand hang on the knob and a hairy arm span the breach, eagle tattoo spread across is. Pants and tidies bundled on ankles, woman's head bobbing between his bare knees.

"Tell them boys we be right out."

The bathroom door shoves closed and I look at Bonnie and then she and I look at Billy. He asks us: "Is that him?"

Billy's filled me in on the ride down here. Rod MacGuffin is a veteran meth cook and underworld businessman. He also ran a motorcycle club in North Missouri. Satan's Grangers. Billy reminded me they were the bikers shooting pool at the Railroad House. Billy says the gang used to run heroin and coke up here out of St. Louis. From what he's heard, MacGuffin got squeezed out by ND&B. Then the club splintered earlier this year when two of its members were convicted of selling cocaine to federal agents. A third was charged with witness tampering. Defectors sung to reporters of the gang's violent supremacist leanings. Billy naturally took an interest.

Here come cats and dogs racing and Bonnie clutches my arm. "What happened that night?"

I know what she means but ask her anyway.

"What night?"

"With that fool boy that cain't bleach his hair?" She brings her voice to the floor. "You hear he got killed? I'll bet that was a time coming."

I can tell she's speeding by the way her jaw clutches as she talks. Like an animatronic out of sync with its dialogue. "You seen what the cat done to my rug? Tearing it up and spraying on it. I'm just going to strangle that bad little boy."

I go back to the couch and plop down. We're not here five minutes and already the frenzy of talk is giving me a headache.

The bathroom door tears open and Rod MacGuffin comes out swinging a thin leather strap in circles around his fist.

Billy stands from the couch as Shake makes the introductions. I give a tip of my head.

Rod MacGuffin wears red hair shocked with gray in a long straight ponytail, his sun-worn face grown with a mustache losing its blond, and beady eyes squinted up. He hitches the waist of his jeans and this reinforces his look as a bad dude from central casting. SS tattoo on his neck and a swastika covers the top of the right hand. Jeans and jackboots, a black t-shirt advertising a death head in a war bonnet, and sleeveless leather patched proper. He takes stock of us and rolls his tongue in his mouth like it's a butterscotch.

Then out from the toilet walks a woman with a face that looks pretty across the dim trailer. Except as she steps into the kitchen light I see she is Letty Fetch and I fold in half on the couch laughing.

"What's so funny, Vicky?"

"I just wasn't expect you is all. I've met your husband."

"We was only promised." She no longer squeaks in the Minnie Mouse voice. Her eyes ride glazed and her feet shuffle-step. She slithers an arm around MacGuffin's waist and with the other points a long, accusatory finger at me. "That hillbilly doesn't know how to dance."

She laughs and laughs and MacGuffin catches her by the elbow to keep her on her feet. Then he tells her to sit at the kitchen table and swats her butt as she toddles off.

"Now there's a woman that does what she's told."

I ask Billy, "Do you know Letty?"

"Nope."

His eyes linger in mine to say that he does.

Dogs and cats race to and fro as Bonnie yells at them to quit. Shake asks if we all want ice tea or a bump of crank or an ice-cream bar.

MacGuffin sits in the available easy chair and grins when he talks. "So you boys're buying a pound of crank, or what?"

Billy turns on Shake, "Did you tell him what we want?"

"They're looking for ammonia, Mac."

"I know it but business is for doing business."

"We don't need any crank," Billy snaps at him.

MacGuffin grins.

"So then what kind of ammonia you want?"

Billy won't answer right off and I can see how he drops his shoulders and tilts his head that he doesn't like MacGuffin. He says, "That kind that fills up a whole tanker."

"Big old white buffalo. I can get you nurse tanks easy."

"None of them small tanks. We want a tanker. And I don't mean commercial ammonia hosed in the back of a milk truck. I mean a D.O.T.-approved MC 331 filled to capacity. There's money in it for everybody." Billy fingers everyone in the room.

"What're you doing with the ammonia?"

"Growing a hundred acres of weed. I got a home kit."

"Ha. You okay, man." Then he points at me. "Your partner here fucks squirrels and can't dance. But you're all right! What kind of money?"

"It's a spot market. I got to see what we can get."

"Farm ammonia goes $1200 a ton right now. About $20,000 wholesale in that tank. What let's say you give me half."

"How do you figure half?"

"Me have ammonia. You no have ammonia."

Billy sighs for these tactics. "How would this work?"

"I got a uncle owns the gas exchange south of here. Tanks get pulled from stock and brought to his station. They linger two or three days waiting on their buyer before getting restocked. In that window, somebody might snatch one."

"When?"

"Monday, maybe Tuesday."

Billy wises his eyes. "Half to you and I can't get it sooner?"

"It's the weekend, sparky. What kind of tractor you got?"

"Don't worry about my end. Worry about the tanker."

Rod MacGuffin sits with elbows bent on his knees and rubs his palms together.

"Only one place round here I think you might sell illegal ammonia off the books. Only one place got that kind of flex. It's that big old warehouse, ain't it? Some big red barn."

Billy won't bite and MacGuffin pushes with another.

"It's a warehouse where they got a black market. What do you know about it?"

Billy shrugs it off.

"How about letting me tag along then?"

"I can't have that, bubba."

MacGuffin lights a cig and sits in the easy chair, thinking.

"If you can't let me help, I want 15 percent more."

"Take your half and we got a deal." Billy says. "We're putting in the work while you got your boots kicked up."

"I need at least 10 percent better. You making an order afterhours and all. And never mind legalities and the risk I take. Say you know what? Maybe I can't get you that tanker after all."

Billy stares at MacGuffin and I can hear him grind his teeth. He says, "Let's call that a deal at 60 percent then."

They all stand and shake hands. Shake and Bonnie smile big and I wonder what cut they get. Letty Fetch is in a kitchen chair nodded out with head down on crossed arms and drooling on the floor.

MacGuffin says the key for the kingpin lock can be gotten from the office Monday morning and that he can get us the right-looking paperwork too.

"There's just one more thing," says Bonnie, and for a moment I think she's going to peel out of her shirt.

"We got to smurf for Mac and need help on the rounds." She means shopping for precursors. "I'm's heading out tonight and there's a thousand Walmarts within two hours of here."

She looks at us and Billy looks my way.

"That ain't my kind of work," I tell him.

"I got this," says Billy. "But y'all can get me home?"

Shake replies, "Why shore!"

They give me hugs and I don't acknowledge MacGuffin. Then Billy walks me out to the Jeep. He follows me across the drain ditch and wants to talk.

"I'll send word to ND&B that we'll have the tank for sale. You going to be all right?"

"I'm fine. You look a little punked."

Billy looks back at the trailer. "I don't like his bitch."

"Letty's bad news," I tell him. "She madams the massage parlor on Dubuque Street."

Billy shakes his head. He knows Letty from somewhere else.

"She's that mystery white girl I saw in Damen's crib the night I robbed him."

Now it's me looking back at the trailer. "Phipps was in on the robbery. So why was she there? Why did she have to be there that night?"

"I'd guessed she was sex trading. But she's got to be why these boys have the same bad intel. Their picture of a big red barn."

I carry it further.

"So Phipps told Letty and Letty told MacGuffin? So then what if it was MacGuffin had planted her with Phipps? You said ND&B cut his business. Maybe biker dude's got the same idea for busting this place as Damen Phipps. That could be why he pushed to come along."

"Maybe."

Billy's freaking out and I enjoy needling him.

"You never should've worked with that snitch. He couldn't keep his mouth to any question I asked."

"Maybe I was counting on the snitch to do what he do."

"So it was you that told Damen it's a big red barn?"

"The words of a secret are like iodine dye." Billy looks off at the trailer again. "And that tells me something about the dude inside. I might stick around a couple days to figure this out."

"You be fucking careful around here."

"I'll be all right," he assures me, giving me a fist bump. "I'll text to let you know. In fact, from here on out, that's our code. I-M-O-K. You got that?"

I CALL PAULIE from the hot tub next afternoon.

"Still sick, bro."

"It's Football Saturday, dickweed. And tell Kinross he don't have to bother coming in anymore. But you're treading the same thin ice, bro. You'll get your ass canned."

"I've been fired before and you wouldn't do it besides. You need all the help you can get, Paulie."

I disco the call and stare at the surface of the hot tub boiling all around me. Weighing wants and needs against shoulds and don'ts, I climb out to towel off and get ready for work.

When I arrive to the shack, I find an alarming post on the door: DUE TO HIGH FUELS AND MAINTNANCE, ALL DRIVER'S COMMISSIONS ARE REDUCED TO 34% AFFECTIVE TONIGHT. THX, *THE OWNERS.*

Historically we've been paid 40 percent commission on all fares. Thx the Owners will undoubtedly sell this as a 6 percent wage reduction. But in reality that translates to a 15 percent reduction in our cut.

Paulie wants to know what I think but he's asking on behalf of Thx the Owners.

"I don't give enough shit to do the math," I tell him.

Tonight I unlock my doors for no one. Heavy rains blow out of the south and I cruise the downtown loop in my green bubble. Endless crowds wave from the curb as I pass to send up showers from the gutter. I feel free and as blank as my tripsheet.

That's when I see our old bus depot has been torn down. The building and its offices and garage have all been scraped off the slab and hauled away. I get out of the taxi in the rain and walk around the sheared-off footings. I shine my Maglite over the exposed floor tiles and broken ground. There's not a doornail left.

I call Captain Jerry right away.

"Ah Jerry," I tell his voicemail. "They tore down our house, man. The bus depot's gone. And give me a call. I was an asshole last we talked and I want you to know you have nothing to feel sorry for. I got no hard feelings."

Soon as I hang up, Paulie calls me.

"Ah buddy, lousy news. The old man. He's dead."

III

BOTTOM FALLS OUT OF THE OCEAN

11

WE BURY HIM on the last day of September. The weather's turned and skies spit light rains. I should've worn a sweatshirt.

Parked beneath the willows is an escort of green taxis. The crowd swells with drivers and regular fares come to see the old man off. Jerry's burial has also drawn alkies and dopeheads who'd call him seeking runway lights. Shaky savages wearing evangelical t-shirts, harsh tattoos on their necks. Leathered riders frowning among the tombstones as if this was a death metal video.

It was the emph that forced Captain Jerry to sleep upright in a recliner. He hadn't answered the phone so his daughter went around the trailer Saturday afternoon. She found him in his knock-off La-Z-Boy with remote in hand, teeth soaking in a glass beside two packs of U.S.A. Golds, a cold butt sticking from under his mustache. No more chatter out of that radio. Gerald R. Nicodemus was 58 years old.

It was his one good daughter that found him and she spills the details while shaking my hand.

"My old man thought the world of you. He said you was helping Billy and that makes you a angel. Is Billy here? I thought I'd seen him."

"I haven't."

All around us I hear the glowing commendations of her dead father. Jerry might've thought a lot of me but I didn't always think much of Jerry. I let him know it too. But I don't like that I was the last to yell at him.

"I knew Billy when we was young," Jerry's kid tells me as she goes on shaking my hand. "He saved me from a mean neighbor dog and then he peed in the neighbor's car for beating that poor thing. He's a special man."

"He sure is."

"And I'm so sorry I had to sign up for the county burial."

She tells me the county option allows for a single grave tucked away from the columbarium and chapel. It was Jerry's wish to get torched and buried with the ashes of Tex and Shelly Feely. All three must be in the hole but I can't get close enough to confirm. The white tent is reserved for Jerry's squabbling brood and their children. Before I got here, a shouting match broke out between his three rotten kids and the one good daughter. Wayne Linder says two of the girls got arrested last night for breaking into Jerry's trailer. He says they were looking for treasure, "Like Jerry had a pot of gold or something."

We all talk angelic about Captain Jerry or bad about Tex Feely or hellfire for our wage cut.

Tex Feely, rapist and creepazoid, will be missed by none. They got on well, Tex and Jerry, preaching the Word to anybody they'd cross, driving hours to their trailer temple and drinking sacramental wine because the Bible said so and never mind the Big Book. They grew old in their sitting chairs playing video golf after Tex's rotten feet no longer allowed him to spoil the walk. Tex claimed he caught the Big C while out shoveling snow because that's when the pain first hit him. He warned everybody against the dangers of what the government isn't telling us about the weather. We all laugh, then and now.

"What a asshole!"

"Too bad he only died once."

Paulie meanwhile makes the rounds spreading news from on high. "The bosses called a mandatory meeting for Thursday.

They want everybody there."

"That's what 'mandatory' means," I tell Paulie. "The note I saw says 'manandatory.' They don't mean the same thing."

"Just please fucking be there, please. Do it for me?"

A brittle old black lady rises from her chair to sing a hymn the words of which we can't hear even after we shut the fuck up. Next a preacher hollers about sin and we can hear his every word as rain drums on the tent.

When the preacher quits, we file up to pay our respects. In the square shallow hole, I see the urn vaults stacked like three sandwich boxes in a to-go bag. Each is marked with a throwaway tin badge that bears the name of the dead.

I leave the shelter of the tent and fire up a cig. The cemetery groundskeeper drives over in a Gator and parks on the edge of our crowd. Itching to throw the dirt in, I guess.

When the taxi escort breaks up and the crowds depart, the last of us drag up folding chairs to sit around the hole and tell the old man's favorite stories. Me, Quiet Chuck, Paulie, Dr. Bob, Helene and Zina.

"Where's Billy?"

"Don't ask me."

A copy of the Big Book has already been thrown in the hole along with a motel Bible. We add a pack of U.S.A. Golds and a few Bic lighters, golf balls, a deck of cards, craps dice and cribbage pegs, old driver badges. The gravedigger climbs off his Gator to shake open a plastic sack and I wonder what for.

But Paulie won't let us leave.

"You got to let it go," he says as he touches me at the elbow. "You got to forgive him, man."

"The gravedigger? Forgive him for what?"

"Forgive Jerry," he says. "And for whatever it is you're mad at him about. For him telling those dudes where you live. For drinking church wine. For not always practicing his preaching. All that business. It's you yelling at him what killed him."

"Fuck off and don't ever say that again."

I stomp off on those sour notes and everyone follows. Half to the cemetery exit, I turn to see the groundskeeper kneeled over the hole picking out the mementos we've thrown in.

So I bust back there, charge the guy, grab belt and collar and lift him ass over head, "What're you doing, gravedigger!"

I drop him and he gets to his feet, wiry and duked for a fight. Everyone hustles back to graveside and gets between us.

"I'm calling the police."

Dr. Bob says, "Our friend is upset and we're leaving now."

"You people been littering on the premises too."

"Fucking jagoff," I flare up. "You're supposed to bury our friends. Not disinter them, asshole."

"Don't asshole me, asshole. This is a show-hole. A display model. That's the county plan."

"Then give us the ashes then."

"Federal law says no. Just like you can't keep your teeth."

"Ah come on," says Dr. Bob, pulling my elbow.

"Then where's he getting buried?"

"County don't handle that. We ship the ashes out to a private company and they handle that."

Zina takes the Mason jar of flowers she'd left for Jerry and we depart. I walk backward so I can eyeball the gravedigger. He tips a board over the hole. Then he loads the bucket of his Gator with the flowers and grave boxes and the trash bag of our mementos until there's no sign of the old man, or his death, and at last the gravedigger climbs on his machine and putters away.

WE ALL SPLIT at the curb. Zina walks me to the Jeep and hands over the jar of wild flowers.

"These're for you."

"They were for Jerry. And I've never been given flowers before. Feels a little weird."

She give me serious eyes. "You out of trouble yet?"

"I'm leaving here to dot the i's and cross the t's."

"I went by your garage, Vic. I saw the door busted open."

"Ah some canners broke in looking for dope money."

Her eyes let go of mine to gaze around the neighborhood.

"I'm all good though. I moved into a house. It's Billy's place and only temporary while we're tying this shit off. I'll be moving into my own apartment after that."

She still won't look at me. "Your life is a nightmare."

"Look. I'm not thrilled either. But aren't these all steps in the right direction? I'm not trying to fix anything anymore. I'm just extracting myself. Getting disentangled. Then I'm out. And I'm being careful."

Now Zina looks at me.

"'Careful' and 'reckless' don't mean the same thing, Vic. After I stopped at your garage, I had two guys knock on my door. Bad guys. They'd followed me home. They said they were looking for you and I told them you split town."

"Was it a dumpy white dude and a big black dude?"

"The big black dude stooped to breathe on me, Vic."

I scan the street and down the curbs. No occupied vehicles, nobody creeping. I should've left with the crowds.

"I'm sorry," I tell her.

"Why did you even come today?" She snaps and hammers a fist on my chest. "How did you know they wouldn't be here? I told them you were gone. That you'd left."

Zina runs off. I won't chase her and she doesn't look back.

THE JEEP CONSOLE has a cup holder big enough for the wild flower jar. I drive and think about Zina. And about the old man. Considering his two ways to go through life. But I don't know any easy ways.

Billy has texted that the ammonia tanker is ready. Following his directions, I take the big road south into Washington County then dead east on a gravel leg. I estimate the trip at 43-6 minutes and it takes 48 for five miles of winding gravel at the end.

Arriving to the gas farm owned by MacGuffin's uncle, I pull in the lot and stop in gear. The gas farm has a house, scale services, and a fenced yard full of white buffalo nurse tanks. Two metal truck barns, one larger than the other. No one around. And no tanker trailer in sight.

I crunch across the gravel and around the rut puddles to make a loop of the larger garage. I can smell the river as it curls nearby. Excavated clay is piled in heaps among the border weeds.

Coming around the corner, I find a bright blue truck rumbling in the thru-way. Its horn rips two mighty yowls. I also see the great white tanker parked inside the larger garage.

Along the apron are two muscle cars, a black van, and a white Buick LeSabre. I slide the Jeep between the muscle cars. Then I empty the glove box, pocketing the Glock and putting the clips in the other. I also take Zina's jar of flowers.

The big rig rumbles and Billy revs the engine, stalling it and causing the hood to shake. Next he turns the engine over, cranks it back to life. The passenger window comes down and Damen Phipps sticks his head out.

"What's going on, dude?"

I keep walking around the truck. It's a Peterbilt 379 with a high-rise sleeper. Electric blue with ice-white flames curling off the nose. Multiple emblems declare its status as a Legacy Class Edition. Custom oval-mesh grill. Chrome everything and chicken lights and a big ugly Texas bumper too.

Seeing Billy at its wheel, I climb the step and yank the door to give him the thumbs out. "Shove over and let me show you what daddy showed me."

The emergency brake hasn't been set and when Billy lets off the pedals I near tumble down, catching myself on the window frame and keeping hold of the flower jar. The engine groans and dies.

Damen Phipps chins at me over the console. "So you came to pitch in, huh?"

"The fuck's in your mouth? Use it again and I'll cut it out."

Billy intervenes. "Go wait in the car, Damen."

After the snitch drops out of the tractor, Billy straddles the console while I settle in the comfy captain's chair. The shifter is crowned with a chrome skull and its eyes are set with blue crystal that matches the dash. I rest the flowers in the cup holder and stow the gun and clips in the door pocket. I restart the truck and punch the brake to observe the air and fuel gauges.

Billy is fresh shaven again like it's the trend with him now. Charcoal suit coat on a sky blue button down shirt, collar open. He unfolds and folds a tactical knife.

"What's the snitch doing here?"

"Playing his part," he says. "And I need him to play right. So cool it."

"I don't like it."

"You liked none of this from the get. So what's wrong with you? This shit makes me feel alive."

"This shit makes me feel like I'm in a barrel of fucking monkeys." I notice the tactical knife has disappeared in Billy's hands. "So where's MacGuffin?"

Billy says he arrived to find us all set up. "We're not meeting him here. But this is easy-peasy. The tanker comes with a remote cutoff switch and the standard HazMat pouch with all the necessary papers."

He says both are in the driver door where I stuck the gun.

"So what's with the other cars? Are they with MacGuffin?"

Billy shakes his head. "Some of his boys drove in but I saw them get in a van and drive off."

"You think they maybe went up the road?"

"Up the road for what?"

"Up the road for hopping on our ass. Maybe that's why he's not here. Because that's his play. Him and his boys waiting to tag along to that big red barn."

Billy shakes his head again. "Mac can't be around when we put the work in. He's keeping with his alibi."

Sounds like bullshit to me. At least the Legacy Edition is a comfortable ride. Custom window cuts and a custom dash with built-in GPS and satellite radio. Microwave and mini-fridge. A premium interior wrapped in quilted powder blue aluminum. Counting the cable dish and PS3, it offers better amenities than Freedom Cove. "I thought you were looking for a trailer jockey. How much did this rig cost?"

"More than you make in a year, bubba."

"Is the DOT on the door legit?"

"The number better be legit. It belongs to ND&B."

"I can presume we got approval to deliver the tanker?"

"Ain't you just full of questions? Well don't worry, boss. We got a late afternoon window for you."

"What's this thing weigh anyhow?"

"Eighteen thou."

"And that's fueled?"

"You can see it's fueled."

"I'm asking if the weight is eighteen when the tanks are full."

"The title says eighteen something."

The tanks look like no-neck buck-fifties. Three hundred gallons or roughly 2100 pounds of dinosaur juice after doing the math. "It's twenty heavy," I tell him. "And that's what'll count on a scale."

Billy throws up his hands. "We're stealing an ammonia tank and you're worried about a scale."

I regard him in that suit and tell him he looks dressed for a funeral. "Everybody was asking where you were today."

"Wasn't me that died."

"What's that supposed to mean?"

"Means I didn't have to be there."

After Paulie called to tell me the bad news, I sent Billy a text that Jerry had passed. Until issuing me directions to this place, all he's sent me are his IMOKs. I can't tell if he's speeding but he is aloof. He's turned his shoulders away and bops his head to an unheard beat.

He says: "At least we're even anyhow."

"Now what the fuck're we even on?"

"I killed Chemo and you killed Jerry."

"Paulie said the same thing and fuck you, too."

"But can you finally take my point? You can't telegraph murder, bubba. You got to walk up and tap a dude. That shit's hands on because it's from the heart."

"I guess so. Like I said, I'm not in the murder business."

Billy scoffs at me.

"Just let's hook this tanker and split."

I drop the brake and wheel the 379 left until I can see the tanker in my enormous side mirror. I double tap the horn and back square with the trailer and into the garage.

Then I stop, set the brake, climb out.

"Where're you going?"

I see Phipps has climbed behind the wheel of the white Buick. He too bops his head, consumed with the thudding radio which I can feel from 50 feet off.

I make a walkaround of the truck and trailer as I would with a taxi I've never driven. I check the fifth wheel and see that it's greased and sitting right.

Billy limps after me.

"Mac's checked all this out. We're all good here."

"What kind of professional do you take me for, Billy?"

My dad had tugged these beasts hauling propane so I'm familiar. Anhydrous ammonia will suck the water out of your eyeballs and flesh and soft respiratory tissues so the transport equipment must be sound. Above the forward shut-off valves, the specs declare a 10,600 water gallon capacity. I tap the temp and pressure dials. Capacity is pegged at 73 percent and I do the weight math in my head. The tanker resembles a long white pill on wheels and with green 1005 DOT placards slapped all over. This one also wears fans of mud along both sides. River clay. The hose rack is filthy with it and I think this trailer was rescued from the flooded fields out back. But the gate and pipe cage and fittings all look intact, and where axles meet wheels looks clean too. The tires and wells look good as does the kingpin once I take the lock off.

I tell him, "We're overweight by 3,000 pounds, at least."

"We're not overweight."

"Your big-ass house tractor weighs 20,000-plus. Legally we can only carry 38 because the tractor-trailer combo's 42."

"That ought to be your nickname. 'Rules 'n Regs.'"

"Just be advised running fat carries enhanced penalties."

"So how much ammonia is it?"

"Better than 20 tons."

He grins. "I can do math, too, bubba. I bet we net 20 g's for the product plus another 20 on sale of the tank. Maybe more."

"I thought all you cared about were the kids."

"I'm not sitting on money because I'm bad at business. So can we get the moving now, boss? Please?"

I climb in the truck and stick for backward to slip my tail under the tanker apron. Then I climb back out to tie in the glad hands and electric pigtail. Then back in the cab to charge the airbags that push the fifth wheel up to the trailer. I reverse slow under the apron until the jaws clap around the kingpin. I shift into gear to test the bite. Then back out again to wind up the feet.

Billy stands in the passenger door of Phipps' Buick, even when I bring the tanker clear of the bay and out into the big lot. I stop and throw on the trailer brake and do another pull test. He bitches at me over the CB.

"ARE WE GOOD YET? OR WHAT THE GODDAMN FUCK?"

"#22 is ready to go. And be advised that FCC rules clearly state there is to be no profanity broadcast via your radio."

We leave the gas farm with the Buick escorting to the warehouse at 45 miles per. I look to Zina's flowers for my good luck charm and keep eyes on my mirrors. The trip should take two-thirds of an hour.

But right off I don't like the way the load feels on my tail. The tank is at three-quarter capacity and even fitted with baffles I should feel the slosh. At the first four-way stop, I give it a hard test and jam the brakes.

The load feels solid as a rock.

Billy on the CB wants to know what's up.

"I think this can's full of dirt. You got fucking hosed."

"JUST LET'S KEEP MOVING."

So I keep driving, both hands on the big wheel. I check the mirrors and watch that no one follows, and I watch that I don't roll over any curbs.

The trip takes 37 minutes. We arrive to the warehouse during shift change and queue up with four-wheelers carrying in the worker bees. Billy talks to the guard and we're waved inside the gate. His voice crackles over the radio. "BRING IT OVER THE SCALES HE SAYS."

The entry to the yard is spacious with clearly marked lanes. As I roll to the scales, the Buick drives past the end of the docks into visitor parking. They send a guy to fetch my paperwork. While I wait, I thumb through the HazMat pouch and its purgatory of information.

"Christ, buddy. You're way overweight."

"How fat am I?"

The scaleman hands me the ticket and grins. "Almost 6,000 pounds. Pull to the mechanics shop and meet a fella there."

The ticket says the truck weighs 85,843#.

I thank him and roll out doing the math in my head trying to cipher where I fucked up.

For a Tuesday afternoon the yard is dead. The laydown yard is lightly occupied by a team of eight rough terrain cranes with 200-ton ratings and 6-axles each, and with off-road tires that are shoulder high. Half the warehouse docks are assigned ND&B trailers. Plain white van trailers with small blue flags painted on rear sides. A few are rigged to yard cabs. The last interior bay is parked with a trailer and its tractor rumbles and hisses, ready to embark.

Cameras watch the docks and service entry. Phipps has parked the white Buick between a company van and a rusted out pickup truck. They must already be inside.

I roll past the docks and visitor lot and follow to the waving fella in gray fatigues. I bring the truck in for a perfect stop and let the air brakes sneeze. He opens the loading gate to expose the tits. Putting on a glove, he turns the valve to let out a hiss of gas. I see a flume of ammonia in the mirror and at last the elephant climbs off my chest. At least I was wrong about the load being bunk.

The receiver directs me to the mechanics bay. "Pull in, uncouple, and pull your rig out the other door. Leave any weapons in the truck or lose them inside."

I steer the beast into the pull-thru bay and park in the spot marked off for repair. I back gently into the kingpin and set the brake. Then I get out to drop the landing gear and yank the fifth wheel safety. Back in the cab I punch the airbag release then back out to pull the hoses. I pull ahead when all clear, park off the apron, and get out of the truck.

The rollup door is already coming down and I hurry to duck under it. Then I'm sealed in the dim hall. I can make out the workbenches and lifts, a torch cage, two big engine gantries. Oil pits in the floor. Smells like grease and diesel, as it should. I don't see any cameras though. If Billy is looking to break in here later, this would be a solid starting point.

I snake to the right and head for the washroom door off a short hall. When I come out, I regard the other door in the hallway. It closes off a space that looks like a paint spray room with curtained windows all around it. But there's no entry big enough for a vehicle.

There's a wall switch beside the door and I throw it. The mysterious space glows behind the curtain. I lift the window skirt and see a room with white tiled walls and floors with a big rusty drain in the center. Next to the drain rises a stainless steel T-post. Shackles dangle from the bars.

"See anything you like?"

My heart jumps but I don't. I turn and see it's my receiver. Giving him the hairy eyeball, I ask, "Is this the sauna? I was told there were driver amenities."

"Showers and beds are upstairs. Let's go."

He flips off the wall switch and I follow him through the shop and past the ammonia tanker. He's handed me a signed lading bill that says I've delivered 30,000# of bananas.

These bays are separated from the warehouse by tall barn doors with a service cutout at the far end. The receiver halts at the cutout to allow me through first.

"Ah what the fuck!"

On the other side of the wall is a trailer loaded with caged tigers, and the nearest, startled by my cursing, pounces against his mesh cage. The receiver giggles like he's pulled this on fools all afternoon and the tiger, playing his part, leans its head with mouth open to show teeth and black lips and its growl.

The interior bays are at ground level. Five of the tigers are already onboard and the sixth is lifted off the floor by a telehandler. The 5 o'clock whistle squawks and causes the tiger to agitate again. The wire cages are open on all faces and too small for the tigers to turn circles though they frustratingly try.

The receiver pats me down for weapons.

"Who the hell sends tigers through a crossdock?"

"I've seen weirder shit, believe you me. Wait here."

The receiver leaves me at the S&R desk and disappears through swinging doors into what looks like the business wing. The tigers won't eyeball me and I stand away from their trailer.

Shipping and Receiving smells like a circus. I spot multiple cameras mounted from the walls and building supports and over the swinging doors too. The area is the rough size of a basketball court and occasioned with loaded pallets. Plus six empty transport cans the cats arrived in. Christ, they switched them into the mesh cages right here on the floor.

The remaining crossdock covers a huge footprint filled with rows of pallet stacks. Above me are the shower and dormitory, and orange sun pours through the high ports.

A catwalk runs around the interior, currently walked by a man in dark gray fatigues. I've noted the floor workers wear beige jumpsuits but I count a few others dressed like the guy in the catwalk, and like my receiver. White dudes in dark gray fatigues and armed with hip pistols. Guard dogs. Country dolts with shaved heads. Six or eight at least, probably more. The one in the catwalk wears a rifle on his shoulder. Armed security isn't out of the ordinary, I guess.

Still, the floor is washed and waxed and the paint looks regularly touched up. Every fixture gleams as if this is a firehouse. So if there's a black market here, I can't see it.

The tiger trailer has a Conestoga top shoved back like a bellows and at last this is pulled closed over the exotic cargo. I've meanwhile perused the S&R desk and find the tiger's bill of lading. They've have been consigned to Heritage Gaming Preserve by Jing Shan Trading Co. of Laramie.

No shit.

With the wagon top fully closed, the Conestoga looks like an ordinary van as it rumbles from the dock and is replaced with the white-out glare of afternoon sun. The bay door claps shuts and the dock falls dark.

I wonder what'd be on that truck if I revealed to Stan my real spirit animal, which is undoubtedly a hippo.

"Hey, bubba."

Billy Kinross leans out of the doors that lead into the business wing. He flashes his teeth like a television stud and I feel the slightest relief to see that he's not dead.

"We've been called to the boardroom. Follow me."

12

I FOLLOW BILLY through the swing doors into a hall that opens at a cube farm and executive offices. Four minutes after 5 p.m. and the place has cleared out.

"Remember," he tells me. "Evidence with teeth."

To our left is a glass boardroom. Phipps is seated inside at a long table made of natural oak. He flips pages of a binder and chats with an Asian guy wearing an iridescent sharkskin suit. The table is spread with black binders and a bookshelf beyond the table holds a library of them.

Billy pushes through the door and we breeze inside. Our host greets us with limpid handshakes. He has leathery skin and grins with teeth too big for his mouth.

"Good afternoon! My name is Joe Hitachi and I will be your representative. How are you today? Would you care for coffee or tea?"

I call for coffee and Hitachi himself goes to the service and push-buttons a Keurig brewer.

Two ball cameras are nested in the ceiling at either end of the room. Phipps lifts out of his binder and sneers at me. "You said this place was red."

"You said this place was red, homie. Not me."

Our host delivers my coffee on a saucer. He wears Italian

loafers, a turtleneck under his shimmering coat, and a gold nugget ring on the hand with which he gestures that I take a seat beside the snitch. He then passes me a binder out of the library.

"These books contain all goods currently on offer. Please consult them at will and feel free to ask whatever questions are in your heart."

Like Wong Fen, Joe Hitachi sounds like he grew up around a lot of white boys. He bustles away to an inner glass chamber that unlocks with a keycard. He enters the chamber and bends over a laptop, dropping the white card in his jacket pocket. Billy's seen this and gives me a look.

We need that keycard.

The black binders are generic but the design is profesh, the pages sleeved in plastic covers, each showing clear photos and a barcode with price tables below. These catalogs are for professional resellers only with minimum bulk purchases beginning at the half-pound. Bopping his head to an unheard beat, Phipps is lost in pages offering high-grade marijuana. My binder offers three grades of Colombian cocaine at two purity tiers; two varieties of crack; and an exotic coca paste from Peru. Eight different cooks of meth from Mexican and stateside super-labs. ND&B also boasts a specialty in Afghan heroin, morphine, opium, and other opiates in addition to two blends of Chinese heroin plus Mexican-made China white and black tar. There's a special on ten strains of marijuana ranging from Cali nugs to Colorado fluff, BC Kind, Cannabis Cup seeds, and hashish by brick and oil. Also on offer are four Afghan-grown indica strains. The photos show the same shipping pillows I'd seen in the Stan's garage. I can almost taste it and rub my fingertips under my nose.

Billy whispers over the table: "I thought it'd look like a gay bar with cases behind purple drapes and buyers drinking champagne. Don't ask me why."

I look through the glass walls and out at the cube farm and feel disappointed. I don't know what I was expecting. Maybe a dock with a truck pulled up and mingling sellers. This marketplace is nothing but a plain old corporate longhouse.

Hitachi emerges from his glass compartment and opens the doors of a frosted cabinet to reveal an apothecary shelved with rows of scientific jars capped with black resin lids. "May we offer you gentlemen a sample of anything from the catalogs? Anything at all?"

He hands out a brass pipe and a glass bulb.

I shake my head. "Just browsing."

Billy declines as well which leaves Phipps to puff weed for all of us before he starts asking dumb questions. "And I can buy whatever I want today?"

"We offer free delivery within three to five days of sale for most catalog items."

I find the next binder is full of club drugs. MDMA, designer stimulants and sedatives, go-pills, amphetamine variants; then a whole sheaf of LSDs and other lysergamides, tryptamines, phenethylamines, psilocybins, mescalines, PCP analogues; lastly a section of Marinol and other synthetic THCs, fentanyl and other opioids, and "Syn" which is also listed as "herbal incense."

There's three fat binders of Mexican-sourced OxyContin, codeine, anabolic steroids, benzodiazepines, Valium, Viagra, Quaaludes, dextromethorphan, hydromorphone, Methaqualone, methadone, mephedrone. The final pages list "mind control drugs" such as Scopolamine, Chlorpromazine, Suboxone, GHB, and Rohypnol. A thinner volume offers exotics like Khat, aphrodisiacs, peyote, DMT, Trichoserus Pachanoi, salvia divinorum; and the paraphernalia shop carries hi-tech gear. Vaporizers, electric pipes, coke mills, grinders and stash boxes, burners, fancy hypo kits.

Hitachi offers three unviewed binders out of the library. "Are you gentlemen interested in arms?"

Inside I find every manner of pistol, revolver, long gun, rifle, Gatling, and mounted cannon for sale, and everything available in bulk. There's pages selling explosives, sound suppressors, extended magazines, auto kits. Czech and Chinese ammunitions, assorted rocketry. The prices are astronomical.

"I don't see anything I like," complains Billy. "I am a man, however, of exquisite taste."

In his suit and manner, Billy plays his role as I've never seen. Like he's a chameleon.

And it works. Our host flashes eyes and curls a Dracula finger, inviting Billy to the private glass office. Hitachi swipes into the chamber and opens an upper cabinet to reveal more binders of what must be ND&B's most illicit offerings. He leaves Billy to peruse the selection and returns to the conference table to propose another coffee.

"I could take a piss," says Phipps.

"Washrooms are in the warehouse just through the doors."

After Phipps goes, Billy comes out with a binder. Hitachi moves to keep that business inside the booth but gets sidestepped as Billy spreads the binder on the table. He wants Hitachi to see this so I'm believed to be a buyer, and he wants me to see this so I know he's not lying.

The binder shows a catalog of young girls that appear under a misspelled heading, PRESCIOUS ANGELS. Each face is attached to vitals like it was a book of cop mugs. Page after page after page of photos and vitals, each with a barcode unique as a snowflake.

"What if the skin's not what I wanted in the picture?"

"There will be others from which you may choose. Or you may enjoy your time with more than one at a special price."

Billy keeps flipping pages for me. "So we do this here?"

"Arrangements are made to suit though we have dormitory facilities on the premises."

I drop my finger on the photo.

"She's the one."

This is the girl I saw in the Kushite's video. I can tell by her hair and eyes, and her smile. The vitals call her Scarlet Rose and give a birth date of 12/12/93. She's fourteen years old.

Seeing her face again, I know I've seen her before but I can't place it.

Billy holds the binder while Hitachi scans her barcode.

"She's in Kansas City," Hitachi reads from the handheld.

"The appointment could be soon as tomorrow evening."

"We got hard-ons for this," says Billy. "Let's do tomorrow."

"I'll make the appointment at once. We offer blocks in four hour increments. But I must tell you if you are unable to meet the appointment for any reason, your deposit is forfeited. I presume you wish to levy this against your credit?"

"Sure, of course," says Billy, flipping to the back of the catalog. "Last thing: What's this?"

He shows us a picture of a room with white tiled walls and floors, the drain in its floor and the tie-down post at center. It's the closed-off room I saw in the mechanics bay.

"That would include a Full Purchase, sir."

"So what's a Full Purchase cost?"

"Pricing of that item is always determined at point of sale. And those activities are most definitely restricted to these premises for obvious reasons."

"I understand. Can we decide during our appointment?"

"Of course."

"Splendid," says Billy, showing his fingers. "I think we're going to want two of them so make sure they send another. Dealer's choice. Weigh that one on the credit too."

Hitachi takes the binder away and slips into the glass chamber to get on the laptop.

"I'm going to kill that guy." Billy whispers at my shoulder. "I'm going to saw his head off."

"Now? In here?"

He regards Hitachi in the glass chamber.

"Tomorrow. I'm going to put his head out front on a stick."

I cannot abide murder and don't want to see Billy saw off any heads. But to consider the girls on sale, the Full Purchase, and having seen the actual room with its tie-down post, I'm feel comfortable turning blind to Billy's plans.

Hitachi confirms for tomorrow, 6:00 p.m. Everything is casual as Billy shakes his hand and thanks him for his time.

Then Billy asks, "Where Damen?"

Speak of the devil, Phipps pushes through the swing doors.

He throws a thumb over his shoulder and talks at us through the boardroom glass. "Something's wrong with the tank."

Hitachi leads us out and we all follow Phipps through the doors onto the warehouse floor.

A dozen guards in fatigues surround the S&R desk and form a wide U to receive us. I see the receiver that inspected the tanker and a few others dressed in street clothes. One of them turns around and I know we're fucked.

Don Salukus.

I pick out his men from Billy's elaborate flowchart. Charley in the wire glasses looks like Radar O'Reilly. The big round black guy is Averil. He killed Chemo Phipps, rousted Hustler out of my cab and harassed Zina. Bunker is the dumpy white driver of the oxblood Caddy. The fake cop in crappy mustache and lame tennis shoes. Fast with his hands though. When I lurch back, he whips a pistol from his waist and warns in a thin voice, "Grow roots, bitch."

Never go into a stranger's house.

The rifleman up in the catwalk is also training on us. I give a wider look around the warehouse and see workers in beige jumpsuits going about their business and ignoring ours.

Damen Phipps, the snitch, stands next to Salukus but hangs his jaw as if he doesn't see where his pals are bringing this.

Charley swings his .45 between us.

"I bet you motherfuckers think you're real smart."

Salukus grinds his eyes on me. "You knew about this."

"I didn't know jack."

Billy agrees. "We're both just regular dumb bitches."

Charley bashes his face and Billy folds to the floor.

Now Charley wags the gun under my nose.

"What you got?"

"Back off, dick breath."

I get socked in the gut. Incredibly, I stay on my feet and see it's Averil, shaved head and big beard with hands enough to crush skulls. I've had the wind knocked from me but find the breath to tell him: "You cut up my stuffed animals. That's low work, buddy. But it fits you. You're a low man, Averil."

His voice rumbles in baritone: "How you know that name?"

I throw my chin at Damen Phipps. "He told me."

Salukus looks at Phipps and Charley lifts Billy by his hair.

"I knew you were chumping me. Those drop offs? So full of shit. Always asking questions. I knew you were smoke."

"That's enough," Salukus orders. He waves at the guard and they open the big barn doors on the mechanics bay to reveal the white ammonia tanker. Our great folly.

Except I spot two manways open on top of the tank. The big nuts holding them shut are purely cosmetic and the doors hang like porthole hatches. Whatever we've delivered to the warehouse isn't ammonia.

A guard climbs the trailer ladder. He dips an arm inside the tank then throws a handful of river clay on the floor.

The receiver pipes up in his own defense. "But the taps blew ammonia when I checked."

"We found a small sleeper tank rigged under the belly," says Salukus. "The tanker's filled with clay."

I figured we were set to get our asses beat. But we're doomed for worse. My hands won't stop shaking. I watch Billy climb to his feet. His face calm and his eyes are full of glory. His hands haven't twitched.

"This isn't the only thing," says Salukus. "These two did all this because they want to rip off the big show."

Charley laughs at us. "Thinking they could hijack the supply boat. Ain't that right, girls?"

Utter seriousness has descended upon the face of Joe Hitachi. Like a priest approaching an altar, he walks deliberately around the S&R dock until he stands beside Don Salukus. His eyes turn mean on Billy.

"I do not believe Mister Kinross and his friend are trying to rob us," he says, and to Salukus, "Sirs ordered two for romance and requested a quote on a Full Purchase."

He returns to Billy. "So who are you, Mister Kinross? You must know the girl? You were hoping to rescue her? She must be precious to have placed yourself at such risk."

Hitachi turns disappointed eyes on me.

"But you chose her. She is your loved one? A child, perhaps? Because I assure that when I cancel your order, I will request this girl receive your Full Purchase nevertheless. Strangulation is, as you say, the dealer's choice. Within a few hours, the three of you will be dead."

"Let's fucking do this then," says Charley.

"We must close down this shift," Hitachi says. He twirls his fingers at a guard. "Send the worker home. Let's have a fire drill."

The guard nods and heads to the alarm pull on the wall. His boots clap across the glazed warehouse floor.

"You all think you control this," Billy announces loudly. "You act like this is your show."

I hear an engine roaring outside the warehouse to the west, and getting closer. Metal screeches as bay door #1 is smashed down by one of the big-ass terrain cranes from the yard. In a scatter we retreat among the pallets as the truck skids blind up the bay and is stopped on a building pole, bringing up the rear wheels and throwing the driver through the spidered windshield and making a terrific clang that shakes my teeth. Charley's glasses are knocked from his face as a thin metal boom swings wild from the crane and pins him through the chest as if he's a specimen.

Everybody breaks up in the dust raining from the rafters. Work halts and forklifts let out a chorus of horns.

Charley, dying, wraps one arm around the pole and reflexively stomps on his own glasses.

Salukus yells in the chaos. "Watch the bay door!"

Half the guards rush the breach as two fighters engage from either side. Shooters with bandanas over their faces.

Next, Salukus fires his gun into the mechanics bay.

Pandemonium in the great cave. Automatic gunfire erupts all around us as Billy yanks me into cover among the pallets. My blood thumps and the floor sways. I follow his gaze behind us and overhead. The rifleman in gray fatigues is flat on the catwalk, one arm dangling. He's been replaced by another rifleman, this one heavily bearded and dressed in leather jacket and jeans, like the fighters at the bay door. We're in full range of him but the shooter doesn't pluck at us.

Now the alarm's pulled. Workers run screaming for the exits and with the herd Damen Phipps escapes toward the front.

"We get out in stages," Billy yells over the racket. "First we get the laptop."

"Back to the boardroom?"

Eight fighters charge out of the mechanics shop firing guns on the fly. Two fall and I yell needlessly, "Where the fuck did they come from?"

Bandanas or bearded, jeans and leathers. Bikers. I reconsider the open manways rigged by hinge and latch. MacGuffin and his gang must've used it as a Trojan horse.

The new shooters keep heat on Salukus and the guards as Averil and Bunker take positions behind the S&R desk. Meanwhile, dead Charley stands in the fight like a scarecrow. I could never enjoy being in a firefight, even if I was armed.

Hitachi has found us in cover.

He lifts his pistol as Billy engages, breaks the gun from his hand, ties an unexpected knot that chokes Hitachi with his own arm. With his other, Hitachi fast elbows Billy twice and breaks the hold, lunges for his dropped pistol.

Billy stomps on the gun and skitters it across the floor into battle. Now he comes out of his sleeve with that tactical knife. The pallet splinters at his feet and he falls into cover as Hitachi breaks for the swing doors.

Then he breaks after Hitachi.

"Billy!"

I fall back at last chance, ears ringing and unsure on my feet. The air is choked with dust and burnt shot.

Hitachi is grazed on the shoulder as he shoves through the doors and Billy, no longer limping, bolts down the hall after him.

Bullets ring along the tanker. Good thing it's filled with dirt. The catwalk shooter now takes aim on a nest of oxyacetylene tanks until gouts of fire roar furious from their crowns. The first tanks flume then blows flashing yellow-white light blinding me out, the bang knocks me down and deaf. The shockwave rolls through my chest and the nest of tanks flares hot as shooters scurry and the S&R desk is wreathed in flames. New overhead alarms blare as sprinklers rain out of the rafters.

Sprinklers mean the fire department is coming. And the cops with them.

I tumble out of cover and hurry at the swing doors, pushing out of the arena as light shooting perks up. My ears sound like I've got a dome over my head.

Right off I see Billy in the glass boardroom. Hitachi supine on the floor below him. I push through the door and see our host pumping blood from the middle of his suit and into the carpet.

Hitachi rolls his glassy eyes on me and lifts a bloody hand to point at nothing.

I tell Billy, "We don't have time to take his head."

Billy dips into the dying man's coat for phone, wallet, and keys which he places beside the knife. His hands are gloved in blood. Coming up with the keycard, he gives it to me.

"Get the laptop."

"The fire department's coming."

Billy shoves me, hard.

"Tick-tock, fucker. The shooters'll get here first."

I swipe into the glass chamber. Seeing the binders left out on the countertop, my mind blanks until I jump to that laptop. I fumble at its cables and one of them leads to the printer on the counter. I go in the cabinet below, dump the paper box, and pile in as many binders as it can carry. Then I clam the laptop shut, shove it in the box sideways, and I leave the booth.

"Let's fucking get," says Billy. He checks his pistol and leads us out of the conference room.

I stumble behind him like a drunken shadow.

We find Damen cowering under a desk.

"They're shooting people in the parking lot! You've got to

get me out of here!"

"Fuck you, snitch-bitch."

"It's all right," counters Billy. "Let's take him."

The front entry slams opens and all three of us drop behind a cubical wall. We see a worker in a beige jumpsuit. He shouts to the others in a language that isn't Spanish and waves his straw hat at the door, adding, "Andale!"

Workers appear from under the desks of other cubicles and herd for the door.

"Must be clear," Billy says. He drags Phipps by the collar, shoving him forward for a shield. I lug the box and stay close, always checking behind us. No one follows.

We spill out the front doors and into the thru-way with frenzied workers. No fire department yet, and no cops.

But even if we evade authorities now, ND&B has us captured on a thousand cameras.

We find two men in the lot dead at each other's feet, one black and gray apiece. No more shooting out here. And no more shooting from inside the warehouse either. I push us harder, yelling, "Truck's around the way!"

We race ahead as three black vans rush from the rear yard. They pay us no mind and screech to halts to extract the workers with practiced maneuvers then rip off for the exit on crying tires.

I lead us around the corner and, with the box of binders under one arm, scramble like a cat up the side of the big blue Peterbilt. I yank the door, throw the box inside, slide in the seat. As I crank the engine, they climb in the passenger side. Phipps hops in the sleeper and screams, "We got to get out of here!"

I drop gear and jump the throttle, throwing Phipps over. I get the Glock from the door and put it in my lap, punching in a clip between gear changes, 20 seconds and eight gears later we are tearing fast across the yard. I whip-slide the 6x6 perfect through the gate and onto the road west with my riders clinging to whatever they can hold and hollering.

No emergency traffic in either highway direction. And no one's chased us out of the warehouse.

"What the fuck is going on, man? Where's the fucking cops?" Phipps pleads with Billy.

"You got to get us out of this! What'd you get me into?"

"Salukus realizes it was a trap," says Billy. "He now suspects you snitched us out because luring him here was the plan."

"Why are you doing this to me?"

"It was Vic that gave them the idea so ask him."

When Phipps turns to pester me, Billy slugs him cold with the butt of his gun.

No traffic in any mirror, no emergency lights. This road should be crawling with fire trucks. Maybe the alarms and sprinklers have been disconnected from the county line.

I turn north at the first gravel and kick up dust for a mile. At the next gravel I turn east and back north at the next. At five miles out, we roll up on Hwy 6 and Billy points me to the roadside. "Damen's getting out."

He opens the door and kicks it wide. I grab the arms and Billy grabs the legs and we lift Damen Phipps over the co-pilot's chair, causing his cellphone to drop out of its pocket. He's starting to rouse when we settle him on the floor. Billy climbs out onto the step and pulls Phipps out of the truck by his belt.

Under the diesel rumble I hear a woozy shout.

Next, Billy climbs in and finds the phone dropped on the floor. He snaps on a blue surgical glove then picks up the phone and tosses it out to Phipps, who's protesting his treatment.

Billy says, "And one more thing."

All day long he's stowed behind my chair his black gear bag. Billy goes inside and comes out with that kilo of brown heroin wrapped in thick plastic with the garish seam. He holds the brick up in his blue glove and gives it a final look.

"You know what this is, Damen? Your get out of jail free card." He tosses the package out to him. "Now we're even."

Billy yanks the door shut without further ado. "Let's hit it."

I rattle off the gravel and turn onto the highway. In the mirror, I see Phipps lift himself out of the wayside grass. Then my quiet bubble pops.

"This shit is blowing up big enough to get on national news, motherfucker. Why'd you bring the snitch with us? And not just now but today at all. What the fuck, man."

"Because I knew he'd tell Salukus. And I knew Salukus would walk into the trap"

I nearly skirt us into the ditch. "What!"

"Look," he says. "Damen's empire got took and they killed his brother. He wanted revenge but more he just wanted his empire back. And ratting us out was his way back into their grace. Except by leaving with us, Damen shows his true spirit. And that's why I gave him the dope. He's afraid of Salukus and he'll go to the cops with that shit. You just watch, bubba."

"I don't want to watch, Billy." My hands shake on the big wheel. "So what do we do when the cops come looking for us?"

"The cops won't buy Damen's shit and he'll take felony possession. End of story."

"So then what do we do when Salukus comes looking?"

"How do we know Salukus got out of there? But let him or whoever come." He tauntingly points a finger at his head. "This hobo's got master plans, asshole. Master fucking plans."

"So you knew MacGuffin's gang was hiding in the tanker."

"Of course I did."

"And you didn't tell me."

"MacGuffin called a new deal or no deal. He bitched how ND&B ran him out of business and how he deserved the score. And I saw how it worked to trap Salukus. So I cut him in."

"Did you help him retrofit that tanker? Was it your plan for hiding those dudes in there? Jesus Christ, Billy. Fuck you for not cutting me in on the details. People got fucking killed. Those tanks exploded and there's a goddamned fire."

"Look at it this way. We got these binders and the laptop. So we got what we went for. Evidence with teeth."

I glance at our box of plunder and I fear what it holds.

"This shit is going to be all over the news, man."

"It's not going to be on the news, bubba. If Salukus is alive, he'll mop it all up. And if not him then somebody else."

Billy orders me to throw on the cabin lights as he thumbs through the binders. He describes the faces to me. Women and children and men in a full range of shapes and colors. "Here's a kid with Down's and another in a wheelchair. They got one of all us. How many binders is this?"

He tilts occasional pages so I can catch glimpses of Hell from the pilot's chair. One kid appears drugged. Another photographed after a beating. Another on the edge of a bed, her face red and puffy. The next boy stares wide as if the light has been blown from his eyes.

Billy goes digging again and when he finds it he folds the binder on its spine. The photo that shows the tiled room that I'd seen in the rear of the terminal. "We can literally lay down money and buy somebody. A kid, a chick, some slim dude. Whatever we can afford. Four hours to do whatever the fuck. Then we kill them."

"I got to pull over."

Too late. I shove the door wide with my boot and puke in the road wind, holding the wheel steady and keeping on the throttle. I slam the door and wipe my mouth across my wrist.

"Son bitch. I ralphed all down the port side. Sorry. That's been building up."

"You kidding me, bubba? You handled that like a boss. But you want me to drive?"

"Got any reefer?"

I rinse my mouth with water from the jar of Zina's flowers and take the window down to spit. He refills his electric pipe with hash oil swiped from Hitachi's frosted glass apothecary.

When we reach the gas farm to get the Jeep, he takes the laptop and binders. He asks to be let off in the road.

"I'll see you at the crib. Get a bunch of beer and we'll run through the laptop together."

Finding my gears, I lumber away on the gravel running west to the big road and catch a chill like I'll never see him again.

13

<u>MANANDATORY DRIVERS MEETING</u> THURS 5 P.M BE THEIR OR <u>FIRED</u>, YOU CHOICE. THX, *THE OWNERS.*

When I turn up at 6 p.m., I learn Thx the Owners failed to show for their own meeting.

"See? 'Manandatory.' It means 'unrequired.'"

"Fuck off," steams Paulie.

Any clout he has is at stake and in care of absentee ownership he's taking the brunt of our bad moods. The pay cut has ginned up threat of a walkout and this has drivers showing too much ass. Lots of direct disobedience from everybody so there's not shit Paulie can do about it.

Business is meanwhile getting bad all over the globe. Our nation's leaders have floated the financial titans with a $700,000,000,000 cash overrun levied on We the People. Television ticker reads: MAYHEM IN THE SQUARE MILE. Meanwhile, Chinese workers report a spike in depression after nets are installed to deter leaping from factory rooftops.

And then murder. State investigators were on Wednesday called to a meth lab explosion in rural Van Buren County. Firefighters discovered three occupants, Jeff Starps, 23, Floyd Cristenden, 28, and Rodney MacGuffin, 56, all of nearby Bonaparte. Autopsy results are pending though police are calling it homicide. They will not, however, elaborate on how the men died.

Conversely there has been no news out of our own rural corner. The warehouse raid has drawn no attention. No reports of bodies. No tank explosions or warehouse fires. No peddling kids and adults for sex work and killing. I even called the mainline from a payphone and got reception. It's business as usual at ND&B.

I'm left to presume MacGuffin and some of his gang got away. Else, they were killed and their bodies moved to Van Buren County. That seems like a lot of work so I'm keeping with the first premise. I can also only presume that Salukus got away too. He must've mopped up the warehouse and torched the biker gang. Him or somebody worse.

In other news tonight, our greenhorn quit. We were all eating drive-thru suppers in the shop when he stormed through to give Paulie the what for. Then he bitched us out for being cocks and for cabs never vacuumed or checked for oil, and finally he got onto the pay cut while the streets have flooded with gypsy cabs. "This bullshit isn't worth it!"

"Amen, brother!"

I'm rapping about this hours later, parked on the empty slab of the old bus depot, eating taco cart burritos with Dr. Bob and Joe Vega on the hood of our taxis. Quiet Chuck rolls up and gets right out.

"I just cleared some dude at the cop shop. He had a brick of heroin on him."

He lifts his hand to show the heft of it.

"Check that lost and found. Where'd you pick him up?"

"Indigo Court," says Chuck. "The guy's scared shitless the boogeyman's after him. I ask him, 'Because of the heroin?' 'No, no,' he says, 'That's why the police are going to protect me.' So I ask him again: 'Because of the heroin?'"

Everybody's laughing but me.

"Did he say why he was bringing it to the cops?"

Quiet Chuck shrugs. "All's I know is he carried out his plan exactly as described. Which was to just waltz into the cop shop, 'Here's my brick of heroin.'"

I make my goodbyes and roll off the old slab, awake and still hungry. I have a growing urge to get on the highway and drive until I'm out of gas. Then leave the cab and start walking.

I haven't seen Billy since dropping him at the gas farm. I managed to pass Tuesday night without freaking out. Then I woke up hungover and convinced he was dead in a ditch. I called his cell and got voicemail 15 times.

Three hours later: IMOK, with added comment: LAPTOP SENT ME OT, BACK LATE THURS. By OT he means out of town.

Then Thursday ends and Friday begins and I haven't heard from him.

Cab driving is tough when you got personal bullshit building up. Especially when nothing's hopping downtown. Nothing but time to pick through strand by terrible strand. I park in an alley behind a church and kill my lights, even my bubble light. Then I sit and watch the shadows and every corner.

THE SUDDEN RADIO startles me in the dark.
"ADVENTURE TIME, #22. TAKE IT TO 1108 PDC."

Dispatch hasn't chirped since midnight. I buy coffee on the way to Prairie Du Chien because I need to stay sharp. I also know the fare will be too wasted to wander off. She's a regular at 1108, a lonely nurse with access to pills. When I arrive, she's waiting at the bottom of her driveway, drunk, her rump dropped on two sacks of dirt, her foot propped on a case of beer. She tips a Silver Bullet overhead. Seeing that dirt, I pop the trunk and step out to load up. It's potting soil with polystyrene beads.

"I'm going up to the cemetery and I need to get all the way in the back."

"I can roll to the gate but not inside. It's after sundown."

She gives me mean eyes. "Oh is it already?"

"Cemetery's closed, lady. It opens again in a few hours."

"First just drive the goddamned taxi."

Three blocks south of her home I halt at the gate and call the minimum fare. She lays into me right away. "I want to go inside. It's inside where I want you to drop me off."

"Ma'am, the cemetery shuts at sundown."

"Then why do they leave the gates open? Smart ass."

The gates never close and this argument can only grow in a circle. So I proceed through the gate and into the boneyard. We take it slow past the chapel and the groundskeeper's garage and over the unlit hills. The dim moon shows above like a round knife.

My fare tells me to stop in the curve of the furthest lane and tosses three sweaty dollars over the seat. I point at the meter. "The big red counter says $4.75."

"That is all you shall receive from me."

I pop the trunk and step out to unload the sacks of potting soil, one of which has been gouged by the tire iron. "And look at what you did to my dirt!"

This while she juggles her case of Silver Bullet from which at least a six-pack rolls off on the macadam as she figures out her cigarettes and purse and lighter. "Aren't you even going to ask me what the dirt's for?"

"Did you want me to?"

"My best friend's mother. She's dead. You clever enough to know what that means? They buried her three weeks ago. But they didn't bury her right and now I got to fix it."

I ask how they buried her wrong.

"They didn't put enough dirt in her hole, stupid."

Leaving the beer on the road with one sack of dirt, the lonely nurse drags the other sack among the tombstones. Fuck it. I rip two of her beers, get back in the cab, and crack one open as I wheel out of the loop, leaving the way we came in.

Then I'm creeping past the groundskeeper's garage. It's a big place with four wide bays and service entries at either end

Two blocks out of the cemetery, I park and finish off the second beer. Next, I pop the trunk to get that tire iron. The air is cool and the wind is blowing as night swells into a singular blackness under the neighborhood oaks.

I slip through the open gates, staying away from the orange entry light and keeping an eye out for the lonely nurse. The brick chapel has a camera bent on the door though I find the garage behind it is afforded no such security. I use the bar to pry through the first service door. The old jamb is spongy enough that I'm able to latch the lock after.

I flip my phone open and get the camera going. It takes shitty pix but the light sensor will pick up the infrared array of any night-vision cameras and make them glow on my screen. I make a pass over every corner before entering each room.

Once I'm certain they've got no cameras, I use the penlight from my purse and walk freely. The Gator is parked in the garage with the keys in it. There's even an unlocked office that contains a safe.

Along the main corridor I find a big closet. Outside the closet door are empty urn vaults, the lids and bottoms stacked as flower pots. Same kind of vault used at Jerry's service. I try the door knob with my shirt and it twists open.

My penlight reveals metal racks running the walls shelved with cans of ashes. The cemetery doesn't send them anywhere. They just go here on the shelf. Not forgotten but abandoned.

I look on the shelf closest to my right hand. Not all the cans have nametags and not all the tags can be read. On my third pass, I find Jerry's aluminum urn next to Tex's Mason jar.

"You're coming with me."

I've almost made the front door when I turn back for Tex and his wife, Shelly. Never mind what I think about Tex Feely. It was Jerry's wish to be buried with his friends, and so be it.

Grabbing a spade off the wall and a tarp off the floor, I go into the chapel's yard away from the light and the camera. With the tip of the spade, I cut out a square yard of grass and roll it back. Then I dig at its center, shoveling hard and fast, and piling spoils on the tarp. I'm soon sweating but don't quit until my arm fits in the hole.

I put the couple in the hole and at last get Jerry settled. I talk to the aluminum can.

"Thanks for all the help you ever tried to give. Even if I was a thorn in your ass. And if my yelling's what killed you, I'd want you to know that I never would intend that. And I'm sorry, I guess. Tell Tinker I says hey."

I shovel the spoils off the tarp and bury the three friends in the chapel lawn. Then I carefully roll the swatch of grass over the spot and stamp it down. Then back to the shed where I stow the shovel, relock the door and reclaim my tire iron.

"What're you doing there!"

The lonely nurse has caught me on my way out. I stay against the garage to scan the lighted edges. Wind scares up the chorus of leaves and I can't see her so I run like hell to the gate.

"Hey!"

I don't turn until I've reached the exit. She's way back in the dark and barely able to walk. She carries her case of beer as if it's a child.

I jog another block then get my phone out. The clock shows 2:53 a.m. Most eventful hour of the night.

I call dispatch and tell him before he answers.

"I quit, Paulie."

"You said you're clear at the cemetery?"

"I said I quit. I'm done."

"Why for? I can't lose two drivers in one shift!"

"I'm fueling and bringing it in."

"But I got a request for you."

"No way. No specials tonight."

"But it's a chick."

"From the massage parlor? Did she talk like Minnie Mouse?"

"Aw naw it wasn't no chick from any massage parlor and I know that for a fact."

Dispatchers get a bad rap for lying, and deservedly so. I'm filthy from the burial detail and need smokes more than I need a shower. But if this is Letty Fetch, I wouldn't mind giving her a chunk of my mind.

"It's is my last one, Paulie. Then I'm done. Where's she at?"

Paulie sends me downtown into the 300 block of College. I draw up curbside and stop in gear. The street is well-lit. My window is half down to let out smoke but the doors are locked and my foot's ready to jump off the brake. Full clearance front and back and street-side.

I call for a punch and keep my eyes on the door that leads to the upper apartments.

A white delivery van wheels around the corner and throws its hazards. The dash clock says it's an hour early for morning deliveries. Or am I just being paranoid? I watch the driver get out. He stuffs a lading bill into his ass pocket and opens the back to retrieve a dolly.

Now she comes out of the building. I can tell Letty by her drug-addled skeleton walk. I should drive off at sight of her. I check the doors are locked and take the window down.

"No fucking way, Letty Fetch."

"Vicky, I didn't do nothing to you. I just need a ride. Billy got with me. We're all cool."

"What the fuck? Everywhere I've looked the last couple weeks, you've been creeping the edges like a roach. And here you are creeping some more."

She comes to the door like she'll try the handle and my idea is to wheel away with her pawing at it.

"Enjoy the good stretch of your legs, bitch."

A flutter on my left, and I look.

The delivery driver is at my window. Something out of his hand bursts on my neck then I'm jiggling in the driver seat pissing myself and stomping my feet. The cab lurches forward, swings wild, hits a parked car and I'm out.

* * *

HANDS BOUND BEHIND me in plastic ties. Ankles bound too. Left eye swelled. I can feel blood on my cheek. Leaning up from the backseat, I see Letty Fetch at the wheel of my cab.

Don Salukus sits in back with me. He pounds on my ribs like a hammer. "Don't you get up. Don't you fucking move."

I lay my face on the bench seat but I've seen a flash of roadside. We're a mile out on the Triple H going east toward Sharpless. The white delivery van is rolling ahead of us. My hippurse, Maglite, phone, Gerber knife and Glock have all been stripped from me.

Less than three miles on, Letty turns north for a bit then east before slewing across a dozen more miles on twisting county gravels. Through the rear window I see the moon, sharp as a mezzaluna, cutting through the broken clouds.

Why is Letty Fetch with Salukus? Could he have planted her with both Phipps and MacGuffin? Or is she with him against her will? Maybe he captured her in the jam. A trophy from the MacGuffin kill.

I ask him: "So what's your deal with her?"

"Everyone's got to survive," says Letty. "Ain't that right, baby?"

Salukus pushes his eyes on me and chews his teeth.

"Letty does what's she's told so Letty gets what she wants."

"Ain't that just like a masseuse?"

That gets Salukus leaning over me, slapping my face until he gets tired. My left ear flares ringing. I feel more blood. He screams at me.

"You two heroes ought to wear Lycra costumes and faggy capes. You cunts have no idea what you fucked with."

He curls a fist like he'll bash my daylights out. But he only stares back at me.

Then a kind of bell goes off in my head. Based on time and track, I feel I've been near this place before. Risking a peep, I see we're along a wooded spread with high brick walls. Letty turns in a driveway to follow the van through a high archway gate.

I remember her. And I have been here before. This is where I've seen the caged girl from the Kushite's video. The first Football Saturday. The caged girl was the crying babysitter and the hundred bucks she gave me came from them. It rained hard that night and it was tough to see more than the raw shape of walls and trees and house. Tonight I see turrets up above and watchtowers too. This also must be the place Phipps described. The country castle. This is where Old Henry lives with his bears. That name occurs to me fresh. Henry. The H in H. Thomas Houston II. The private zoo like Phipps called it isn't a zoo at all.

This is Heritage Gaming Preserve.

Salukus glances out the window. "Won't be long."

I roll back on the bench, knees to chest, and mule kick his face with both feet, twice. Third time his head bounces on the window. Letty screams. I scissor my bound legs over his head and roll into the floor well, crushing his neck between my knees. Salukus, pinned, faces away and slugs my leg with his free arm and I choke harder with the ball of my knee. His slugs begin to fall off their mark and I roll deeper into the floor well.

Letty tears across the property honking and running us through a second narrower gate to smash Cab #90 into the ass end of the white delivery van. Crush of metal, splashing glass. Salukus and I roll together against the front seats and he falls out of my death grip. I've hit the floor facedown and he's slugging me hard again.

Letty lifts her head off the horn. The door opens and I get dragged out into a wide pea gravel lot behind the fortress home. The lot is hemmed in the rear by a third high wall.

Salukus has gotten out of the cab and stands over me brandishing my Glock. He swings with it, smashes my cheek. I hear the slide snapping back.

But a familiar voice warns him off.

"Henry wants him breathing. Besides I get a turn with him."

Stan the Kushite stands over me in his workaday coveralls

and stomps my left hand. Sounds like sticks breaking. He pummels me with big round fists and kicks my sides. "I trusted you, fuckface. Now I'm going to fuck up your face!"

Salukus breaks it up and I roll off to spit blood. The knuckles of my left hand swell hot. Then I hear growling behind the third wall.

Somebody cuts the binds on my ankles and I'm dragged to my feet. The man who freed my legs is the same little man I saw at the exotic animal auction. The Indonesian in safari getup that welcomed us in the lobby. Tonight he wears a relaxed form of the same outfit.

Salukus orders Letty to my taxi. "Dump it in town and wait to hear from me. Nobody can see you with that cab."

"I understand."

Letty coaxes the taxi back to life and backs out of the narrow gate. Spidered glass drops out of the broken passenger window and I hear rattling in the drive train as the cab rolls off.

They drag me through the third wall at an iron gate. My left hand burns and it hurts too much to bend the fingers. We halt in the unlit yard and I see the amber lamps of a control board glowing in the entry hut. The safari man throws switches on the board and lights bang on across a broad flat pitch.

Brick animal houses light up right and left. Six cages to either side and every other one pens a tiger. Straight ahead of us is a grand fourth gate shuttered with tall wooden doors. High lighting towers glow in the dark beyond. Must be the entrance to the hunting grounds.

Stan bangs a wooden rod along the cage bars, taunting the cats so that I'm paraded past riled beasts.

"I wouldn't want to be you, you walking meat. These tigers? Henry told us we're going to cut you apart and make them do tricks for the pieces. I've seen him do this with bears, boy. Ugly way to go but entertaining to watch. Just talking about it gives me a hard on. How about it, Donny?"

Laughing and laughing, howling at the sliver of the moon. He comes behind me for a bear hug. "My heart's beating in my cock. Can you feel that?"

I halt and stomp my heel on his ankle, twisting, hoping to break it. Stan yells and butts his head into mine. Boxes my ears on my way down. Then he pounds and pounds on my head and each landing makes the inside of my skull light up. A nearby tiger growls for the fight.

Again Salukus breaks it up. "Go take a walk."

"Get his pants down."

"I said go take a walk."

The Kushite skulks off and Salukus guides me to the last cage on the left. He whirls his hand to the little man at the other end of the barracks. A bell rings and a red beacon rotates over the cage door. Electro motor whirs and lock claps open. A second bell rings and the cage door creaks wide. Salukus cuts the binds on my hands, shoves me inside. He signals again. The bell rings once and the cage door pulls closed, sighing on its hinges.

The lock claps shut. I can hear it out of my left ear but my right buzzes and the pain of it shuts my eyes.

"They'll only rape you a little bit," Salukus says. "Then they'll feed you to the tigers. It won't last as long as you think. Henry wants you gone by dawn."

He leaves me to think on that.

The animal house stinks of the piss and shit of every animal tromped through. Under blazing overheads I can tell these are the same cages where Stan shot his amateur sex video. The same cages that'd held Chemo Phipps, and every animal led to slaughter on the gaming preserve. It's as weird a death as diving off a parking garage.

The tiger in the cage beside me hasn't stirred. Old and wore out, she lazes against our adjoining bars.

Across the yard, the Kushite leans on the cage opposite mine. He's got his coveralls open and is working his cock in his hands. I turn my back on the gate and flop to the ground, wincing for the head twinge. This position leaves me staring in my old neighbor's face. The tigress stretches front paws and sits on her rump staring back at me. She's used to seeing and smelling humans. Jing Shan Trading Co. must capture their stock from the circus.

Something causes her to stand and I instinctively stand with her. Except the head rush is killer and then my tailbone rings because I've tumbled back on my ass.

I just want to lay here a minute.

But the yard jumps with commotion and I climb the cage bars to drag onto my feet. I'm wobbly as the 'Yota and can't hear anything on my right.

First off, Stan has properly dressed. He and Salukus approach my cage followed by the little helper. And then the man I recognize as Henry Thomas Houston II. Old Henry.

"Where's his partner?"

Salukus replies, "We think he split town."

Removing his pith helmet, the old hunter creeps on my cage door. He gets so close that he touches his nose to the iron. "You and your friend are as miserable as the Golden Horde."

Like his little man, the old hunter is costumed for his role wearing gaiters on khakis and bearing a leather quirt he swishes about. Old Henry's full of theatrical affectations too. Old dusties though. He overacts with his hands like a bygone star of silent film.

"I am Henry Thomas Houston the Second. Do you know who I am?"

"You're a skin-trader and a fucking worm."

"Condemnation!" Old Henry grins with black teeth. "What is the plan then? Escape! Crawl through my home with a knife in your teeth? Kill me!"

"It won't be me that kills you."

A hot yellow wave of nausea rolls through me and I tip, catching myself on the bars. I go to a knee and hold onto the cage door. I feel like I'm going to puke.

"Ah just look at yourself. Oblivious to the predicaments you cause, which includes the whole of your life. I could free you from where you are and you would still be a caged man. Living as a derelict in a garage. A drunk and a drug user. The only use I have of you is your money. And though I can afford not having you as a customer, I cannot afford your thieving and meddling and exposures. Do you understand? Killing you will resolve an issue for both of us, my friend. No more of your scrambling and suffering. No more unbearable dawns."

He stoops to his knee as I do so that we can see eye to eye.

"As this wasted life is chewed out of you, do not hate that you were oblivious. Do not focus on your routine failures. Simply run into the light and fucking die."

The yard light above us claps out as if on cue. Theatrics to go with his monologue, I guess.

"Must be killing me is a bad idea."

"Jinjee, the light. And get his cage open."

The helper is already off to bug-hunt the trouble. Except trouble finds him first and his little voice breaks out.

"Danger, sirs! Danger! Hatari!"

The lights above the yard begin to bang off one by one. Then the towers beyond the high gate fall dark. Stan yells and Old Henry curses, "Happy Hitler's birthday, what now?"

The cell lights are cut and we're in the dark as a bell rings and the electro box above my cage door whirs. I hear the lock clap open. And I hear this sound echo in my head a dozen times before realizing this is all of the cage locks opening in sequence.

The second bell rings and the doors rattle. All is dark save for the red beacons rotating over the cell doors. In the thin red waves I can see my gate remains shut though the others begin to open wide in creaking concert. Every time the red light bubbles across my eye I feel it crush me over. My ear hurts so bad I want to cut it off.

The skin-trader and his lieutenants bewail their bad luck and my neighbor cat startles to her feet. She growls low and paces and rushes out of the cage. Once the cage doors are open, the revolving lights stop and it's dark again. It feels better in the dark. Cooler. The completeness of this unseeable world takes the edge off my nausea.

Flash and bang of a gun and I puke all over my shoes as Stan panics, hollering what the fucks and firing twice more.

My ear blazes in pain and I cover it with a hand. With my good ear, I hear Old Henry ordering to hold their fire.

"What the devil are you shooting at?"

Nearer by snarling causes the Kushite to yell and his gun muzzle flashes loud over and over. My cage door is hit and sings unearthly while the bullet cracks on the wall behind me. He dry fires, *click-click*. "I'm empty!"

The old hunter cries out, "Jinjee!"

Maybe I've passed out. I rouse lying on my side though the world feels right side up. With my good ear, I can hear Stan scrambling over ground, moaning like he's wounded and scared. He grunts and bays. Yells become shrills muted with his mouth covered over. I hear the melon split and heels kicking the dirt until there is nothing left to motor them.

The old hunter cries out, "Jinjee!"

The little voice carries from the front of the yard. Explaining he has made his way to the light switches. He whinnies like a caught rabbit.

"I am wounded, sir! They attack!"

I hear growling closer by.

Feet thump in the grass, and wrestling sounds, a man holding back until he can't and then he's screaming. Brutal fast swiping. Like a kitty kicking a bunny to death. Salukus moans aloud. I hear their feet shuffling.

And then: "Not two of you bastards!"

The old hunter cries out, "Jinjee!"

Jinjee doesn't reply. But Old Henry has attracted predators. I hear his feet lighting away until he stumbles and falls, or is tackled, and then he howls terribly until he's out of breaths.

Afterward, I hear prowling feet and meat dragging and I give myself to the completeness of the void.

* * *

SQUARE OF STARLIGHT opens overhead. I can see better in the dark now. My tiger growls on her feet. I can make her shape outside my cage door. She laid down in front of it. Guarding me.

A rope ladder unfurls into my cage and a silhouette shows in the square of starlight. I can hear Billy's voice.

"On your feet, bubba. I can climb down and get you up. But I can't carry you on the rope ladder. You got to move."

Rung by rung I pull myself upright against the unsteady rungs and my feet can't find where to land. My head aches and bad ear feels like a fist of hot glass. I don't know if I can make the top but I climb one rung after another with one good hand. When I'm within reach Billy drags me clear.

He shines a light in my face and I see he's wearing his NVGs.

"Ah your face. We got to get you to the clinic."

"Get the tiger in the cage. Shut the tiger in the cage."

"What for?"

"She's tame. Like a circus cat. Not like the other ones."

"She's just like the other ones, bubba. And we got to go."

"You shut that cage door and I'll let you pull me off this roof."

Then I shut my eyes.

When I open them, I'm lying on my side feeling uncomfortable and sick. My face in pea gravel. The world no longer feels right side up in this position but half upside down.

Next, Billy's dragging me away from the third gate.

Good. We're leaving.

"Stay awake, bubba."

"When did you get here?"

Now we've reached my taxi. He drags me into the back seat and then gets behind the wheel. I can hear the drive train rattling under us as he drives off.

But I don't understand. Letty already left my taxi.

Wind and rain blow through the busted window and heat blasts from the vents. I puke on the floor. I taste blood.

"Did I ever tell you about the poppies?" asks Billy. "I always think about the poppies after putting work in."

I ask, "Did you get that tiger in her cage?"

"Granddad always got us those red paper poppies to remember the vets. And the Veteran's Day Ethan got snatched, granddad drove all night to be with us. He gave my sister Mo a poppy and me a poppy and Ma got one too like he'd gotten her since she was a kid."

Highway lights pass above the window like a pendulum that moves in a single direction. I can feel darkness closing in. Why am I in the backseat of my cab?

Suddenly I can no longer breathe.

"I knew he got one for Ethan too but he didn't show us. Like he didn't want the poppy sitting out unclaimed. I even went through granddad's coat but the poppy wasn't there."

14

THE ROARING CROWDS awake me.

I'm in a hospital bed and hurt like I've been run through a washer. The lights are low and pulled venetians slit the glow of the window. And there it is again. Tens of thousands crying out. A nurse passes the door and I call to her. She keeps moving.

A guard, however, pokes his grinning face in the doorway. "What's up, buddy?"

"Do I hear screaming?"

"It's a close game," he says. "Hawks are down by two."

He then resumes his post and my eyes fall shut.

WHEN I ROUSE again, the venetians are yanked high and orange sun pours over the foot of my bed. The orderly says it's Monday afternoon, "You're awake just in time!"

She's brought a flower delivery. But it's Monday already? Doesn't feel like Monday. The orderly places the flowers on my bedside stand then exchanges my garbage bags.

I spot a Z on the flower tag and lean for them, groaning. My left hand is taped in a splint and the breath is cut from me to pull the stand closer.

"The tag says these're for Zimmerman."

"Ah he's next door. So sorry!"

Hurrying off with the flowers, the orderly is crushed in the doorway by the doctor and two blue coats.

"Welcome back!"

The doc is an older woman in glasses with salted black hair.

"Do you know what's happened to you, Mister Pasternak? You're at the university hospital. You've sustained a serious injury. Can you hear me?"

"Not so well out of my right."

She takes my vitals and the resident fetches me ice chips.

"You're pretty well banged up. We literally found you wandering outside the emergency room early Friday morning. You've suffered a traumatic brain injury consistent with assault. Do you have any recall of what's happened?"

"It doesn't feel like three days." I'm deaf on my right from getting my ears boxed. I've got two fingers splinted. She hands me a mirror and I see 12 stitches in my right eyebrow from getting skull-bashed. Sixteen more in my left cheek from a pistol grip, a Glock 17 9mm, which can be determined from the underlying bruise. My knuckles are busted up from fighting back, my arms in scratches. Both eyes are blacked and I've got a contact burn on my neck from getting tased. But I tell the doctor, "I don't remember anything."

"Amnesia is likely."

Next, she startles me with noises and walks to the corners of the room to check my stereo hearing. The buzzing in my right ear is making me dizzy so she writes an otology referral.

"Where can I smoke?"

"No smoking on the hospital campus. One more thing. The police wanted to talk as soon as you woke up."

I check the open door and spy the round blue edge of uniform posted out there.

"Is that why the guard?"

"They want to talk about an investigation, Mister Pasternak.

Do you feel up to it?"

I shrug. "I'm awake anyway."

Then the doc leaves with her residents.

The cops don't give me any time to sweat it. They must've been hanging around the nurse's station. Two plainclothes dicks, beefy and lean, mustachioed and not. The lean one carries a laptop and the beefy one makes the introductions.

"Detective Gary Davis, ICPD, and from state DCI, Special Agent Steven Vaughan. May we talk?"

The skin of my neck pricks and I get an insta-headache. They can only be here because of Damen's brick of heroin.

I recognize the beefy cop with the broom 'stache. He was at Chemo's murder and among the gang that escorted Dorothy to my taxi. The state cop is wiry and athletic, wears an orthodox black suit with a red tie. I sense they have no truck together. Repelling one another like a pair of the same pole.

"I remember you." The city cop smiles at me. "I was still on patrol. We had a guy at Memories stabbed in the neck with a pint glass. You were the cabbie that picked up the guy that did it. I remember you stalled him so we could make an arrest."

"Regular hero," the state dick grumbles.

"Yup. That's me."

What he's talking about happened during my second year driving a cab. Back when I was a healthful sport. I find it disconcerting that he's remembered me this long.

"We're here today to talk about an incident that occurred Friday during early morning hours. We talked to your dispatcher and other witnesses to get a rough picture of what happened. Do you mind if we ask you a few questions?"

I tell them: "All right."

The beefy cop licks his thumb and pages through a cheap notebook. He starts fresh and takes down where I'm living, and how long; where my family lives; where we came from. He wants leads on where to look if I run.

"Somebody really gave you a work over," he says. "Can you tell us what happened?"

The state cop meanwhile unpacks a laptop and situates it on the stand so that its sleeping screen faces me.

"I dropped a lady off at the cemetery," I tell them. "She was drunk and complicated. It must've pushed me over the edge because I remember that I called my dispatcher and quit."

"You quit your job? Your job of ten years?"

Cop looks at cop and I jump to my case. "My quitting didn't have anything to do with anything. The cemetery lady was just a regular crazy drunk and I'm burned out. Stick a fork in me, I'm done. You know?"

Stick a fork in me because if they talked to Paulie they already know all this. Even the state dick holds out a hand.

"Got it."

He stands off in the room, a lingering observer. As if he's going to catch something missed by me and the mustache cop.

"So if you quit your job why pick up another fare?"

"Dispatch must've talked me into a final call, per usual."

"So you don't remember that?"

"Sure is ironic what happened considering you just quit," says the city cop. "We got a surveillance tape. Would you mind taking a look?"

The other one brings the laptop out of sleep and the video is already cued. "Your doctor's given us the go-ahead. But this video may disturb you."

My voice comes out dry and hard. "Let's have at it."

The security camera gazes into the middle of the 300 block of College, shot from above and behind. It offers an oblique profile of the passenger side of my cab as I roll to the curb. The white van isn't seen except for the swing of its headlights when it rounds the corner. The timestamp rolls another 40 seconds before the woman appears from right of frame. She halts on the sidewalk and stoops to talk through my open window. The video shows I briefly let off the brake. Taking my time to give her the what for. Baiting her to grab the handle.

Dropping in through top of frame, creeping out between cars, a man in coveralls hurries toward my side of the cab. One arm extended. The other hand is brought up over his face.

Next, the taxi lurches ahead, swings wild, and quarterpanels a parked car.

A second man comes from right of frame and stands behind the woman. Like the first man, he keeps his face away from the camera. The men remove me from the front of the taxi to the rear. Then the first runs out of frame while the other climbs in back with me. The woman at last bustles around to the driver door. This is the only time the video shows her face. She gets in, backs out of the crash, and drives out of frame.

The state cop asks: "Can you tell us what was happening inside the cab during that video?"

"I don't remember any of that. Not pulling up or waiting or talking with her."

"The woman's name is Letty Fetch. Do you know her?"

"Sure. I've known Letty 15 years. I keep my distance."

"Why's that?"

"She's a junkie. She runs the massage parlor on Dubuque."

"She got a beef with you?"

"None I know of."

"This looks coordinated to me," says the city cop. "Do you have any idea why these people targeted you or your taxicab? Anybody that'd want to hurt you, or see you hurt?"

"I'm a cab driver and will pile chips on anybody's shoulder. But nobody specific." I shrug it out. "Drivers've been getting robbed all season. So maybe this is part of that?"

The state cop pins his eyes on me. He looks like Encyclopedia Brown all grown up.

"We're in the process of getting other video," he warns "Are we going to find out that you know these guys when we get another look? Because we can make it a whole lot easier if you can tell us what happened."

"I can't tell from this video. And seeing it doesn't jar anything loose. I just don't remember."

The mustache cop grins like we're buddies.

"All right," he says. Now I must ask you to brace yourself,

bud. Because this has become a homicide case."

I let that settle then tip my chin. "All right."

"Your taxicab wasn't located until yesterday morning. Which was Sunday, if you're blurry on that. Where the quarry road passes under the interstate? Parked up in there between the pylons. Ms Fetch was found in the trunk."

"Ah jeez."

He balls his big fists and leans on the foot of my bed. "The tox screens aren't back but like you say: Junkie. My guess is she was given a hot shot and then put in that trunk."

"The quarry workers say the taxi wasn't there as of Saturday afternoon," the state cop adds. "The vehicle had been in a wreck with a window broken out and an exchange of paint. Your blood was found on the backseat and floor. But the vehicle had been wiped of any fingerprints."

I look to the window full of Monday morning sun and remember Friday night wind blowing through the busted window as the drive train rattled and the heater roared.

I remember puking on the floor and Billy at the wheel going on about poppy flowers. I also remember Letty departing in the cab before all that. How Billy got it between those points, and whatever happened thereafter, I don't know.

And I don't want to know.

"I want to help. But it's like I was blackout drunk. Sorry."

THE COPS THANK me for my time and wish a speedy recovery, leaving business cards on the bed stand in case I remember anything. They relieve the guard from my door and clear me for visitors.

But I'm also served a warning: "Don't leave town because we'll want to talk again."

Soon as they go, I punch the call-button for the nurse. I ask to use the phone and have her dial the sideline to Emerald Cab.

Paulie answers.

I ask him, "What're you doing there on a Monday?"

"Jerry's shift needed covered. By the way, you're fired."

"You can't fire me, I quit. And what the fuck was with you putting me into this bullshit? I'm still in the hospital."

Paulie sours.

"I don't know what it was. I put you into that call and didn't think anything of it. Then you disappeared until I got a call from the ER. Fuck, man. That's twice in a month I put a driver in the jackpot. I'm losing my radar for this shit."

"Technically it's three times. And you can't fire me."

"I got standing orders from the new owner that I got to fire you next time you called in."

"Did you tell him I already quit? And what new owner?"

"The 'manandatory' meeting? Thx the Owners were going to break it to us then. They've sold the company."

"When'd that happen? And who'd buy their shit anyway?"

"You know that Turkish guy running UniCab? He became owner as of midnight Saturday."

Paulie means the guy whose tires I stabbed out. The dude that warned me there'd be a greater price. In buying Emerald Cab, he now owns the largest taxi fleet in town.

"He just up and bought it?"

"Thx the Owners have already split for the coast."

Paulie has worse news.

"The new boss is suing you for damages to Cab #90."

"The cops got video of me getting jacked so fuck that guy. Is he standing next to you? Put that son bitch on the speaker."

The phone whines in my good ear.

"Mister Pasternak, I want you to listen. You are finished, do you hear? You will never drive a taxicab in this town ever again. If you drive for another company, I shall buy that one too. You will be hearing from my lawyers, sir. Good day to you."

The line breaks off but I yell into the phone anyway.

"You're going to sue me? I'll countersue. Oh yeah? It'll be

called Pasternak Cab, you hear me?"

Blowing my top gives me a headache and I hand the phone back to the nurse.

"He hung up."

DRIVERS SHOW UP before the 9 o'clock kick out, Dr. Bob and Quiet Chuck and Wayne, one after the other. They pick at the cold cafeteria vittles that I haven't touched and I ask them to bring real food next time. Everybody's heard what happened and about dead Letty Fetch in the trunk of our cab and the rumors that I died. I tell them I almost did.

"So where's Zina? How's she doing?"

All they want to talk about is the new ownership and how our pay cut was a big conspiracy previous to sale. Dr. Bob says, "Quitting like you and the rookie did should inspire us all."

Even Leon Bath drops by to stink up my room with farts and lies. He does tell one true tale, which I'm later able to confirm: "Shake and Bonnie got busted with precursors."

This happened last Wednesday, the day after MacGuffin and his crew were blown up in a meth lab. I wonder if Salukus had anything to do with it, or if this was just regular fate.

After they've gone, I watch cable news and see the president has signed off on that big check for the banks. Whatevs.

In other news tonight, I'm told there's been an incident on an estate northeast of town. In fact, this segment is a follow-up.

"Over the weekend we reported on the deaths of four men killed in a tragic accident on a private hunting reserve. Tonight comes disturbing allegations regarding the property's owner."

Cut to a daytime press conference held in the pea gravel lot at Heritage Gaming Preserve. A somber man in big glasses tells cameras that the ensuing death investigation at the estate has uncovered a cache of child pornography. "There is evidence to suggest Mister Houston was not only a consumer of this media but potentially a distributor of this media as well."

Cut to footage of jacketed agents carrying boxed evidence and desktop computers as the voiceover resumes: "Police would not say if any charges are pending. Houston was one of four men killed Friday by Bengal tigers when a gate separating them from the animals apparently malfunctioned.

"Henry Houston built quiet renown as a developer and an as advocate of what detractors call 'captive hunting.' These shocking allegations are certain to tarnish that image."

Cut to a parting shot of the law enforcement and media vehicles that occupy the driveway, and parked, I am certain, atop of bunches of my DNA.

Next day, regular fares and more drivers drop by my room until I get to feeling like Jerry at his funeral.

But Zina doesn't visit or call. And she doesn't return the messages I've left on her phone, or at the taxi shack. Next day, I call Paulie: "Can you at least tell me if she's doing all right?"

This forces him to break the news. "She doesn't want to talk to you, bro. And she doesn't want us talking to you about her. That's just the way it is."

My next call is answered by a male. "If you dial this number one more time, we will call the police and have a restraining order placed on you for harassment."

The man disengages and I don't call back.

I AM RETURNED to my room the next day following a bad ear exam and a good CT scan. A lunch of cold meatloaf has been left for me. I snarf the lime gelatin, cover the rest, and fall into the afternoon cable news cycle, listening to the crumble of the world economy and peering at my busted face in a hand mirror.

I startle at the shutting of my door. Billy has slipped in like a ghost and he's wearing a brand new KC Royals hoodie.

"Didn't know you liked baseball."

He replies, "How you feeling, bubba?"

"Like somebody busted my face, stole my ear, and gave me a concussion. You're looking good though."

"Glad to see you haven't lost your asshole."

Billy grins as he flops in the visitor's chair. He's brought my knapsack of clothes and kicks it over. The stink of his mansion emanates about the room.

"The cops have been around asking about Letty Fetch."

But Billy doesn't want to talk about the cops.

"And I don't want to talk about her. Not yet."

"So then what happened? After the gas farm. Start there."

"I had to go back to ND&B," he says, nonchalant. "I had to do something about those security cameras. And you got me worrying if Salukus made it or not."

"Did he?"

Billy shrugs. "His crew didn't. I found those dudes left behind with bikers and guards, and Hitachi. Hey, I found your guns too. They were in the trunk of the oxblood Caddy. I've hidden them in your garage under the bottom bunk bed."

In my haze of mind, I've managed to forget all about Billy's scheme to Trojan horse MacGuffin's gang into the warehouse. Thinking about it makes me mad all over again and getting mad makes my head hurt like hell.

Billy keeps rolling. "The cameras fed to a server in Kansas City and its physical address matched the one slugged in Hitachi's laptop. So I took the trip."

"Did you find the girl?"

He shakes his head. "I found Hitachi's server room though. And once I got into the servers, I got Hitachi's accounting files. Now I got a list of a dozen of firms that've laid out money for ND&B and I confirmed a familiar one—DevGRO. Drilling into the record, I found the purchase of those tigers in the loading dock. 'Consignee: Heritage Gaming Preserve.' So I blew out from KC before midnight and from 300 miles out landed at the spread just as that bitch was leaving in your cab."

"D equals RT," I tell him and Billy gives me a fist-bump.

Then I throw a bomb.

"Right before I got jumped, Letty said you two had gotten together. She said we were cool. So why'd you kill her?"

Billy holds me in his gaze a moment as if he's going to tell me something other than a lie.

"When I arrived, your cab was parked at the end of that driveway. Lights off except the bubble on top. She was behind the wheel nodded out with a needle in her arm. It could've been Salukus that gave her a hot mix."

"Or maybe you made sure she got a heroic dose."

"What doesn't kill you makes you stronger. And why do you give a shit about Letty Fetch anyway?"

"Did you stuff her in the trunk?"

"I had to put her somewhere. And I'm trying to tell you the story of how I saved your lunk ass—which, by the way, you're welcome—and you're going on like she's some prize catch. So what the fuck?"

My heart pounds in my broken fingers and face.

"Fine, Billy. Tell your story."

"So I hid the cars and crept across the yard and I saw the back lot didn't even have but two yard cameras and those didn't catch me. I got there in time to see you get stuffed in that cage and I saw the lion tamer work the door valves. That's how I got all them cage doors to open all at the same time."

He beams like the winning quarterback.

"Did you use the valves to cage my tiger?"

"Just like your prized bitch nobody gives a fuck about those cats, bubba. Damn. Look at you. You're alive. You ought to be celebrating, shit. And look—it's payday."

Billy leans back in the visitor's chair to pluck from the belly of his Royals hoodie a brown policy envelope. He gets to his feet and slides the thick envelope under my hand.

"You should know your uninsured ass is covered by an escrow medical account up to half a mil. The card and info are in there. I drew a collection too and put it with a little clean pay for driving the tanker. I also signed the title of that Peterbilt over to you. Just bring it in for registration." He drops the keys to the truck on my bedside stand. "I parked it for you in Welby's truck lot. Over near the taxi shack."

Welby's. I know where he means. But I don't know what to say. Recuperating these days in the hospital, I've clung to the fear that blind retribution is sniffing me out and as it fails to find me I've instead been left to carry the burden of knowing. It might not have taken my body, maybe it's carrying another part of me away.

Billy won't ever know that fear. Because the stake I've put to hazard he's already lost. Or he might've been born without it.

"I was getting my head scanned an hour ago," I tell him. "This bald little kid wheelchairs into the lobby and says, 'Hey, pardner. How're you feeling?' I tell him I got beat up and was almost eaten by tigers. That seemed to cheer him up. 'I'm sick with cancer,' he said. 'I'm going to die.'

"He put such ease on those heavy words. 'Me too, kid.' I told him. 'You're just beating me to it.' And I tried to laugh but I got like this. Crying like. And you don't have that."

With hands burrowed in the belly of his hoodie, Billy looms like a royal blue monolith while I sob on the bed.

"So what that I don't cry?"

"You don't cry because the part of you that's supposed to be human doesn't work. You tie in with the rest of us. But you're not one of us, Billy."

"It ain't like that."

"It sure as fuck is. You and your Nazi tattoo and bad ideas. I don't think we can be friends anymore."

I mean this sarcastically. In my book of friends, the name BILLY K. has twice been struck.

Yet his face collapses as if I'd stomped to death a box of a puppies. The voice that comes out of him is hard and strained.

"Sure we're friends. What we been through. We'll be friends forever. We're different, no doubt. But we get on like a shadow of the other. I told you shit I don't ever tell nobody."

I bring my words out hard as if each is a hammer.

"You lied to me. You lied when we robbed the drug dealers. You lied when I confronted you on the dead brother and you lied when I confronted the brother that lives. I never would've called on you again except I felt for a girl I saw in a video. And because I needed Salukus off my ass."

"There you go," he throws in. "You need me."

"I need you like a hole needs another hole, Billy. And you're like that hole in the bottom of your brother's globe. A great black void that sucks everything in with it."

He goes on that we could make it if we tried except he hasn't any spirit to leverage behind these pleas. "We could scale back to pals. Or bump into each other for drinks."

"I'll take the cash and the truck and the healthcare. But we can't be friends anymore."

He looks at me like I'm a just right rock. Like he wants to pick me up and throw me.

"You're right, bubba," he says at last. "You earned every bit of your take. And with that truck, I don't know what I'd do with that damn thing but sell it. So I'm happy you'll be getting use of it. Or you could sell it for weed. Whatever.

"But I want you to know this isn't the first time I been turned away by somebody I'd call a friend."

"And what's that tell you?"

"Tells me I can live with it. Except it's not me I'm worried about. You better get dressed. I'll tell you more along the way."

"What? Along what way?"

"We got unfinished business," he says. "That girl is out there and I know where she's at. Tonight. So get dressed. Now, bubba. We got to get back to Kansas City."

"I'm not going anywhere, you dumb son bitch."

He grins like a kid with hands stuffed in the tummy of his sweatshirt. "All right. You'd at least better get dressed and leave the hospital."

"And why the fuck?"

"Get somewhere you can watch a TV. Watch for the bombshell on the afternoon news." He points at the television mounted on the wall. "You got one here. Heck, you could just sit tight. You only got less than an hour."

He opens the door and hospital noise rushes inside.

"You care more about a tiger and a dead junkie hooker than you ever cared for that little girl. You actually enjoyed watching that video, didn't you?"

"Fuck you, Billy. I hope Kansas City eats you alive."

He leaves and shuts the door and closes me in the quiet purgatory of cable news.

I've only got less than an hour. What does he mean? The girl is alive and still in trouble and needs our help. Bombshell on the news. What does he mean by any of it when everything he says is a lie?

Less than an hour.

I have no want to believe Billy Kinross but I've got to listen to my gut and my gut's telling me to get out of the hospital.

I ease out of bed and discover my body doesn't hurt as bad as I expect. I yank the tubes and pull off the hospital gown.

The cops took my clothes for testing but they missed my Redwing boots. Everything else is in the knapsack except it all needs washed. The toes of the socks are stiff and the cleanest shirt smells like three cab shifts and a night at Billy's.

Once I'm dressed, I exit the room with the knapsack over my shoulder. I have no problems walking off the unit and even tip my cap to a nurse. She's glanced at me and I have no choice except to play cool and I think she'll catch on for sure.

Except I keep walking and nobody stops me. Past the first bank of elevators and the next bank and all the way to the south end of the hospital. Then down the stairs and I'm out.

15

I ORDER BREAKFAST for dinner and read the 5 o'clock news in closed captions on a muted big screen. Village Inn is nearest to the hospital for dining with a TV. The place got flooded with everything else along Riverside Drive. It's been gutted and given the full makeover in a hurry.

My waitress is the Sex Dungeon Lady, which is why I avoid coming here. She too has survived the Great Flood and gives me the kid glove treatment, "Aw shore, hon!" She's noted my hobbled walk and busted face and black eye fading to blood ocher. Yet she shows no recollect that I'm the cabbie that dragged her into court. She's short and bird-boned and I cannot unthink the idea of her riding in that sex swing as she clucks through put-on smile and lays out my spread, "And with a side of pancakes. Anything else I can getcha, hon?"

"No thanks."

"Awlright!"

Away she goes and I turn back to the big screen where I recognize right off the facade of the ND&B warehouse. Already in progress, the captions read: AFTER A MAN IN CUSTODY MADE SHOCKING ALLEGATIONS THE BUILDING IS A FRONT FOR A BLACK MARKET DRUG RING.

CUT TO: Wide view of the S&R desk. The torched area has been cleaned up, repaired, repainted. It's as if the news is broadcast for me alone. The bombshell. I get to wolfing down eggs and potatoes and pancakes, everything all at once.

WANTED FOR QUESTIONING IS JOSEPH HITACHI SOLE OWNER OF THE OPERATION. EMPLOYEES OF THE COMPANY SAID HITACHI HAS NOT BEEN TO WORK IN A WEEK CITING FAMILY EMERGENCY.

CUT TO: Exterior of visitor's parking. Investigators leave the scene with more boxes of evidence. Did they grab the binders left behind? The drug samples? Carpet cut out of the longhouse floor? The camera angle shows that between a company van and rusted out pickup truck is an empty slot. Damen's Buick is gone.

CUT TO: Mugshot of the snitch and I can't get the cakes down fast enough.

FACING TWENTY FIVE YEARS IN PRISON IS DAMEN PHIPPS WHO ALLEGES TO HAVE WORKED WITH WEALTHY BUSINESSMEN TO DISTRIBUTE LARGE AMOUNTS OF COCAINE AND HEROIN IN THE EASTERN PART OF THE STATE. LOCAL BUSINESS LEADERS NOT AFFILIATED WITH THE COMPANY UNDER SCRUTINY HAVE CALLED THE ALLEGATIONS A HOAX AIMED AT KEEPING A HARDENED CRIMINAL OUT OF PRISON.

CUT TO: My mugshot from a public intox ten years ago.

POLICE HAVE NO FURTHER COMMENT THOUGH THEY ARE LOOKING FOR VICTOR PASTERNAK A LOCAL CAB DRIVER WANTED FOR QUESTIONING IN A RELATED INCIDENT.

What shit did Billy pull to keep his name out of this? I climb from the booth and wave cash at the Sex Dungeon Lady.

"But don't you want your check, hon?"

Now I wave my phone at her to distract from the television. I should've greased the cakes better. They've bunched in my gullet so that my misdirection comes out as an imperiled hiss.

"Bad news. I got to get back to the hospital."

* * *

FREEDOM COVE IS officially a no-go zone.

Two squad cars are parked catawampus on the apron. An officer talks to my landlord Clyde. The others enter my unit through the busted front door. I watch from across the road, mourning. The cops have my guns and the 'Yota and everything that isn't in my knapsack.

I sneak away the way I've come, climbing back over the fence to rejoin the riverside bike path. I cross the highway underpass due south and keep my eyes peeled. I've never seen a bike cop out here but they could have a squad car snooping for me at Emerald Cab.

Billy said he parked the truck in back of Welby's lot, next to the taxi shack, and I've got to take the chance. That truck is my way out of here. First I get the truck and then I get Billy. If I'm going to be jammed up with the law over this, I'm taking him with me.

My hurt body throbs hot as if my wash cycle has been followed-up on tumble dry. My footsteps pound in my hand and ear and I keep a sure march into falling twilight. Soon I hustle along and then get up to a jog. My headache kills this pace but the A.P.B. for my arrest has strongly provoked my instinct to flee the fuck out of here.

A mile south of the highway, I cross the river on the train bridge. Welby's truck lot, like Emerald Cab, has its back to the water and I know where to snake through the riverbank trees. Except this means I've got to divert the hobo camp and cross the rear of the taxi lot.

I crouch at the edge of Emerald Cab property and have a look. No cops lurking. The pop machine silhouettes two drivers smoking and laughing. Through the open office door, Paulie hunches at the desk and yells at a phone.

I move quick so nobody spies me.

Long ago somebody busted the wooden fence between the lots. I leg through the breach and find the big blue Peterbilt like Billy said I would. Early moon glows along its lines and shines the chrome and causes the ice-white hood flames to sparkle. Not an optimal getaway car but it's the one I got.

Nobody stirs at Welby's when I turn the big engine over. I topped off the tanks after the ND&B run and the other dials look good. Next I need a reference on rural Missouri highways.

The Legacy 379 comes equipped with GPS. I punch it up and find a treasure map left by Billy. Coordinates to a location in Kansas City, a midblock location west of downtown. The navs are the interstate equivalent of a drunk route. South into Missouri and across the state's northern barrens until the interstate south into Kansas City. A good way for a wanted man.

I also google the address on my phone and find a matched listing for "Plato," though googling that gives me nothing but chaff and soft hits.

Fuck it. It's not like I've never driven to a strange address. I punch on the lights, grind out of Welby's lot and turn the big wheel toward the highway. I pass light traffic on the roads and see no cops parked up around the corners. On the entrance ramp, I paddle the chrome skull shifter and ease into the throttle and let the truck carry me out of Iowa City.

At last I've found my bridge to burn and the fucker's ablaze. This place has for me always been salted ground. Four days after we arrived, Mom went to the hospital puking blood. She was dead 12 weeks later. Nearly 20 years gone and it's not that I've meanwhile failed to thrive. It's that I failed to take the hint and leave with my brothers. Hey look, Ma. I'm finally on TV....Seeing my mug broadcast in criminal red-and-blue on local news and on that big screen has made everything clear.

There's no coming back here. Not ever.

And until ever, I'll be in a horror waiting for the other shoes to drop. What the report didn't tie together are the connections between ND&B and DevGRO and bikers executed in a meth lab and four hunters mauled by illegal tigers, or what any of that has to do with kiddie porn found at the Houston estate. What the report also didn't say is that I'm an accessory to murder, felonious assault and robbery, and property thefts in excess of $50,000. And I can probably catch three counts of fucking with a corpse.

None of that causes me to wince. I only cringe that what we did led to the killing of a punk kid. It will never matter if he had it coming, or if his brother set him up. Or if that noisy orange-headed jagoff with the pants hanging down made me want to run his ass over. Still never enough reasons to get him dead.

Not that it matters now. Because a girl whose slave name is Scarlet Rose is still in trouble. I'll never feel right about Chemo Phipps. But until the girl is safe, for all we've done wrong we will have accomplished no good.

The evening traffic thins the further south I drive and I see no state cops. Yet the panic doesn't lift until I cross into Missouri. Hwy 136 is another five miles. I take the western exit and five miles further my phone chirps.

C? KNEW U'D COME. U WANT TO BE FRIENDS. U NEED ME.

Billy's waited to make contact until I made the turn to the west. He knows I'm headed his way. So he's got a GPS marker on the truck, or my phone, or my clothes.

My phone chirps again.

MIDNITE SHARP BACK DOOR THAT ADDRESS. & QUIT BEING A LAME AZZ BITCH.

I glance the dashboard clock. I got to hammer down to keep a good D=RT. I've only blown through Kansas City on its freeways and I want time to get my boots on the ground. I also got a bit of shopping to do and make a mental list of items that can be bought in a truck stop.

Then another text from Billy.

I PICKED DAMEN FOR HIS FLAWS & SO I PICKED U. U R WEAK & MORALLY CONFUSED. U CANT EVEN STAND BY YR OWN WORDS. DISGUSTING.

I've never forgotten how he first struck me. From that miserable crumb, Billy cultivated our sliver of trust until it was large enough to manipulate and abuse. Even after that he's wanted to see our friendship thrive so he could abuse it further. And it wounds him that I've killed the friendship.

I don't want to kill him. I don't even want to hurt Billy. He's committed the crimes to which I'm an accessory and my only defense stands with him. So I need him alive.

I would, however, let him run headlong into a metaphorical brick wall. And I need to lead him into it. I don't need any gun for that. I only need the sliver of his trust. And I'm going to roll him up and I'm going to trap him in it and we'll go down with the law together.

THE RADIANT BUBBLE of Kansas City nightlights shine against the outer dark as I roar under the interchange lights among wolf packs of four-wheelers. My belly tickles nervous but I adjust my grip on the big wheel and keep driving.

I follow the GPS off the big road into West Bottoms, an area heavy with old tracks, truck repair, antique shops in antique buildings and a few hip bars. Neglected just long enough to have ripened for outside investment. The apartments above look to be inhabited by artists, hip lawyers, junkies and remainders of urban poor.

Driving past the address, I see it's called Plato's Mattress Emporium. The OPEN sign is off. Nobody's parked out front. Both sides of the street are likewise empty though I'm passed by a taxi zooming to a bar two corners up.

I park the truck four blocks away then wipe the wheel and chrome skull shifter and the GPS and anything else I might've touched. Finally I lock the truck and walk away. Two blocks on, I trash the keys in a sewer.

The road hums in my busted hand and body. Yet despite the pedal mashing on foreign roads, my legs feel fresh and I hike back to the shop with a jump in my new boots. The

October evening is a comfortable mid-60's with scattered clouds. Night traffic is lean in this neighborhood, by foot or wheel. I'm armed only with a fresh Maglite, Gerber tool and boot knife. I've also got plastic binds to tie him up. The cash he's given me totals $10,000 and I wear it stuffed in a money belt that keeps sneaking above my waistline. I've also shed the last of my janitorial wardrobe and dumpstered everything, even my Redwing boots. Those have been traded for a black hat, a chambray, jeans fastened with a silver buckle, and black Tony Lamas with silver toes that look kind of bad ass. I may be an imposter truck stop cowboy but I know it works because nobody looks at me twice.

The mattress shop is in the middle of the empty block. A once stately firm built in an American heyday. I can make out the skeleton of a rooftop sign, FARAMA OIL CO, each burned out letter lighted only by the moon.

The upper stories are boarded over and the retail foot is occupied by the bed shop. Foregoing any displays of actual furniture, Plato's has instead plastered catalog adverts over its windows. The shop is shut up tight. Peeking in the doors, I see the foyer is aligned to obscure the view.

I keep walking and turn at the corner, checking down to the alleyway. There's a taxi oncoming but no other traffic. The taxi slows to trawl me so I come ahead at a brisk walk.

The alley leading to the rear features a long and narrow vestibule. A lumpy old cobble paved over and potholed. Overhead floods throw ample light. Too late I see a camera poised to watch this entry. Good thing it hangs from its perch, disabled.

I slink along the alley's narrow part and halt at the far edge. It dead-ends in a parking square behind Plato's. At least that jives with my plan to run Billy into a trap. Half the slots are taken by black sedans and a couple SUVs. The bed shop has a two-bay garage with tall roll-ups and the rear service entry where Billy wants me at midnight sharp.

My phone shows I've got eleven minutes though as soon as I stuff it away it vibrates. Another message from Billy.

COME THRU TO THE SHOWROOM WHENEVER U GET HERE. THE WAY IS CLEAR & THE WATER IS BLOOD WARM.

I break from the corner and keep to the edge of the parking square and go around the outside of the cars. I check the rooftops and scaffolds of fire stairs and spot another disabled camera over the service entry.

When I reach the door, I see its peephole has been punched out. The lock has also been zipped clean and the deadbolt dropped open. The unlocked door sits half an inch out of jamb and I toe it further with my cowboy boot. It stops on something so, damn the resistance, I shoulder it wide as it'll go and squeeze inside Plato's Mattress Emporium.

The door has stopped on the boot of a body lying backward from the entry. A dead kid with a red beard and a peephole cylinder for a right eye.

I take a quick scan of the garage. Two black vans are backed to a pair of double doors leading into an unlit area. To the right is a closet office brightly lit from the floor.

The man inside has gotten worse that the kid at the door. A spatter trail leads the way and I find him toppled over a chair. Arterial blood shines under the fallen table lamp. Gunshot wounds in chest and tattooed neck, and the stubby end of a tire iron tapped in his brain.

I sense movement behind me and whip about. The service entry has closed itself. But no one's there.

The dead lifer grips a pistol in his right hand, a pissant 9mm. I lift the barrel with my boot. The gun had been brandished but the safety's still on. I grasp the barrel of the gun and pry it from the hand. The lifer's mouth hangs ghastly and the eyes stare out crossed as if yet pondering the improbability of that tire iron.

I check the pistol. The clip is full though its chamber is empty. I quietly pull the slide back and feed one in. Better to be readier than the dead.

Sweeping out of the office with gun high, I see a room previously obscured by the black vans. A break lounge for

Plato's employees. I peek inside but it's empty.

Next, I head back to the double doors and peer through the window. On the far end of the unlit area, two rectangles of pale yellow light mark the doors to the showroom. That's where Billy is. And that's where I'm going to trap him.

I elbow the door open and garage light spills into the stockroom. On the far end, beside the next set of doors, a body sits upright against the wall. To my immediate right, another man has ragdolled to the floor, hands buried under torso, head encircled by a corona of blood. Beside him, another gun dropped unused.

The door won't stay open on its own and I don't want to give myself away shining the Maglite. So keeping the door open with a boot, I grab the collar of the ragdoll and I lug him into the entryway for a doorstop. And that's four counts of fucking with a corpse.

But now the stockroom is filled with enough ambient light for me to move ahead between upright mattresses stacked to either side like dominoes. As I creep I watch the light on the ceiling for the play of any shadows other than my own. At the feet of the body sitting beside the showroom doors, I see a discarded .45 with an oil can suppressor screwed on its snout. That's got to be Billy's. The dead guy has no gun. Lifting his coat tail, I see an empty buckshot sleeve on his belt. This must be where Billy switched to heavier firepower.

The windows on the showroom doors are frosted over so I can't know what's on the other side without swinging through. I put my left ear at the crack between the doors. Nothing but the endless exhale from the HVAC. My heart pounds. I breathe sharply to steel myself and I adjust my grip on the gun. It feels sweaty and heavy and wrong in my hands.

Then I push through the doors.

The aftermath of a fierce battle unfolds around me with the lifeless splayed among the beds and slid to the floor. The floor is tacky with blood and the air stinks of burnt cotton and spent powder. I keep my eyes sprung as I move into the showroom.

There's not a whimper from the casualties. A busted fluorescent hangs and throws sparks. Weapons are littered about. I see bodies piled in the trenches between display beds. A dozen men, or more. A glass end table has been shattered into a sharp wedge and jammed into one defender's collar. He sprawls across the tiled lane that divides ahead to carry shoppers around a crowning display of three king-sized beds.

Each bed is dressed in high-end plush as indicated by the banner above: EVERYTHING'S GOING TO BE ALL WHITE.

Except the display has been liberally restyled in crimson reds and muzzle-flash blacks. A fire has been started and extinguished on the left bed. The right bed is occupied by two men soaking a designer comforter with precious fluids.

And occupying the central bed as if it's a raft are eight minors, ages 10 through 16.

They wear costumes as if somebody's dressed them out of the Halloween aisle. Princess. Cowboy and sailor. Schoolgirl and stripper. A sporto in a LeBron jersey.

They give slack looks as if waiting for an explanation from me, or an order. All this blood and mayhem is not enough to ripple their dark ocean.

Behind them, across the hanging display walls, I see words painted in blood.

WE CAN'T BE FRIENDS ANYMORE

Another message for me secreted in a global broadcast. I've chased Billy from Welby's truck lot and I've followed his route and showed up exactly when and where he wanted. And this is what he wants me to see.

I now recognize Scarlet Rose among the other kids. I feel sudden joy beaming on my face and wave at her as if to say: It's me.

She breathes through her mouth and stares as if drugged.

I ask her, "Is he still here?"

"He's gone. He left before they got here."

I hear a hammer cock behind me. It sounds velvety and

warm, like a revolver.

"Easy with your hands, bubba. Let's drop the piece."

Billy's words but not Billy's voice.

I put my arms out and make a show of thumbing the safety as a man comes around to level his revolver in my face. Latino, in his 50's, glasses. Looks like a cop in his no-tie suit.

A fucking hulk winds on my opposite flank. Muscles outsized like rocks stuffed up under the skin of his arms. Even his veins cast shadows in the flickering light. He snatches the gun from my hand like swatting a fly.

He hands the pistol off to a fellow soldier who goes about collecting weapons from the floor into a duffel bag. Now from behind the mattress displays, other soldiers appear. Men in balaclavas and ceramic vests. Professionals bearing M4s with pro silencers and scopes. And a few women soldiers too.

The hulk frisks me while I watch the tactical scrubbing. The other soldiers have broken into teams. Four of them handle a prelim intake on the children. The others lay the dead in rows on the floor like the day's catch.

The hulk removes my Maglite and hand tool and the boot knife. Plastic binds scatter out of my ass pocket. But I protest when he rips at the Velcro money belt.

"Let him keep all of it," says the man that could be a cop.

He's lowered the revolver but gives me the stink eye through unassuming grandpa glasses. "You must be Pasternak."

"Pasternak couldn't make it. I'm Zhivago."

The hulk gathers up the fingers of one paw and taps me hard on the chest. A slight move yet it causes me to yelp. He's tagged the soft meat between my shoulder and breast. The pain blooms incredible and he leans to bark in my face.

"Nobody around here likes cute dicks."

The first man says, "People call me J-Bob. Maybe you've heard. We have a mutual acquaintance. William Kinross."

I remember hearing the name around the hot tub, tucked in among Billy's outrageous stories. Maybe the bit about J-Bob and his vigilante gang isn't bullshit. But more than a gang they look like special forces. I get myself upright and find my breath.

"It rings a bell."

"We should talk."

The four soldiers now escort the children toward the garage as the dead are piled onto mattress movers wheeled in from the stockroom. I follow J-Bob and the hulk follows me out of the bloodbath back through the overstock. The children are gathered in one of the vans. The rear doors of the other hang open and wait for the dead.

We enter the break room and the hulk is put on point. He breaks off from us and has an announcement for the others.

"Listen up: We got 10 minutes. Let's figure out how to make a fire."

The break lounge features crappy lighting and a leaning refrigerator and a table with metal chairs. I smell an ashtray and dig out my smokes before taking a seat.

J-Bob comes out of the fridge with a six-pack of Bud heavy, courtesy of Plato's. He wrenches one from the plastic yoke and hands over the balance.

"William Kinross." His voice sounds at once wistful and hurt. "We met after he got out of Huntsville and worked a long time together. He has a weird spirit for what we do. But always teetering to the dark side." He tips his hand to show it. "I thought it'd be me to steer him right. So I kept him under my wing until he broke it."

On that note, we crack our beers and J-Bob lifts his can.

"To a most dangerous man."

"Fuck him. Let's drink to having survived that son bitch."

"So it's true you fell out. You really come to shoot him?"

I shake my head.

"If you know we fell out, what else do you know?"

"William reached out to me this afternoon. Said there was a meet tonight here in Kansas City. He didn't say what it was but I'd guess a sale given the number of children, the lack of johns and everybody armed. Did you know about the children?"

"He only said he was coming for the girl. But are you

working with him? Is he with you?"

J-Bob gives an adamant shake of his head, swallows a slug and sets the can on the table.

"We haven't spoken in two years. Last we saw William, I had a gun in his cheek and he convinced me to let him go. Our bridge is burned on both shores. We only keep tabs so as to steer clear of his games. Tonight is a special exception, given the children in need.

"But you just missed him," J-Bob informs me. "He left out of here in a cab he stole around same time you were spotted out front. William warned you might show up to gun him down."

I deny it again.

"I'd only come here to trap him."

"To trap him?"

"So I could hand him over to the law," I admit. "The cops squeezed me because a dead hooker in the trunk of my cab. Now I got this warrant because of a snitch. And Billy, with his magical fucking touch, has erased himself from both threads."

Too late, I see that I've played a major role in Billy's plot. This is why he dumped Letty Fetch in my cab. This is why he brought me into ND&B. Why he had me drive the ammonia tanker and why he wanted me at the meeting with biker fuckhead. Why he had kept his secret deals with Damen Phipps and why he had me creep through the Coronets during the fake robbery. And having me stab out those cab tires. That was his test. Breaking my seal. He's tied me into every angle of his scheme. He's had me walk alongside his footsteps and turned me into his foil. I am Billy's long game, and he's won. He's clean and I'm trapped. My only way to survive is to keep no home.

A light in my brain burns behind my eyeballs and my skull feels like its bursting from the inside.

"You all right?"

"I want to know about the kids. What's going to happen with those kids?"

"We work with an organization that takes them in. They're private, like us. That girl. She must be important to you. But you two put her in considerable danger. I think you wanted to play the big hero."

"No hero. I saw that video and just wanted her safe."

J-Bob rounds his hands as if trying to grasp an invisible beach ball. "And so did William ever explain to you the global impact behind your games?"

"Everything I saw was pretty local."

"On the purchasing end, sure. The gambling side of it. But I mean on the business side. Are you aware of its ownership?"

"Billy told me ND&B was running the show."

"ND&B is third party."

"Then Billy wasn't sure. We met a dude named Hitachi that worked in the brokerage. But he said it was all tied to a dead guy in Florida."

J-Bob laughs until he's coughs.

"I like you, man. Fearless."

"What's that supposed to mean?"

"William has been climbing the underground corporate ladder this whole time," he says. "Robbing dope dealers to put himself in with the snitch. The snitch got him into ND&B and the money backing it up. And all that has put him within reach of the ownership class. The bodies here? William has tonight bloodied the nose of some very nasty people."

J-Bob tips his head the other way and peers through glasses.

"The cops are the least of your trouble, bubba. These nasty people will think they can use you to find William, even though they can't. It's because of this that William asked we look after you. He said you need all the help you can get. Except, not one of us trusts you given your reference and work history. William Kinross, as I'm certain you learned, is an unprofessional rogue. Untrustworthy. He'll work with anybody to get what he wants. And what's this say about you?"

J-Bob shakes his head theatrically.

"Truth is, we won't help you. Not directly. There's an organization though. The people that take care of the children. They have a remote facility. They'd keep you hid just to have your hand around the ranch." He tips his empty can at me. "Play by the house rules and you'll get all the help you need."

He yanks another beer out of the ring and cracks it open. Mine sweats on the table, untouched.

"You're saying they can protect me from him?"

J-Bob tips his head and says, "He couldn't find out."

"I think he would. Going with them puts me one step from you. Which means they can't hide me from him. I'm safer in a West Memphis truck stop."

"You're taking your chances if you run. Running means living over your shoulder, bubba."

"If everybody made good on threats to kill me, I'd be dead a bunch of times. What's more, I'm good on hard road. I don't live over the shoulder, *bubba*. I'm a turn-around motherfucker."

I startle at a shuffle behind me and twist to see the hulk has filled the doorway. "We're ready on your order, sir."

"Do it," says J-Bob.

The hulk gives us back the room and J-Bob looks sour.

He asks, "So's that it?"

"Is there supposed to be something else?"

"Well," he says to rise from the table. "*Eso es todo, amigos.* That means, 'Good luck, you dumb son of a bitch.'"

I follow him out of the break room just as the vans exit the garage one after the other. J-Bob and his huge lieutenant trot to a sedan that pulls ahead of the SUVs. I leave the parking square as the last vehicle departs. Through the opened doors of the stockroom, I see a great fire has overtaken the showroom.

My Tony Lamas clap underfoot as I hustle down the alley and out. I look for a cab. I feel a great need to get to the airport, or disappear into downtown before sneaking away in small steps. Two paths and no good choices, per usual.

I should go a mile before finding a cab. Except there's one rolling to the corner and he couldn't have seen that I've come from the alley. I wave him down and climb in and slide across the bench until I'm behind the driver.

"Where we headed, cowboy?"

"I'm working on that," I tell him, waving my phone. "Just get me out of here."

He dutifully burps away from the curb and then asks, "Weird night, huh?"

"It's been a weird few weeks. This whole year actually. And why don't you take me downtown. Any strip of bars works."

I need to figure this out. I need a plan. I'll have him drop me off somewhere busy. Then I'll get a new cab and start a fresh getaway and decide on my ultimate destination then.

Through the rear window, I watch the face of Plato's Mattress Emporium, and I wait for it.

"So tell me then. You lose your job? Or discover you're a woman? What's making your time-bomb tick?"

"Nothing to tell, really."

I keep watching, waiting for windows to explode into the street, or fire to burst from the upper stories. None of that happens before the driver takes his first turn and we lose line of sight.

Then, a silent orange flash obscured in the quarter like lightning behind clouds. I sink back into the seat and drop my head on the rest. I need to figure out what I'm doing. I need to figure out what my plan is.

The driver presses me. "C'mon man, everybody's got a story. That's why I became a hack. I'm here to collect the stories of the street."

"Quit this job then and go be a garbage man. There are no good taxi stories."

AUTHOR'S NOTE

People are like, "Wait—you're Vic Pasternak?"
 Turns out, I'm not. But I understand the confusion. When Matt Steele, publisher of *Little Village* magazine, asked me to write a taxi-lifestyle column, I was still in that line of work and so requested they cut my byline. I am forever grateful that Matt let me run free with the material, which provided a foundation for this book.
 I also have a mercenary army of folks from the cab universe to thank, notably Alan R. Martin, #19, the old and new #22s, the new #17, #5, old #88, #86, #54, SNAFU23, #55 and old #50, #21, DIRTY30, #Jared, #34, #67, #74, #96, #11 and #98, Norb Schulte, the taxi gods, and #666. Plus Candace, Mark G., and The Player.
 I'd at last like to thank draft readers Roy, Marcy, and John; my cop procedural coach, Bill Genell; editors, Todd Jackson and Brent Johnson; my longtime wingmen, Matt Sweesy and Bob Hall; Mom and Da, my sister, Aimee, and all my family, and my wife Liz for listening to every word that didn't make the lifeboat.

SPG - July 2015

© Sandra L. Dyas

Sean Preciado Genell received his MFA from New York University and is author of "Haulin' Ass" and "Business as Usual" for *Little Village*. He lives with his wife, Liz Preciado Genell, and daughter in Iowa City where he also fronts punk blues band Illinois John Fever. *All the Help You Need* is his first novel.

Also from Slow Collision …

The Best Part by Brent Johnson

The good people of Quantrill County live in a fairy tale of quiet optimism and prosperity, but when a sudden outbreak of methamphetamine ravishes their sleepy communities, that optimism quickly erodes. Brent Johnson's incendiary second novel follows a loose collection of bored, dead-end locals through the ghost towns, the trailer parks and the secret turmoil of Kansas in the 1990s.

Detroit Trip by Todd Jackson

In Todd Jackson's savage second novel, Zack Edwards (*Zack's Summer Break*) is stuck in a boring manufacturing job in the suburbs of Minneapolis until a frenzied mushroom trip and a crumbling marriage force him to reassess his life. He flees for Detroit where he lands a job in the automotive industry, destroying crash test dummies.

Slow Collision Mixtape

What would you get if the funniest, weirdest dudes you know started a literary press with nothing but a dirty thirty of PBR and a hundred bucks in loose change? Slow Collision's *Mixtape* is the answer, featuring excerpts from *Detroit Trip* and *The Best Part*, as well as hot-wired passages from early drafts of *All the Help You Need* by Sean Preciado Genell and Brent Johnson's *Genesoid*, a verse-by-verse retelling of the *Book of Genesis* set in a hallucinogenic, mutating nightclub.